Post Hill PRESS

MORE BY ABRAHAMS

SEDITION

In the vacuum of a constitutional crisis, self-described American Neo-Patriots seek to seize power. They have the will. They already have someone on the inside. And they have the explosives.

Standing in their way is a woman who listens to conversations not meant for her to hear. She reads mail not intended for her to see. She knows their intention. But can she stop them in time?

ALLEGIANCE

★ TOM ABRAHAMS ★

A POST HILL PRESS book

ISBN (Hardcover): 978-1-61868-9-955
ISBN (eBook): 978-1-61868-9-962

Allegiance copyright © 2013
by Tom Abrahams
All Rights Reserved.
Cover art by Jason Farmand

Post Hill
PRESS

For Courtney and our nanobots; Samantha and Luke

PROLOGUE

"It's always a battle between anarchy and tyranny – always has
been."
TEXAS GOVERNOR RICK PERRY, FEBRUARY 18, 2010

The sniper never missed. Never.

The job was always simple: target, breathe, pull, and kill.

No emotion. No second thoughts.

This target, this place, this job, though, were different.

The mark was not some nameless insurgent or foreign ally
turned enemy. He was one of the wealthiest men in the world.

The location wasn't a frozen mountain perch on the Afghani-
Pakistani border or the humid, tangled jungles of Central America.
This was on U.S. soil.

There was no payment on the other end of the bullet. This was
a favor; a freebie the sniper didn't typically grant.

All of it was irregular, the sniper thought, lying belly down on
the roof of the George R. Brown Convention Center in downtown
Houston, Texas. The crowd on the grassy area below was small.
The sky was clear. The wind was slight and from the south.

It was the loud rush of traffic on highway 59 from behind that
was distracting. The sniper slipped in a pair of earbuds and pressed
play on a small black iPod. The electric guitar licked into rhythm,
followed by the beat of the drum.

AC/DC always helped clear the sniper's mind and focus on the task ahead.

The sniper thumbed the volume up a click and took a deep breath. Eyes closed, the sniper didn't see the figure to the left approaching with purpose.

A large man, his muscular frame was hidden by the gray Ghillie suit used to disguise his presence on the convention center's roof. His dark, polarized sunglasses hid his eyes and his muscles flexed as he crouched low, moving to the shooter.

The sniper spun as the man approached.

"Where have you been?" whispered the shooter, pulling out the earbuds.

"Checking the escape route." The man was the sniper's spotter. He was the senior, more experienced member of the team. "You want coffee?" He nodded at a large stainless canister to the sniper's left.

"Thanks." The sniper reached for the caffeine.

"You set?" The spotter inched onto his belly next to the sniper. "Crowd's beginning to fill in."

"A bit." The sniper took a sip of the coffee without making a sound.

"That road noise sucks," the spotter said, glancing back toward the highway behind and below them.

"That's why I'm amping up with music. Helps me focus."

"This I know," the spotter smiled. The pair had been through a lot in their time together; Parachinar, Al Fashir, Benque Ceiba, Tampico. They were always in and out. They always hit their mark. They knew each other as well as they knew themselves. Hours, or days, in a snow drift or mud hole had accelerated their personal learning curves.

"*Shoot To Thrill?* AC/DC?" The spotter knew he was right.

"You know it." The sniper felt the wind shift.

"Trite." The spotter adjusted his elbows.

Another silent sip from the cup.

"Okay," the spotter rolled his eyes and reached into a small gray sack and pulled out a scope. "Time to get serious. I see the car approaching."

"Roger that." The sniper set the coffee to the side and scanned the crowd, which now numbered at least two hundred people.

High above the target, the sniper team quietly pressed forward with their pre-shot routine, despite using a new weapon given to them for this assignment.

The M110 rifle was longer and heavier than the sniper's weapon of choice, the thirty-six inch, nine pound CSASS. Still, it would do. There was, after all, no such thing as a single best sniper rifle. Any rifle in the hand of a sniper was equally effective.

The spotter put his eye to his adjustable power scope. He zoomed in to 45x and spun it back to 20x, giving him a wide field of view and the ability to trace the bullet once fired. As he scanned left, he saw the target getting out of a vehicle.

"Target spotted," he whispered above the swoosh of the traffic. "Dark suit, near intersection three. Waving hands. Smiling."

"Roger," answered the shooter. "Got him." The sniper moved the rifle from right to left, following the target. "Now approaching intersection one."

The target shook hands with a handful of men and women lining the path to the hurriedly assembled stage. He looked at the skyline to his right and extended his arms as if to embrace the city. He turned to the crowd, clapped his hands, and bounded up the steps to the lectern. Every move was choreographed.

The spotter checked his range finder. He lifted up his head and looked, without aid, at the scene below them. "That intersection is 350 meters. I laze him at 351 meters. Come up to six plus four."

"Roger that," the sniper adjusted again. "Elevation six plus four."

"We have right to left wind now. Come right 1.3 M.O.A," the spotter looked at the flags blowing to either side of the target. The gusts were slight, but they'd switched from south to north.

"Roger that," the sniper made the adjustment. "Right 1.3 M.O.A."

The crowd below them was cheering. They were waving signs. The target was relatively still. He was in a single spot. Not working the crowd as he normally did.

Through their scopes, the team saw the target remove his dark suit jacket and tug at his tie. He was wearing a white shirt, making the mark increasingly visible against the reflective glass and steel of the downtown buildings behind him.

The spotter and sniper exchanged knowing looks. The two were telepathic, almost. They were ready.

"Spotter up." The spotter shifted on his elbows. He'd done this countless times before. With each one, the moment before the shot, he felt the adrenaline course through his body. He was anxious, ready to pull the trigger himself and see the extraordinary result of his godforsaken skill. He was the eyes, not the muscle. He looked to his right at his partner's hand on the trigger and returned to the scope.

The target had his finger to his lips, quieting the chanting crowd.

The shooter exhaled and settled in for the pull. Everything around the target blurred. Concentration was critical. One last breath before the shot.

"Aaaahhhhh," the sniper exhaled audibly, signaling the spotter.

"Send it." The data was good. The target was there.

At that moment, the sniper pulled the trigger which, in turn, engaged the sear. Instantly the sear released the firing pin, which struck the back of the bullet primer. A small, internal explosion propelled the 7.62 x 51 millimeter bullet down the barrel and into the air toward the mark.

Traveling at 2,600 feet per second, the bullet tore through the flesh, muscle, and bone of the target before the sniper released the pressure on the trigger.

"One o'clock, three inches," the sniper said softly.

"Roger that," the spotter confirmed with the scope. "Target hit."

The sniper chambered another round as the spotter scanned the field one last time. Both were motionless until the spotter, out of habit, picked up the brass casing to his right and dropped it into his bag. It was still hot.

By the time the target's blood began pooling around him on the stage, the sniper and the spotter were off of the roof. Within minutes they'd easily merged into the whirring traffic on highway 59.

The M110 was in a dumpster on the rear loading dock of the convention center. It was wiped clean and dropped onto a stack of corrugated cardboard, the team making no effort to hide it.

PART I
COME AND TAKE IT

"Texas is the obsession, the proper study, and the passionate possession of all Texans."
---JOHN STEINBECK

CHAPTER 1

The last I remember, I was at a bar on Sixth Street.

It smelled like a Thursday; a mix of cloves, hairspray, spilled beer, and sweat. Thursdays are big in Austin, a jump on the weekends that lie ahead.

My girlfriend, Charlie, left me sitting in a small red vinyl booth while she went to the bathroom. Charlie always likes hitting the clubs on Thursdays. She says it makes getting through the week easier when she knows she has an extra night of dancing and drinking.

She's as tall as I am; maybe 5'11", with red hair and bright green eyes, like Nicole Kidman after she got famous, but before she denied having plastic surgery.

She is *Days of Thunder* hot and whip smart. I've dated attractive women before, but I've never fallen for one until Charlie. I always run when things get too serious.

I had a busy Friday planned and hadn't slept lately, but given how much I'd been traveling it was great to spend time with her.

The band 139 played on a small stage at the far end of the cramped pub. The rhythmic strum of the bass guitar vibrated in my hand wrapped around the glass mug on the table in front of me. I thumbed the condensation off of the glass and nodded to the beat.

Through the cigarette smoke haze hanging in the air there was the regular mix of college kids, politicos like Charlie and me, and Austin free spirits.

At the large black granite bar on the other side of the room, a group of gel-headed fraternity guys wearing Polo shirts clinging tightly to their biceps laughed and playfully punched the testosterone out of each other. Next to them were a couple of men in dark business suits, their bright silk ties loosened but still knotted beneath the collars of their pressed white cotton shirts. They worked at the Capitol. I didn't recognize them, but their attitude and attire gave them away. They leaned against the granite, holding hi-ball glasses and whispering to each other about the women who passed by them. They ogled Charlie until she disappeared into the bathroom. Men were always looking at her. She pretended not to notice, but I knew she did.

Near the stage, in front of the band, about twenty people were bouncing to the music. They'd occasionally hold their glasses above their heads as they swayed back and forth. It seemed spontaneously choreographed; like a mosh pit without the slam-dancing.

I took a swig from the sweaty, vibrating glass of Shiner Bock. It was saltier than usual, and bitter. I remember thinking the bartender didn't know how to pour a beer as I wiped foam from my lips with the back of my arm.

139 finished its set. I think. I don't remember much after swigging the beer.

***

I am seated and chained to the floor.

Where is this place?

There's a man standing over me, insisting I reveal whatever it is I know. His voice is deep and gravelly, as though he needs to clear his throat. He's British.

What does he want?

"I don't know anything." I swallow past the dryness in my mouth.

"Are you hungry?" The voice behind me is calm this time. It's almost a sympathetic whisper behind my right ear. Almost but not really. "How long has it been since you've eaten, good boy?"

My head aches at my temples from dehydration. My vision is blurred, my tongue is thick, and my lips are chapped and feel as though the dryness has glued them shut. I shake my head.

"Come along," the voice says. "We'll get you something to eat, a little water to drink. Perhaps that'll help your memory. I know how hard it can be to concentrate."

It's obvious to me he's done this before. He's a professional extractor of information, standing a step outside my foggy line of sight. He sounds simultaneously proper and evil.

He walks away. There's the sound of a door unlocking, opening, shutting, and finally being relocked from the outside. I've heard the series of clicks and creaks too many times to count. I imagine the door is thick and riveted. It has that sound to it when it slams closed.

I'm not sure of where or when I am.

When I'm not chained to the chair, I'm in my cell.

It's cement floored, next to the much larger interrogation room, and is sized such that I cannot stand fully upright or lay down completely. The joints in my hips ache. My knees are killing me. I can't fall asleep because of the throbbing in my head. Instead, I find myself in a constant haze where I begin to dream while fully aware of the noises around me.

There is loud, distorted music blasted into the cell for seconds or minutes or hours at a time. It's speed metal that pounds with a pulsing light that, at times, is so blinding I swear I can feel the heat from it.

When the light is on consistently, I can only see by squinting though my swollen eyes. Then the room will go black. With the lights off, I can't see anything. I can, however, smell the mess I've made of myself; the constant stink of body odor and worse. I can't ever completely catch my breath.

In the larger room there are constant threats of pain, but very rarely pain itself. The threats are worse.

This is torture.

Sometimes there's the sound of metal scraping against metal behind my ear, or maybe it's a boiling pot of water held close enough to my face the steam makes snot drip my from my nose.

The only breaks are the occasional moments during which I black out from hunger or lack of sleep. I can't keep track of it. Each time I wake from the painful twilight, I'm wearing a new jumpsuit. Some of them are too big. Others are uncomfortably tight. Whoever it is that has me here is trying to keep me off-balance. Despite my best efforts to catch clues of my surroundings, I'm too disoriented to do it.

"I must apologize," the voice says as he spoons something toward my mouth. "I dropped a jar from the counter and it shattered." He knows exactly what he's doing. "So sorry."

I take a mouthful and swallow what tastes like warm baby food. Carrots. Maybe beets.

The voice pauses as he shovels the goop. "I believe I removed all the glass, but some of it may have gotten into your food here. Chew carefully, good man."

I suck down the beet/carrots as though some little functioning corner of my mind is telling me I am hungry. I should stop eating. I should refuse, but I slurp another spoonful, tasting the cold metal of the spoon and vague sweetness of the mush.

Another slurp. And another. Until a small shard of glass stabs the roof of my mouth. It sticks into the soft skin.

The blood pooling in my mouth tastes warm. I wince and try to remove the glass with my tongue before spitting it out onto the floor.

"Ooh!" The voice seems amused now, reacting to the pained face in front of him. "Perhaps I missed a shard? My apologies. I gather you're finished." He drops the spoon into the bowl and places it on a table next to him.

"Now," the voice slows and deepens. "You were clumsily suggesting you don't know anything. I suggest I don't believe you." The last four words hang in the air between us.

The blood pools in my mouth behind my lower front teeth. It's warm and thick. I inhale and, with the strength I have, spit. The mix of blood and saliva sprays onto the Voice and drips down my chin. It's hanging there from my lips.

"Who are you?" I try to suck back in the pink spittle and lick my lower lip with the back of my tongue.

"My friends," he begins, "what few I have of them, prefer to call me a saint. Or rather *The* Saint."

"Like that crappy 1990s Val Kilmer movie?"

"No. That film was horrid. I prefer the 1962 Roger Moore incarnation. It was on the telly," he laughs and sits quietly awaiting another sarcastic remark. I give him nothing.

The Saint grabs the chain between the thick iron cuffs on my wrists, the rough edge of the hammered cuff digging into my skin at the point where the bones in my wrist widen. I can feel the existing bruises deepening, as though I had been punched in the same spot repeatedly.

"Stand!" he commands. He is both the good cop and the bad cop.

He adjusts the leg irons attached to a metal eye hook in the floor. I lurch forward suddenly, feeling a yank on my arms as the chain between my hands is locked to the eye hook. I'm bent at the waist, doubled over in a sadistic involuntary yoga pose; my ankles and wrists bound to the same spot. The pressure on my lower back is spreading through my torso. The muscles along my spine and shoulders are screaming at me to stand. I can't. I whimper at the impossibility of this and it echoes against the concrete in the room. It's a sound I don't recognize as anything that would ever come from my mouth.

The Saint says nothing and leaves the room with a series of clicks and creaks at the door. It's quiet.

The lights go out.

Without sight, my sense of smell intensifies almost instantaneously. I can smell the carrots. I am sure I ate carrots. It's mixed with the odor of mildew and bleach. It's such an odd combination of smells. It's a welcome distraction.

How long have I been here? Somebody must be looking for me. My boss, my friends, Charlie...

From above me there's a long, inhuman moan and within seconds, an open-ended six inch pipe that drops a foot from the ceiling croaks to life and begins spitting water. I can't see the pipe from my yoga pose, but it's there. We've met before.

This time the water is cold and hits me in uncomfortable spurts. Large exhaust fans begin to spin and the air chills. There's a crackle from the intercom system.

"I forgot your water." The Saint is relentless.

Tensing against the rustle of the intercom, my back seizes. The thickness of the cramped muscle along the right side of my spine hardens. The suddenness of it makes me laugh in pain and reflexively wince.

He wants me to talk.

***

I wake up to a sting on my right cheek. I've been slapped conscious.

"What?" I ask with every bit of defiant anger I can muster. He doesn't answer me.

My eyes are watering and trying to adjust to the light, and I can see he's connecting something to an electrical cord in front me. He's plugging something into a socket. I can't see exactly what it is. My heartbeat accelerates and I am having trouble catching my breath. It's definitely something electrical. There's water. There's electricity.

What is he going to do to me now?

My eyes dart around the room again. *This is where I am going to die? Electrocuted in a dungeon? My body burned, tossed, and never found?*

"What do you want from me?" This time my question is more of a whimper.

Directly in front of me, on a small rolling table is a laptop computer.

On the screen is the website from a Houston television station. Channel 4. In the large video box at the center of the screen is what appears to be news footage of a speech by the man challenging my boss for the Governor's office. I can see an empty stage and lectern against the skyline of downtown Houston. The camera pans to the left to catch a group of dark colored SUV's slowing to the curb near the stage.

"I'd like for you to watch this." The Saint was again behind me. From over my shoulder he clicked the keyboard to bring the video full-screen. His breath warms my neck behind my ear. I exhale and the tension in my shoulders relaxes. The electricity is not for me.

On the screen is gubernatorial candidate Don Carlos Buell. He's a tall man with broad shoulders and an angular jaw. He appears deeply tanned with a shock of gray hair atop his head as he steps from an SUV and onto the grass flanked by shorter, lesser bespoke aides. As he crosses the grass with his long, effortless strides, he turns his body to the crowd and waves with both hands above his head.

Buell climbs the half dozen steps onto the temporary stage that fronts the downtown eastern skyline. It's elevated such that television and still photographers have to angle their cameras up at Buell, adding to his curb appeal.

Buell glad-hands a handful of local politicians and walks onto the stage and steps up to the lectern without an introduction.

Why does The Saint want me watching this? I start to shift in my seat and The Saint moves me.

"Watch."

Buell is quieting the crowd. The camera zooms in to focus more clearly on the candidate.

"*Thank you,*" he says, motioning again for the cheering crowd to lessen its enthusiasm. He shifts the flexible arm holding the mic. "*Muchas gracias amigos!*"

Someone in the crowd yells back an unintelligible encouragement. Buell smiles and points. He's a formidable opponent despite his lack of political experience. My boss is right to be worried about him.

"*My good friends,*" Buell eases into his prepared remarks. No TelePrompTer, no notes. "*It is so good to be back here in the wonderful city of Houston!*" He pauses and turns to admire the skyline that frames him. He turns back to the congregation. "*Look at this beacon of American ingenuity; the city known for energy and space exploration, technology and medical advancement. If this campaign gives me a heart attack I know where I'm heading. Right over there!*" The crowd laughs with him as he points southwest toward the Texas Medical Center. The camera widens and tightens again. There's a glint in Buell's eyes.

"*I have made this campaign about being an American. It's about Texas values and American idealism. I know both still exist in abundance here in Houston. I want to be the one who harnesses that capital which exists within every one of you. With your help we can, together, improve the lives of our families and neighbors. We can lift up those who need help without sacrificing that which we've worked hard to accumulate.*"

He pulls a white handkerchief from his jacket pocket and dabs away at the shine glistening on his forehead, waiting for the applause to stop before he continues.

"I am the son of a poor farmhand and a schoolteacher in the Valley. I did not always have the wealth I enjoy today. My riches are the very reason I choose to serve. I know there are other poor sons and daughters out there who have dreams. I want to help them realize those dreams. I want to give back to you what Texas and the United States of America has given to me." More applause. *"My daughter, Bella, said to me, 'Papa'—that's what she calls me—Papa, why should I vote for you?"*

The crowd laughs again. They seem enraptured.

"She tells me she knows I am a good father and businessperson. She wonders what would make me a good Governor."

Buell steps back from the mic, pauses, and bites his lower lip gently. He takes off his Italian cut suit jacket and hands it to an aide. He unbuttons his custom fit white cotton shirt at the collar and loosens the double Windsor knot of his tie. This is show. This is theatre. And I am his captive audience.

"I will be a good Governor because I will help Texans from the bottom up and not from the top down. From the bottom up! I have ninety days to convince you and your friends and your coworkers and your neighbors and anyone who will listen I should be your next Governor. I need your help. Will you help me?"

The crowd cheers and chants "BU-ELL, BU-ELL" affirming their willingness to follow and support their candidate. It lasts for two full minutes before Buell quiets them with a finger to his lips.

"Now, I know," his tone is softer and less excited, *"there are those out there who will tell you I cannot do what I promise. There are naysayers who believe Texas is better off with the cronyism and favoritism that exists today in Austin. You know what they don't know?"*

"What?" yells the crowd in unison.

"Do you know?"

"What?" This time louder.

"They don't know about you! They don't know about your concerns and worries. They don't know about how difficult it is to make a mortgage and pay for milk at the store. They don't know

about making a difference through hard work. *They don't know about working from the bottom up. They don't know these things because they don't listen! They haven't heard you. They don't want to hear you.*"

Buell raises his arms, expecting another cheer, but suddenly wrenches and collapses to the floor of the stage, like someone invisible punched him to the ground. There's a spray of what looks like blood coming from his chest. The delayed sound of a gunshot cracks like a backyard lightning strike.

What the hell???

My eyes involuntarily widen from the shock, hurting from the influx of light. The cheers are replaced with screams as the blood pools from underneath Buell's back. I don't think the cheap speakers on the laptop convey the terror in those voices.

The Saint, his breath on my neck again, reaches from behind me to stop the video and close the lid of the laptop. "Tell me about the iPod, Jackson," he whispers.

The iPod? *The iPod?* What does the iPod have to do with what I saw? How is the iPod connected to the assassination of a political candidate? How does he know about the iPod? Nobody is supposed to know about it. Nobody. I've done everything asked of me to keep it secret; to give it only to those for whom it is intended.

"What iPod?" I say, playing stupid.

"*The* iPod."

The lights are bright, and I think The Saint has turned on the heat. Maybe it's not the heat. There's sweat dripping down my back.

"I can't help you." *I won't help you.*

"London, Caracas, Omaha, Anchorage, Baton Rouge, Oklahoma City, Tallahassee, Rio. Can you help me now?" The Saint is snarling and he knows where I've been.

"If you're not going to tell me what you know about the iPod," he said, his breath hot against my left ear, "I am going to tell you what it is *I* know."

What does he know?

"You've taken at least eight trips in the last six months and on each said trip you carried a different iPod."

I say nothing.

***

I saw the first iPod months ago.

"I have a job for you," my boss told me. "It's an important job that requires a certain amount of discretion." My boss, the Governor of Texas, has a penchant for the dramatic. It's what makes him an effective politician.

"Okay," I told him. What else *would* I tell him? I value my job. At least I did six months ago when I accepted the assignment.

We were at the Governor's ranch located about an hour northwest of Austin. The sprawling 1500 acre estate ran along the Lampasas River in between Lampasas and Copperas Cove. It's a beautiful piece of rolling land dotted with mesquite, oak, pecan, and cedar trees.

It was my first time at the ranch and I was surprised by the invitation. There I was, sitting on the back porch of his Texas limestone retreat. It was one of two houses on the property. This was the main house. He'd brought us each a glass of blood red wine from the climate controlled closet. I refused his offer of a Cohiba, but he indulged. He puffed and sipped and we talked about the weather and the white tailed deer which ate the garden day lilies at night.

I fell into my job working for the Governor. He was in his second term and, through a friend of a friend, he hired me as part of his communications staff. In another life, I was a television reporter in Tyler, Texas and in San Antonio. I liked TV, but not enough. I didn't like being a radio deejay either, or a website sales representative, or the host of other jobs I tried. I always found myself restless and needing to move. After falling off of the grid for a couple of years, I made the jump to politics. It was either that or public relations. I picked what I believed was the lesser of two evils.

Within a couple of months, I was taken out of the press department and moved to the Governor's personal staff. I ran errands for him. I returned phone calls. I did whatever he needed me to do. I didn't question it. He told me I reminded him of himself when he was my age; ambitious but without direction.

I work hard. I'm thorough and dependable. I don't have any

family obligations to preoccupy me.

"I need there to be some communications with various friends of ours," the Governor said. He smiled and leaned into me, the cigar in the right corner of his mouth. "I can't really talk to these people in public, put them on the official calendar, or have them sign the guest register at the mansion. Understood?"

I nodded.

"Now I promise you there is nothing illegal here," he winked as he said it. "It's sensitive stuff. This could be good for you, you know. Maybe a promotion, more responsibility down the line." His Texas drawl curled the vowels, making his words sound almost lyrical. His tone reminded me of Andy Griffith in that old TV courtroom show, *Matlock*. The lawyer was always a step ahead, even if he seemed a beat behind. It was the drawl. It was the perfect cover for his brilliance.

"What is it?" I couldn't help but ask.

"Paperwork. Some digital documentation." He looked at me intently and licked a spot of wine from his upper lip. No smile. No pretense. I understood no follow up question was necessary.

He pulled the latest generation iPod from his pocket.

"So, you'll be doing some travel. You'll be taking an iPod like this one to a handful of places. When there's a trip to make, you'll know about it."

The word iPod sounded like 'ah-Pawd'. Lyrical. Almost.

The Governor sure knew how to spin a phrase, and the accent when always thicker when he was trying to sell something.

CHAPTER 2

My first trip was to London. It was a ten hour nonstop flight from Houston to London Heathrow. After the tiring early morning drive from Austin to Houston, I slept through most of the flight. I was next to the window, cramped and uncomfortable with the narrow seat. I had with me a carry-on bag with my laptop, a change of clothes, and the Governor's iPod. I'd also brought a small duffel bag with enough clothing and toiletries to last me the 48-hour length of the trip.

Once I cleared passport control, I walked down the stairs to baggage claim. At the bottom of the steps was an ATM. I withdrew a couple hundred British Pounds and waited for my bag. It was the last one off of the carousel.

I followed the signs to the exit and ground transportation. As I left baggage claim, I was hit by a mob of limo drivers holding signs. They were held back by a velvet rope, like paparazzi at a movie premiere. I unconsciously puffed my chest, stood a little straighter. I found the man holding the sign with my name: JACKSON QUICK.

"That's me," I said, pointing at the sign. The man, who looked to be of Middle Eastern descent, nodded and waved me around the rope. I followed him to the garage outside the terminal. He had a Bluetooth earpiece in his left ear and was chattering in Arabic.

He didn't offer to take either of my bags.

His car was a two-door Citroën DS3. It was small for a taxi, but whatever. It didn't matter. I was traveling light.

"Where you want me take you?" His English was broken but intelligible.

"Admiralty Arch."

"Okay," the driver said. "Good." He continued his conversation in Arabic.

Within minutes we were on the M4 traveling east into London's city center. At Brentford we merged onto the A4 into town. I was amazed by the amount of construction on the southern side of the highway. It looked like a series of life-sized Erector sets with one large contemporary office building after another. The skies were gray, almost blending into the steel of the construction.

Forty-five minutes after I climbed into the back of the DS3, I was climbing out. My right knee was stiff and ached from the long trip.

"Sixty." The driver was holding out his hand. "Cash." The light on his Bluetooth headset was flashing. He was still in the midst of a conversation.

I gave him seventy and grabbed my bags. The arch was directly ahead of me to my left, a beautiful old office building that marked one end of the Mall near Trafalgar Square. After looking at it for a moment to take it in, I slung my duffel onto my back and walked northeast toward Trafalgar.

I had to remind myself to look right before crossing the street. A small car whirred past me as I balanced myself on a curb.

Navigating the streets wasn't difficult. They were well-labeled: Spring Gardens, Kennard, and then Cockspur.

I laughed at the gold painted lettering above the large glass doors.

"THE TEXAS EMBASSY"

The large limestone building was once the home office of the White Star shipping line, owners of the Titanic. Now it was London's finest Tex-Mex cantina. I'd thought the Governor was joking when he told me the meeting place.

"You know," the Governor had said days earlier in between bites of a sausage and cheese kolache, "Texas did have an embassy in London for a while."

We were walking from the Governor's mansion to the Capitol

when he'd asked me to take the first trip. It was warm outside and he was wearing a polo shirt with khakis. Four Texas DPS troopers were following a half dozen steps behind providing security.

"From 1836 to 1845 The Republic of Texas had its own delegation in London, Paris, and Washington. We were our own country. The British even offered to guarantee our borders with the United States and with Mexico. Of course, we folded into the U.S., became a state, and the embassies shut down." The Governor was finished with the kolache and he'd slipped his hands into his pants pockets. His stride was effortless and he talked as if he'd lived through the events he now recalled with some nostalgic lamentation. This was an important trip he had told me.

Now I stood looking at the cantina for a moment before crossing the street and walking into its roughhewn interior. It was early for lunch and the tables were empty. Martina McBride's *Independence Day* was playing over the speakers in the high ceilings:

In front of the open kitchen were two large stucco columns. One read, "Caliente Y Fresco". Hot and Fresh. The other, "Tortillas". From the décor and smell of grilled steak, I thought for a moment I was back in Austin at Z'Tejas or Trudy's.

I sat at a table near the tortilla column next to a potted tree decorated with little white Christmas lights. I rubbed my hands on the lacquered pine table. My palms were sweaty.

On the table, there was a small tin holding packets of sugar and artificial sweetener and a drink menu. I decided to skip the drink. I needed my wits about me.

My bags were in the chair next to me. I wanted them close to me.

The waitress brought me a menu. My stomach warned me I wasn't particularly hungry. I settled for a chimichanga and a bottle of mineral water.

Since I'd sat down, two couples had entered the restaurant and found seats. Both of them looked like American tourists; the men in their golf shirts and shorts, the women in their cotton blouses and Capri pants. I took a sip of the water, its carbonation bubbled in my mouth. Then I saw him.

A well-dressed man with short gray hair and reflective aviator sunglasses walked in from the street and stood in the entry. He pulled the glasses from his eyes and stuck them in the breast pocket of his suit jacket, squinting as he scanned the room. His eyes settled on me, he nodded the half-nod of recognition men often share, and made his way to my table.

I could tell he was British before he spoke. His jacket and pants were tailored slim. His shirt was a tight checkerboard of blue and white, his tie a solid green. He smiled and his stained, crowded teeth gave it away.

"Mr. Quick?" he asked, sliding into the seat across from me. He kept on his jacket. I assumed the meeting would be short.

"Yes." I rubbed the dampness from my palm and extended a handshake. His grip was firm but non-threatening. He looked me in the eyes. I always measure a man by how he shakes hands. If he looks me in the eyes, he's off to a good start. "And you are?" I ask.

"Mr. Davis." I assumed it was not his real name. "First time in London?"

"Yes."

I'd always imagined a trip here, though under far different circumstances. I'd gotten my passport because Charlie and I were planning a vacation through Europe after the election was over. It was her idea. London, Paris, Rome, Barcelona. We'd buy Eurail passes and stay in cheap hotels. I felt a tinge of guilt being here without her, but it was my job. I couldn't tell her about it. I told her I was in El Paso meeting with the county party chairperson.

"Where are you staying?" Davis asked, but I don't think he really cared.

"Kensington," I said. "Near Earl's Court."

"Nice." He leaned his woolen elbows on the table. "Many wonderful hotels there. It's convenient if not centrally located."

"What do you do, Mr. Davis?"

The waitress arrived with my plate and warned me it was hot. I touched the plate anyway. It *was* hot. Seeing me ignore her warning, she smiled and rolled her eyes.

"Everybody does that," she laughed and asked Davis what he'd like, if anything.

"A margarita please," he smiled at me as he ordered. It sounded odd hearing someone with a British accent order a *mah-*

gah-reeter. "I hear they're not to be missed," he leaned back in his chair and adjusted his coat. Maybe his visit with me would be longer than I thought.

"You asked me something, Mr. Quick?"

I studied his expression, which gave away nothing. His face was smooth, the pores small. He took good care of himself, apart from neglected orthodonture. His eyes were bright, telling me he knew more about me than I would ever learn about him.

"What do you do?"

"Hmmm," he tapped his fingers on the edge of the table as though he were playing piano. "I suppose whatever it is needs doing, Mr. Quick."

"Must keep you busy," I remarked. I took my fork and dug into the shell of the chimichanga. Steam rose from the shredded chicken inside the fried shell. The waitress brought his margarita, on the rocks, salted on the rim of the glass.

"It depends on the season young man." Davis smiled and took a sip of his drink. "Quite good. Never too early in the morning for a good drink, wouldn't you say?"

I nodded and chewed the chimichanga, burning the roof of my mouth. Davis thumbed the salt from above his lip. He licked it off as though he were preparing to turn the page of a book.

"So, Mr. Quick," he pushed his drink toward the middle of the table and began his concerto again with his fingers, "you have something for me?"

I could hear the condescension in his voice. He was much older than I, and obviously more experienced in cloak and dagger exchanges performed over late morning alcohol and European Tex-Mex.

"Yes, I guess I do." I put down my fork, wiped my mouth, and turned to my carry-on. I unzipped it and pulled out the iPod, turning it on for the first time since receiving it.

Davis reached across the table with an open hand. I hesitated.

"There's a code, Mr. Davis," I reminded him. "You need to give me the code. I will unlock it, then it's yours."

"Of course." A crocodile smile. "Zero, Three, Zero, Two."

I tapped the numbers onto the screen and the device unlocked.

I passed the iPod to Davis. "It's yours."

Without saying another word, Davis slipped the iPod into his interior breast pocket and pushed back from the table. He fixed his jacket and turned to leave. I half expected him to turn around as he walked out of the restaurant. He didn't. He was gone and it was as if we'd never met.

***

"Each trip was financed through a bank account connected to some powerful people."

I say nothing.

"What you're doing would be considered," The Saint pauses for effect, "sedition."

Sedition? What does he mean?

I flinch as he moves behind me.

"I want to know what was on those iPods." The Saint is behind my right ear now. "What did you give to your contacts? I know *you* know what was on them. At least one of them was synched to a computer before you delivered them to your contacts."

Synched? He's knows 'at least one of them was synched'? How can he know this?

Somewhere I am finding the strength to resist the temptation to talk. Part of it is that I am so tired I don't have the energy. Part of it is I'm expecting death regardless. It doesn't matter.

I shake my hanging head and sigh. I catch a whiff of licorice and bleach before I exhale. Without thinking about it, I talk. I refuse to die a victim.

"Lyle Lovett," I mumble.

"What?"

"The iPod. Maybe it's Lyle Lovett," I chuckle without looking at him. "You know, *You're not from Texas, but Texas wants you anyway?*" I ape in my best crooner's voice.

"You can play these ridiculous games," he sneers. "Let's remember I am the one with the information here. I know you, you don't know me. I know about the iPods, I know about Charlie, about your childhood friend Hank, and those couple of years after college you'd rather forget."

Hank? How does he know about Hank? Nobody is supposed

to know. Nobody.

"You might think you know me," I snap through my quickening pulse. "Obviously you've got connections. If you knew half as much as you claim to know, you wouldn't be trying to get information from me now. There's clearly stuff you *don't* know. I'm not helping you figure out what that stuff is. Do to me whatever you want."

"Okay." His thick mitt of a hand pats me on right shoulder. I jerk involuntarily. Despite my verbal bravado, the constant threat of pain frightens me.

"I'm going to need you to hold still," he warns a moment before there's the pinch of a needle in my neck and the slight burn of whatever it is he's injecting into my bloodstream. I don't have to time to react before I'm disoriented. He's saying something to me, but I can't really understand him.

Who is this man? What does he really want from me? Who is he working for?

I was a courier. That's all. I did what was asked of me. Now I find myself losing consciousness again. The room begins to wobble. He's pressing numbers on a cell phone. He mumbles.

Is he talking to someone on the phone?

The lights go out. It's quiet. I'm falling asleep. Or dying.

***

In the twilight between deep sleep and waking up, a series of images flash through my mind: Charlie laughing that throaty giggle of hers, Don Carlos Buell being shot, an empty airport lounge in Caracas, me banging on the metal of a small enclosed space and screaming for help, the Governor handing me a stack of iPods almost too big to carry, my parents catching fire, Sir Laurence Olivier as Szell drilling into my tooth and asking me, "Is it safe?"

I jerk awake at the moment Szell's drill hits my tooth. I'm groggy and have a pounding headache. My tongue is thick and pasty. There's an ache in my lower back.

I'm in a burnt orange UT T-shirt and white boxers, lying on my back staring at the white wainscoting which covers the ceiling. The flush mounted fan is spinning slowly, the pull chain tapping against the housing. I can feel the breeze on my legs. Sunlight is slipping in through the gaps in the open mini-blinds on the pair of double hung windows to my right, reflecting off of the dust floating in the air and the white exposed brick walls of the room

I'm in my apartment.

My apartment? How did I get here? Was it all a dream? Maybe it was a dream. Maybe I had some bad beer, some weird dreams, and now I have a horrible hangover. It's gotta be a dream.

I sit up in my bed and spin to put my feet on the worn pine floor. The thin planks are scratched and pock marked. The stain is uneven and faded, but the floor feels good on my bare feet. As I stand I lose my balance. Man, they need to clean the tap lines at the bar. The beer was something nasty.

I walk the short distance to my bathroom and drop my boxers to sit on the toilet. I'm too dizzy to stand. I rub my toes against the grout in the two inch tile that lines the bathroom floor. I'm home. I am safe.

I stand up, flush, and shuffle to the sink. I flip the tap and bend over to cup the cool water in my hands. I splash it on my face and feel my skin tighten against the chill.

Still hunched at the waist I blindly grab a clean towel from the rack next to the mirrored cabinet in front of me. I dry my face and exhale. My knees feel weak, my lower back hurts, and my head pounds with each heartbeat. I can feel it in my temples.

I drop the towel to the edge of the sink and look at myself in the mirror. My eyes are bloodshot and I have deep, dark circles that run from the bridge of my nose to the edges of my face near my throbbing temples. I'm thinner somehow. Maybe it's the thick stubble on my chin and along my jaw line. I thought I shaved yesterday.

My thick wavy mop of brown hair is unkempt and seems darker. I rub my hands through it. The strands are heavy with oil and grease. I'll need to take a shower before I go anywhere.

There's a small circular bruise on the left side of my neck. I rub it. It's sore.

I open the mirror and pull out a bottle of migraine medicine. I push down on the cap and spin it open, shake out two caplets, and pop them in my mouth. After putting the bottle back in the medicine cabinet, I bend over to slurp from the faucet.

I don't think I've ever been this hung-over.

My apartment is a two bedroom near downtown Austin. It's expensive. I don't spend money on much else, and I like living so close to work. I still have a lot of the money my parents left to me when they died. It got me through the lean years as a $12,000 a year reporter in Tyler. I've got maybe $350,000 left. I only use a little of it here and there. I feel guilty spending it.

I walk out into the combination family room/kitchen and yank open the refrigerator. There's a carton of orange juice, a tub of margarine, a small can of Red Bull, and some leftover takeout from Iron Works Barbecue. I pull the carton of juice to my mouth and take a couple of gulps before I taste its bitterness. It's sour. I smell it and wince. The expiration date tells me it's got three days. *What the hell?*

The phone rings.

I trudge back to my bed and sit on its edge to pick up my cell, which apparently I left on the oak nightstand. San Antonio area code.

"Hello?" I rub my temples with my left hand as I hold the phone in my right. I'm looking at the digital clock next to the bed. The LED numbers announce 3:45.

It's that late?

"Jackson Quick?" I immediately recognize the voice. *The Saint.*

I can't speak.

"Okay, Jackson, my good man," The Saint continues in an even, disturbing tone. "I'm going to explain this to you slowly. You are not to hang up. You are not to take notes. I want you to remember what it is I am about to tell you."

I say nothing. I can't. I physically can't. The pounding at my temples is suddenly blinding.

"I'll assume your silence implies your consent."

What is going on?

"I am aware of everything you do, Jackson." There is the sound of street traffic in the background. "I am watching you. You are not to tell anyone."

This is not a dream, is it?

"I will know if you *snitch*, as they say," he makes the word *snitch* sound particularly vile. "I will not be pleased with you. As for your whereabouts for the last five days..."

Five days? I've lost five days?

"You've been ill," he explained. "While you were with me, I sent text messages from your phone to anyone who tried to contact you."

He had my phone and my keys.

"If you fail to comply..." The Saint pauses, in the distance there's what sounds like the air brakes of city bus, "...we'll repeat our question and answer session."

"Why did you let me go?"

It's the only thing I can think to say. I can feel a clammy sweat forming on my forehead. My stomach feels tight. There's an acidic ache in my chest. Bullies have always made me want to puke.

"You'll be of more use to me this way."

"Useful for what?"

There's the honk of a car horn and the line goes silent. He's hung up. I check the number on my phone and hit redial. Maybe he'll answer.

It rings five times.

"Hello?" It's a woman's voice on the other end. She has a thick Texas drawl which catches me off guard.

I'm not sure what to say. "Uh, yeah. Where am I calling?"

"Dude," the woman sounds incredulous. "This is a pay phone at the Stop N Go on Sahara Drive. You probably have the wrong number."

"Are you in San Antonio?"

"No, Sahara Drive in Austin." She hangs up.

I sit on the edge of my bed holding the phone. My mind is racing through my options, though it seems I have none. Unconsciously rubbing the soreness from my right knee, I try to evaluate my situation.

I can't tell anyone where I've been for five days. I'm in danger of being kidnapped again. The iPods I've been faithfully delivering all over the world are somehow connected to the assassination of the man who wants my boss's job. Whatever information is downloaded onto those iPods is treasonous.

I've got to figure out what is on those iPods. I need to draw the connection between that information and the shooting. Maybe, if I can do that, The Saint will leave me alone. He, and whoever he is working for, will let me go back to my life. I can focus on my future with Charlie.

Charlie!

It seems like more than five days since I've seen her. It feels more like a year. Actually, I feel like I haven't slept in a year. I fall back onto the bed and stare up at the spinning fan. If I focus on a single spot long enough, I can see the individual blades as they turn counterclockwise. It's a welcome distraction.

I need to see Charlie.

***

"I have missed you sooo much!" Charlie's grip around my neck is tight. I don't want her to let go. "I'm glad you're feeling better." Charlie loosens her hold and moves back to look me in the eyes. She brushes my hair off my forehead. Her fingernails tickle.

"I've missed you too." I have. She has no idea how much. "I'm sorry about leaving you at the bar on Thursday. I—"

"I know," she interrupts and turns to lead me to her sofa. Her left hand grabs my right. "You felt sick. I got your text when I was still in the Ladies' room. I was a little pissed off you left me there, but I got over it."

I sit on the soft chenille of her overstuffed sofa and she straddles me, sitting on my lap with her legs tucked behind her. I rest my hands on her hips. She's wearing a gray T-shirt and jeans. I thumb the copper rivets on the pockets of her jeans. It's good to be with her.

She has her hands on my shoulders. Her T-shirt reads "Bush Cheney '04". She's more politically conservative than I am. I'm right-leaning moderate. We both, though, found our way onto the Governor's staff ahead of his reelection.

"You look like you've lost weight, poor baby," she noted. She pouts her lips and frowns, running the back of her hand along the right side of my face. "I wish you'd have let me come and nurse you back to health."

"Yeah, well, I didn't want you to see me like that." I'm guessing my kidnapper had dissuaded her.

She leans forward and slides her hands onto my chest. Her lips meet mine and we kiss for a few moments. She's an aggressive kisser and I like it. She can tell.

Twenty minutes later we're cuddled together under a blanket on the sofa. I'm lying on my back and she's curled around me, her left leg draped over me. We're holding hands, playing with our fingers.

It's dark outside and the soft lamplight in her apartment radiates warmth. There are framed reproductions of French impressionists and wrought iron sconces boasting thick candles. The walls are beige with thick crown molding. Her furniture is a mix of antique, glass, and overstuffed, floral-patterned chairs. I call it ultra-feminine. She calls it shabby chic.

"You broke a nail," I pointed out. The index finger on her right hand is missing its usual manicure. I rub the top of her finger with mine.

"Yeah," she sighs. "I'm going to need to get a fill." She shifts on the sofa and lays her head on my chest. I missed her. Before I get to figuring out what the hell happened to me and what I have to do with an assassination, I need a minute to decompress.

"Hey," I ask as nonchalantly as I can muster, "what's going to happen to the race now that Buell is dead? I guess the debate is cancelled?"

Charlie whips her head around to face me with a look of disbelief on her face. "What do you mean Buell is *dead?*" Her eyebrows are scrunched together and her eyes are drilling holes into mine. I can feel the immediate tension in her body.

"Wasn't he shot at a rally in Houston? Wasn't he killed?"

"Oh," she relaxes. "No. You freaked me out. He's alive."

"But I thought..."

"No," she lays her head back down. "He was hit in the shoulder. He was hurt bad but he lived. He's already out of the hospital and campaigning again. He's got this huge sling on his arm. It was on the news this morning."

"Wow, I'm glad he's not dead. Do they know who did it?"

"Yeah," Charlie bites at the stub of a nail on her index finger. "A guy who is part of the Texas Independence movement. He has a website dedicated to secession."

"What?" *Secession? Is that the connection?*

"Some guy with a website who talks about Texas seceding from the United States. He thinks Buell would be a federal lapdog if he gets elected."

"So...?"

"So he shot Buell." She pats my stomach with her hand. "You really *were* out of the loop."

"Guess so," I said, only half listening to her as she talks about her policy struggles on the Capitol floor.

Secession. The iPods. My boss. My *treacherous* trips. I need to get some sleep so I can more clearly process all of this.

First thing in the morning I have work to do.

***

Charlie mumbles goodbye to me as I snake my body out from under hers on the sofa. I kiss her on the head. I want to stay with her, but know I can't.

"Going for a run?" she asks groggily through her fog.

"Something like that," I mumble.

I slip on some khakis, a Kinky Friedman T-shirt, and a pair of comfortable Merrell shoes. I grab my backpack and trot down the stairs to the sidewalk. My back still aches and I have to slow my pace. I walk a few blocks to the McDonald's on MLK north of the Capitol and order a coffee. It's a little out of the way, but it's a lot cheaper than Starbucks and equally good. I grab a seat in a beige plastic booth and pull my netbook from the backpack. I pop open the screen and connect to the free Wi-Fi network, then pull a set of ear buds from the backpack and pop them in my ears.

I go to Google and type DON CARLOS BUELL SHOOTER.

A series of recent news articles fill the screen. I move the cursor to VIDEO and click. A new list appears; the first link is from Channel 4 in Houston, the same station that carried the shooting, so I click it.

My netbook's processor isn't the best around. It takes a few seconds to load the new page with a large video player in the middle of the screen. The caption beneath the player reads, RIPLEY

DENIES SHOOTING GUBERNATORIAL CANDIDATE.

I press the play button, hit the full screen tab, and wait for the video to buffer. There are two anchors on the screen. I vaguely recognize the woman. She's blonde and older than I remember her. The man speaks first.

"*Our top story tonight on 4 News is an exclusive interview with the man charged with trying to assassinate gubernatorial candidate Don Carlos Buell.*"

"*4 News reporter George Townsend,*" the woman anchor cut in, "*sat down with suspect Roswell Ripley for his first televised interview since being arrested hours after the shooting. He joins us live from outside the Harris County jail downtown. George?*"

The reporter is standing in front of the jail, his shirt sleeves rolled up to his elbows. His tie is knotted but loosened, a contrived look to make it appear he's been working hard, gathering the news. He has thick blonde hair he parts to the side and wears round, frameless eyeglasses. He looks tall, though that's always hard to tell on television without a frame of reference. People always told me I looked heavier and shorter on T.V. I never knew how to respond.

"*Roswell Ripley says he's being framed. He says he's a target of the federal government and the liberal media and he had nothing to do with the attempted assassination of Don Carlos Buell.*" The reporter stands still for a moment, holding his position until the taped portion of his story rolls.

The video begins with a shot of Ripley in leg irons and handcuffs, being led into the small interview room at the jail. The reporter is talking about how *exclusive* the on-camera meeting is. News people like that word, *exclusive*. There's a sound bite with Ripley.

"*I didn't do it,*" Ripley shuffles in his chair, seemingly uncomfortable with the restraints. He bangs his wrists on the small plastic table in front of him. "*They know I didn't do it. They need a fall guy. I am that guy. Pure and simple.*"

"*Who is 'they' Mr. Ripley?*" the reporter asks. "Who *wants you to be a fall guy?*"

"*The government, boy!*" Ripley seems irritated with the question, as though the reporter should have known the answer. His face is long and gaunt. I can tell he's a smoker from the yellow in his graying hair. *"The damn government. I'm telling you, anybody who speaks their mind against the federal government better watch out. They'll get you."*

The video switches from the interview room to a full-screen shot of a website. The reporter explains the website is run by Ripley and it advocates Texas seceding from the United States.

"TEXASECESSION dot com is Ripley's online contribution to a growing underground movement that challenges the constitutionality of certain federal laws as they relate to state's rights."

"If I didn't have a website," Ripley says as the video returns to a close-up of his face, *"they'd never have known about me. I wouldn't be here."*

The reporter's voice continues underneath more pictures from Ripley's website and file video from the shooting scene. *"4 News has learned that Roswell Ripley is a U.S. Army veteran. He served in the first Gulf War and he was a sniper."*

On the screen now is what looks like a police report. *"We have also learned forensic testing of the weapon believed to have been used in the shooting revealed fingerprints belonging to Ripley. The weapon, a Knights SR-XM110 Rifle, was registered to Ripley five years ago. Ripley contends it was stolen a week before the shooting, but he admits he did not file a police report."*

"That rifle cost me $20,000," Ripley says in the video, leaning forward at the desk, snarling at the reporter. *"If I go tell the cops I'm missing a weapon that costs half as much as they make in a year, they're gonna ask me a ton of questions and they ain't gonna help me find it. It wouldn't be worth reporting."*

The video ends with the reporter standing live outside the jail, figuratively patting himself on the back for his *exclusive*, and mentioning Ripley's next court appearance. The video ends and the 4 News Houston website offers me a chance to share the report on Facebook and Twitter.

I move the cursor to the search bar on the top left of the screen and type TEXASECESSION. A list of options descends on the screen. I click on the first option which takes me to the homepage for Ripley's site.

There's a flash animation featuring a waving Texas flag with accompanying audio of a fife and drum composition. Ripley's face slowly replaces the flag. He has a solemn look on his face.

"*Honor the Texas flag,*" he says. He's staring directly into the camera and it's a little uncomfortable to watch. "*I pledge allegiance to thee, Texas, one state under God, one and indivisible.*" It's the Texas pledge. Children in Texas public schools always recite it right after saying the pledge of allegiance to the U.S. flag.

Ripley disappears and gives way to the white background of the homepage, with a photograph of the San Jacinto monument, which commemorates Texas' victory over Mexico in its battle for independence. It lists a series of options along the top of the screen:

HOME   FAQ   FACTS   HOW TO HELP   STORE

I choose FACTS and the screen changes. At the top of the screen the site gives credit to "Brother Secessionist Site TexasSecede.com" and lists a series of "facts" about the secessionist movement in Texas.

The first explains, contrary to popular myth, Texas does not reserve the right to secede in its constitution. It does state, however, "*Texas is a free and independent State, subject only to the Constitution of the United States...*" (note it does *not* state "*...subject to the President of the United States...*" or "*...subject to the Congress of the United States...*" or "*...subject to the collective will of one or more of the other States...*").

It's interesting but not earth shattering. I scroll through the arguments for secession until I near the bottom of the list. There's a question that asks how Texas would benefit from secession.

The website answers it by contending, "In many ways. Over the past century-and-a-half the United States government has awarded itself ever more power to meddle with the lives, liberty, and property of the People of Texas. Sapping Texans' wealth into a myriad of bureaucratic, socialist schemes both in the U.S. and abroad, the bipartisan despots in Washington persist in expanding the federal debt and budget deficits every year. Texans would indeed gain much by reclaiming control of their State, their property, their liberty, and their very lives, by refusing to participate further in the fraud perpetrated by the Washington politicians and bureaucrats. By restoring Texas to an independent republic, Texans would truly reclaim a treasure for themselves and their progeny."

Wow. Is that what this is about? Do the iPods have something to do with preparing Texas for a secession attempt?

Am I helping arrange the downfall of my country?

The Governor has half-jokingly hinted at secession, as former Governor Rick Perry did in 2009. That can't be what he's really planning. I always assumed it to be rhetoric on both sides. It's distraction politics to talk about secession.

Isn't it?

I click the back button a couple of times and go to News 4 Houston's news team link, locate reporter George Townsend's picture and click again. In the midst of his self-aggrandizing biography I find his email address and his direct phone line. I type them into my cell phone, save them, and drop my small laptop back into my bag.

There's more to this. It can't be this simple. Since Townsend is the only one who's talked to Ripley, he may be the only one who can help me put the pieces together.

***

"Is this George Townsend?" I ask. I'm leaning against a parking meter on the corner of MLK and San Antonio and the traffic is noisy. I should have stayed inside the McDonalds.

"Yes," he says. "Who is this?"

"I need to talk to you about the interview you did with Roswell Ripley."

"What about it?" he asks. It sounds like he is typing on a keyboard.

"Is there a way I can see the whole interview, you know, the parts you didn't air?"

"Probably not," he says, sounding a little irritated. "Are you an attorney?"

"No."

"Well, we don't keep unused portions of interviews and we certainly don't send them out to viewers."

"I understand, but I am gonna guess you wouldn't get rid of that interview. You probably have an unedited copy on your desk alongside other big interviews you don't want to erase."

"Fair enough," he says. The typing has stopped. "Who did you say you are?"

"What?" A truck passes by me and I can't hear.

"Who are you?"

"I can't tell you that yet."

"Look, I don't have time to play games with you. If you have information you think might help me on this story, maybe I can help you. This mysterious stranger act is overdone."

"Okay," I relent, sensing he's about to hang up on me. "I'm a former TV reporter. I now work in state government, and I may have some information for you. I need to know if Ripley said anything of interest you cut from the story."

Silence. Another truck passes me and turns onto MLK. The puff of exhaust from its tailpipe is suffocating. I cough.

"I can't let you see the unaired portion," he says finally. "I could get in trouble for that. I can tell you he rambled on about his son being the key to everything."

"His son?"

"Yes," he says. He's typing again. "His son. He kept telling me his son was the real reason behind the shooting. He said his secession website was a convenient cover for the government. It made him an easy scapegoat. His son was the real story and if I could find his son, I could find the real shooter."

"Have you talked to his son?" I walk back towards the McDonalds, noticing the large bronze longhorn that sits in front of the façade. I'm not sure how I missed it before. It's an enormous homage to the UT mascot Bevo.

"No."

"Why not?"

"Because the guy is crazy," Townsend answers. "He's a conspiracy theorist and fringe thinker. All the evidence points to him. He's a loon who's grasping at straws. I don't know if he even has a son."

"You need to find out," I tell him. "When you do, you can call me back."

"Wait!" he almost shouts at me. "I thought you had information for me. This is a quid-pro-quo thing, right?"

"Find the son, and I'll help you." I stop at the door to the

McDonalds, my hand on the handle. "You have my cell from caller ID right?"

"Yeah, I've got it."

He hangs up and I find the end of the line at the counter. I need more coffee.

***

Caracas Maiquetía International Airport is about 15 miles north of the city on the edge of the Caribbean Sea. It was my second trip for the Governor and I'd hoped to get into the city, but my instructions were to meet my contact at the airport and catch the next flight back to Miami and Texas.

Still groggy from my nap on the flight, I passed by rows of blue cushioned seats at the departure gates lining the international terminal. Beyond the floor-to-ceiling glass panels that framed the long hallway, I could see the sloping green foothills which separated the coast from the steep Cerro El Avila Mountains.

I rolled my carry-on past a Duty Free Shop and noticed its shelves were empty. The shop was open, there was an attendant at the cash register, but he had nothing to sell.

Embargo?

I kept moving toward customs.

After checking through immigration and withdrawing a few thousand Bolivar from an ATM, I found a small Venezuelan Café and sat at an empty table. I watched the people passing by, rolling their luggage along the reflective white floor tile. The large metal lettering on the wall read "Simon Bolivar", the airport's official namesake. Bolivar was the George Washington of South America. He'd freed six countries from Spanish rule. His nickname was El Liberator.

He was a secessionist.

I'd burned my tongue on a small cup of dark coffee when I felt his tap on my shoulder.

"*Hola mi amigo,*" he said as I turned to face him. "Hello my friend. My name is Juan Garcia." My contact was short and overweight, his black hair combed back and gelled. His skin was bronze; tanned but not excessively so, and he was clean shaven. His eyes were bright and his smile was nicely framed by his full cheeks.

Juan was wearing brown leather sandals, tan linen pants, and a loose fitting sky blue T-shirt. On his wrist was what looked like an expensive stainless steel watch. He had large gold rings on his middle and index fingers. I could feel their weight as I shook his hand. "*Mucho gusto*," I told him I was pleased to meet him and offered him the empty chair at the table. "*Me llamo* Jackson."

"*Yo se*," he knew. "*Habla Espanol?*"

"Only enough to get me into trouble," I admitted. I ran the tip of my tongue against the back of my teeth and felt the tiny blisters that had already formed.

"*Esta bien.* I speak English well enough."

"Your English *esta muy bueno*, Senor Garcia."

"You are drinking our fine café?" he asked and turned to get the attention of the waitress. He ordered two more drinks and turned back around.

"You know, Jackson, that café used to be our biggest product here." He leaned on the table with both elbows. He was still smiling. "But as we became more of a place for petróleo, our café became less important. Still, we have outstanding café, especially from our border with Colombia."

The waitress arrived with two small cups, steam rising from the bone china.

"I order for you the best of Venezuela. This is Tachira. *Esta muy fuerte.* It is very strong and rich. It's hard to find in your country. There are many things your country does not get," he said, leaning back in his seat.

"What do you mean?"

"*Petroleo por ejemplo.* For example you make ten percent of the world's oil but you consume a quarter of it. You are the planet's biggest user of fossil fuels, and yet you are the ones who complain the most about using it. Maybe your Governor is on to something."

"I don't understand," I said. "What do you mean?"

"Let's try the Tachira," he said, changing the subject.

Juan picked up the china from the small saucer and toasted me with his cup. I followed his lead and burned my tongue a second time. He saw me wince.

"*Caliente*, no?" He smirked, blew the steam from the café, and

41

took a small sip. His smile wasn't quite as engaging and the light melted from his eyes as he pulled the cup from his lips and gently set it on the saucer.

"Now, Mr. Jackson Quick," his accent was suddenly gone and his English diction was flawless. "I believe you have something for me."

I reached down to unzip my backpack, pulled out the iPod and asked him for the code.

"One Two One Nine," he said. The amiability was gone, and I could tell Mr. Juan Garcia was a man of business first, a genial host second.

I punched the numbers on the screen, slid the UNLOCK bar with my index finger and handed him the iPod. He flipped it over to look at the back, ran his thumb across it and stood to slip it in his pants pocket.

"*Muchas gracias,*" he said and walked away. By the time I turned to watch him leave, he'd already disappeared into the crowd of travelers crossing the terminal. He never explained what he meant about my Governor and, like my contact in London, he stiffed me for the check.

CHAPTER 3

I shift on the uncomfortable seat at my fast food booth. My right knee aches. McDonald's coffee may be as good as Starbucks, but the decor isn't nearly as comfortable. Maybe if I were into jazz fusion and the rainforest I'd put up with the expensive java in exchange for more plush seating.

After twenty minutes of searching variations of Ripley's name, I can't find anything that would help me find his son. I'm getting frustrated and ready to head back to my apartment, when my phone rings.

The number is restricted. I figure it might be the reporter, George Townsend calling me back. Sometimes newsrooms will have blocked numbers.

"What did you find out about Ripley?" I ask, fully expecting to hear Townsend's voice on the other end.

"What do you want with Mr. Ripley?" The voice is deep and resonant. It's him. Again. *The Saint.*

"Uh, I uh, I-I want to know how I'm connected to the shooting. He's the shooter. I want to know what's going on." I gulp past the thick lump that's instantaneously formed in my throat. I can feel a cool sweat forming on my forehead. I push what's left of the coffee toward the edge of the table.

"What do you want to know?" Matter of fact. Like he's going to help me now.

Right.

"He claims his son is involved. Who is his son?" I have

nothing to lose by asking.

"How is it you know?" A change in tone. Surprise maybe?

"I just do."

"Has that reporter, George Townsend, been feeding you this information?"

"How did *you* know *that?*"

"I told you, Jackson," he pauses, "I am watching everything you do, my good man. From your phone calls, to your work on the internet in a booth at McDonalds, I know what you're doing. Might I suggest McDonalds is not particularly healthy. Eating there too much could shorten your life."

I whip around to look over my shoulder toward the front counter. There's a young couple and an elderly man sitting here. Where is he?

"I'm outside, Jackson." He can see me. Holy crap. He can *see* me.

I'm white-knuckling the phone and turn to look out the window toward MLK. On the corner, near the parking meter where I stood a half hour ago, he is there. A big man, wearing a long sleeve black shirt or jacket with dark pants. The sun is behind him and so I can only make out his figure. He waves at me.

"Why are you asking me any questions if you already know what I'm doing?" I can feel my knee bouncing up and down reflexively. I'm biting the inside of my cheek. I turn away from the window. I can't look at him.

"Old habit, I guess." He laughs. "Look, chap. Ripley may *not* be the shooter. You're onto something there. His son has nothing to do with this. Stay away from him."

"Who are you? Why should I believe you?"

"I am your guardian angel, Jackson. *Your* saint, so to speak. You really don't have a choice."

I turn back around to look out the window. He's gone.

I have got to figure out a way to lose him and find Ripley's son.

***

I call Charlie from a pay phone four blocks south of the Capitol near the corner of Congress and Eighth. "I need to get to

Houston." It's not easy finding a payphone anymore. I left my cell phone in the bottom of a trash bin in McDonalds. I'm due for an upgrade anyway and, right now, I can't take any chances.

"Why?" She sounds confused or maybe annoyed I am asking her to drop what she's doing and drive me 3 hours southeast. "Don't you need to be at work or something?"

"No," I lie. I've completely forgotten about work. I'll need to call in sick again or something. "I've got another day off. I need to get to Houston."

"Why not take your car?" She makes a good point. I don't want to tell her than I can't take my car because I'm being followed and tracked.

"I need new tires," I lie again. "Can't risk getting a flat." I don't think I am a very convincing liar.

"Well," she sighs. "I wish I could, Jackson, but I can't. I've got too much to do here at the Capitol."

"Okay," I try to sound dejected. "I'll figure it out. I'll call you later. Love you."

"Love you too," she purrs. "Hey, what number is this you're calling me from? I don't recognize it."

"I lost my cell," I say. "I'll explain later. Gotta go."

I say goodbye again, hang up, and weigh my options. I could take a bus. There are plenty of options there, but once I get to Houston, I am stuck at the terminal. I drop in another thirty-five cents and dial my friend Bobby.

"Dude," I say in as pathetically friendly a voice as I can muster. "I need your help."

"Of course you do," he laughs. Bobby is a good guy. He works for a state representative from Lufkin and is as loyal as the day is long. We met shortly after I started working for the Governor and, when I am not with Charlie, we hang out a lot. He loves football and gets me great seats to UT games. I buy him a lot of beer.

"I've got to get to Houston today and can't take my car."

"What about Charlie?"

I knew he'd ask me that. He doesn't like her. He says he doesn't trust her and tells me often any girl *that* hot cannot be good news.

Bobby and I could be brothers. We often get mistaken for one another. Women who look like Charlie have never been interested in him, while I've had my share of attractive girlfriends. He's jealous. If Charlie had liked him instead of me, it would be a different story.

"She's got too much work," I tell him.

"Sure," he grunts. "What's in Houston?"

"I have a meeting." I'm being honest with him. Sort of. I do need to meet with the reporter, George Townsend. I'm hopeful that by the time I get to Houston, he'll have found Ripley's son. "It can't wait. It's at a television station."

"Campaign thing?" "You could say that." I don't want to tell him any more than what he needs to know. No need to risk his safety further than I'm doing by asking him for a ride. "Meet me in an hour?"

He agrees and hangs up. Hurriedly, I walk a couple of blocks west to Lavaca Street, and spend the next thirty minutes at a cell phone store. I need a cheap phone with a new phone number. The salesperson doesn't seem to understand my sense of urgency, but I manage to get everything set up in time to grab a couple of sandwiches and Dr. Peppers and meet Bobby at the corner of Guadalupe and West Eleventh. He's on time and seems grateful for the lunch.

"Ain't nothin' dude," I say, sliding into the passenger seat of his 2009 Mazda 3.

It's a comfortable car. It fits Bobby; sensible with a slight edge of cool. Though, like him, the car pretends to be cooler than it really is.

I pull my sandwich from the bag and peel back the wax paper. I take a bite and suddenly realize how hungry I am. I can't remember the last time I ate. Between bites I uncap the Dr. Pepper and swallow a couple of gulps. I wipe my mouth with a napkin, ball it up, and put it in the cup holder.

"Don't mess up my car," Bobby says, looking at the crumpled napkin. "I had it detailed." He smiles and spins the steering wheel to merge onto Highway 290 towards Houston.

"I'll clean up my mess," I say. "And I'll pay for gas."

"That was a given," Bobby states. He takes a bite of his sandwich, drops it onto the wax paper on his lap and cranks the music on his aftermarket sound system, a punk rock band from Austin called "16 Hour Drive".

Bobby starts bouncing his head up and down to the rapid beat of the drums, the speed of the electric guitar. I recognize the song. It's called "Call to Arms".

He's shouting along with the lyrics, alternating bites of food and swigs of his drink. I laugh to myself at the absurdity of it: a left-leaning aide, driving a sensible car, effectively slam dancing to politically conservative, sardonic punk rock. For a second, I forget the trouble into which I've fallen.

I finish my sandwich and stuff the wax paper, along with the crumpled napkin, into a bag and place it on the floor between my legs. I put what's left of my Dr. Pepper in the cup holder and settle in. I'm looking out the window, when Bobby turns down the music.

"Dude, have you been watching *The Walking Dead?*" We are both fans of the television epic on AMC. It's based on a graphic novel and follows a group of survivors in a post-apocalyptic, zombie infested world. We were late to get on board, after the show had gained an enormous cult-like following, and we watch the series online.

"Yeah," I say. "I'm way behind. I've got it on Netflix and I'm only a couple of episodes into season two."

"What part is that? I'm already in season four," he says as if it's a point of pride.

"Um," I think back to the last time I watched an episode. It seems forever ago, given the recent changes in my life. "The last episode I watched was the one where Carol's daughter goes missing and Rick's son gets shot."

"Dude, you are behind, but man, what's coming up for you is awesome."

"Don't spoil it." I spin the cap off the Dr. Pepper and gulp down another swig.

"Okay," he laughs. "I won't. It's good." He's quiet for a moment before he looks over at me with a smirk, his right hand draped over the steering wheel, his left on the driver's door armrest. "Hey, Jackson, what happened the other night?"

I play dumb. "What do you mean?"

"I heard you got sick or something and ditched Charlie."

"You heard that?" I fidget in my seat and turn toward Bobby. He's speeding at about 80 miles per hour. I have to speak up over the hum of the road noise.

"Yeah," he picks at his teeth with his free hand. "A couple of guys I know were there at the bar and recognized her. They didn't know you." He looks at me for a second, smiles, and laughs.

"That figures." I remember the two guys standing at the bar. I pegged them for Capitol staffers.

"They said she was walking around asking where you were, if anybody had seen you. They told her you hobbled out of the joint with some guy, some big dude carried you out. They thought you were drunk and the bouncer was making you leave. She seemed pissed off." Bobby checks the rearview mirror. He eases the car into the right lane to let a faster car pass. A black sedan with dark tinted windows zooms by us and merges right again in front of us. "They said she finally left with some other dude."

"What?" I can feel my cheeks getting flush and my chest ache. A wave of nausea slams into my gut.

"Yeah..." Bobby must sense my discomfort but does nothing to ease it. "My friends said she made a couple of phone calls and some guy came to pick her up. He was a good looking guy. Older. My guys said he looked official, like a douche Jean Claude Van Damme."

"Okay," I half-chuckle. "That's redundant. How do they know it was Charlie?"

"Dude," Bobby looks at me like I am an idiot. "How could it *not* be her? They described her to a tee. The same way I described her to them." Bobby pushed the gas and moves back into the fast lane. He passes the black sedan and moves back to the right.

"You described them to her?"

"Well, yeah." Bobby checks his rearview mirror again. "I mean we were talking. I don't remember when, but I told them about you and Charlie. I guess I described her accurately, because they knew it was her."

"How did you describe her?" I am going to puke. I roll down the window to get some air. It makes it harder to hear Bobby. At this point, I am not sure I want to hear him.

"Hot," his eyes grow wide as if he's picturing her in his dirty mind. "Tall, leggy redhead. Awesome rack. Looks like she could kick a dude's ass if she wasn't so fine."

Bobby switches hands on the steering wheel and punches me in the shoulder. "Dude, why are you so bothered? I mean *you* ditched *her*. How else was she supposed to get home?"

He has a point. I did *ditch* her as far as everyone's concerned. Maybe she called someone from the office to get her. No big deal. I am panicking over nothing. With everything else going on right now, I am overreacting to the one thing in my life I know is safe.

***

After a half hour of silence, Bobby tells me he has to go to the bathroom. His Mazda also needs gas. He pulls into a service station and up to the pump. The gas station shares a large parking lot with a Pizza Hut and a Dairy Queen.

I pull out my wallet and try the credit card reader. It doesn't work. Probably better anyhow; I don't want to have my credit card traced. Thankfully, I have some cash in my wallet.

"Hey, Bobby!" I yell after him before he gets to the door of the station. "Take my wallet and pay inside. Give her the twenty."

He runs about halfway back and I toss him my worn leather wallet. He catches it and acts as though he's caught a touchdown as he dances to the station.

I wait for him to pay and when the pump grinds to life, I drop the nozzle into the fuel tank, lock it, and lean back against the car. I watch the analog numbers slowly spin on the old pump as the car fills up. My mind feels like those numbers. It's spinning. It's too full. I'm not sure what to make of everything.

I take mental inventory: I was kidnapped; I was interrogated and let go; I'm being stalked; I'm somehow part of an attempted assassination plot; I've been complicit in something treasonous by delivering iPods around the world; my girlfriend may be cheating on me; and I am busy chasing the invisible son of a secessionist sniper.

I would laugh at the ridiculousness of it all if I didn't feel as though my world is unraveling.

The pump finally clicks to a stop. I replace the nozzle, screw the cap back on the tank and shut the little door.

I decide I might as well go to the bathroom while we're stopped. I could use another Dr. Pepper anyway. I cross the parking lot to the store, stopping for a second to let a dark colored sedan with tinted windows squeal its way out of the parking lot. I think it's the same car we passed on Highway 290 about a half hour earlier but I'm not sure.

The rush of air conditioning feels good as I walk into the store. I walk past the register and down an aisle of candy to the cooler on the back wall. There are shelves full of twenty ounce bottles: water, flavored water, sports drinks, energy drinks, and soft drinks. I have to double back a couple of times before I spot the Dr. Pepper.

I look behind me and over the other aisles. I don't see Bobby; he must still be in the bathroom. I grab a couple of drinks from the cooler and walk them back to the register.

"I'll pay for these in a minute," I tell the clerk, who seems not to care.

I walk back to the bathroom and knock on the door marked *MEN*. There's no answer. I knock again and try the brass door knob. It turns clockwise and I push the door, but it won't open. There's something leaning against it.

"Bobby?"

Again no answer. My pulse quickens and I start pushing harder against the resistance. I lean my left shoulder into the door and push. I can feel something sliding along the floor as I shove my way into the small bathroom. There's a stall and the urinal on the wall opposite the door. I look down.

Bobby's eyes are fixed and distant. The bullet holes between them are deep and round.

The bathroom door is locked behind me and I'm cradling Bobby's head in my lap. His pants are unbuttoned and his belt unbuckled. His pant legs are soaked. They shot him while he was taking a leak. My wallet is on the floor next to him.

I move to lay his head gently on the bathroom floor and notice there's blood all over my left hand. On the wall to the left, there's red spatter mixed with the graffiti; two holes drilled into the drywall amidst the mess. The bullets went through his head and lodged in the wall.

I stand up, holding my bloody hand away from me. It drips on the floor as I step over Bobby and turn on the sink. There's a cracked bar of green soap next to a roll of white paper towels. I wash my hands up to my wrists and dry them. There's blood under the fingernails of my left hand but I can't do anything about it. I can sense I'm moving almost robotically, dispassionately, as I pick up my wallet.

With Bobby on the floor beneath me, a pool of blood expanding beneath his head, the driver's license photo stares at me from behind a protective, clear plastic sleeve in my wallet. It's me. I look down at Bobby, struck by our resemblance to each other.

They thought he was me.

This jolts me back to the moment. The blood on the floor is about to seep beneath the bathroom door and into the store. I grab Bobby's keys from his front pocket and the roll of paper towels. I unwrap half of the roll and stuff it on the floor underneath the door and slip out into the store.

As calmly as I can, I walk to the exit past the glass-enclosed register. The cashier doesn't even look up as I make my way back to Bobby's Mazda 3. As I am about to jump into the driver's seat and leave, I notice a bus in the parking lot next to the Dairy Queen. Its marquee reads HOUSTON.

A group of people start to make their way back to the bus. I reach into Bobby's car and grab my new cell phone. I also get *his* phone, his wallet, a worn UT baseball cap, my backpack and lock the keys in the car.

The group shuffles back to the bus and I merge with them as the driver opens the door. She's writing on a clipboard and doesn't even look up at me. I find a seat in the back by the bathroom, sit next to the window, and pull the hat low over my head.

As the bus pulls away, I call 9-1-1 from Bobby's phone. In a voice barely above a whisper I tell the operator about Bobby. He's dead in a bathroom at a gas station next to a Dairy Queen. His car and his keys are in the parking lot at a pump.

I hang up before giving her any more information, slip the window open, and toss the phone out of the window.

I get up quickly and open the accordion door to the bathroom at the rear of the bus, close it behind me, and lock it. I turn around to face the toilet, and puke into it. I keep vomiting until there's nothing left and my stomach muscles burn from the contractions. The mirror above the small sink shows me that my eyes are sunken and my skin is pale, almost green.

I got him killed. It's my fault.

I fill the small sink with cold water and splash it on my face. I'm cleaner but not cleansed. I grab a handful of paper towels and wipe the area around the toilet seat, wiping up residual vomit. I wash my hands again before I return to my seat.

Bobby's wallet is holding a hundred dollars in twenties. Mine has blood on it. There's still forty dollars in it. My credit cards are no good. Neither are Bobby's. I toss them out the window, hoping someone might find them and use them. That might throw off whoever it is that wants me dead. It'll keep the police from finding me until I can sort this out.

It's only a matter of time before they see me on the surveillance video in the store. They'll trace me to the car. My fingerprints are everywhere in the vehicle and in the bathroom. I need to hurry.

The bus is half empty. Nobody seems to notice me. I tilt the baseball cap back on my head and stare out the window.

We pass a mileage marker on the side of the highway. HOUSTON 94 MILES. That buys a little time to think.

***

I'm sick to my stomach. My throat burns. Whoever killed Bobby wants me dead.

Slouching in my seat on the Houston-bound bus, I dial 4-1-1 on my new phone and tell the operator I need the number and address for Channel 4 in Houston. I have the information texted to my phone and wait for the operator to connect me.

"News 4 Houston," the voice answers. People who work the assignment desks in newsrooms are either old and homicidal or young and stressed. This woman sounds young and stressed. I ask her for George Townsend. She sighs loudly and her yell for George gets cut off when she puts me on hold.

"George Townsend."

"George, this is...I'm the guy who called you earlier about Ripley."

"Yeah," he says. "I've been trying to get a hold of you. Your phone goes straight to voicemail."

I had forgotten my discarded phone was his only way to reach me. "This is my new number, sorry. The old one's no good anymore."

"Okay," he says. I can hear him typing. He's always typing. "I have good news."

"Really?" I could use some good news.

"I found Ripley's son."

"You did?"

"He's here in Houston." Townsend stops typing. I assume he's waiting to hear my response.

"Good," I say. "I'm on my way to you right now."

"What?" He sounds surprised. "Why?"

"Someone is trying to kill me. Whoever it is has something to do with Ripley."

Townsend says nothing.

"George?"

"Yes."

"Did you hear me?"

"I heard you."

"Say something."

"That's not the quid pro quo I was hoping for."

I tell him I'll meet him when I get into town and that he needs to have a place for us to meet privately. He hesitates.

"Look," I say, "my name is Jackson Quick. I work for the Governor. Google me. I am legit. I am not crazy. I am telling you I am connected to the attempt on Don Carlos Buell's life, Ripley, and his son. I need to find out how. You can help me."

"Okay," he sighs. "I'll get us a place to talk. I'll see you when you get here"

He hangs up and it takes everything in me to press the END button on my phone. I am spent. I send Charlie a quick text message from the phone. I don't want her to worry:

it's jackson. have new temp phone. taking bus. lots to tell u. will call l8r from houston. <3

I close the phone and lean my head against the window. The adrenaline rush has faded. I need some sleep.

***

The dream is always the same.

I'm trapped in a school locker. I bang on the door and scream for help. There's nobody there, and I am running out of air.

Through the slits, I can see my mom. She's in the distance, maybe a hundred yards from me, running toward me as fast as she can.

My dad joins her from out of nowhere. Side by side, they're coming. They're on their way to rescue me.

I bang harder and harder against the door of the locker. My hands are bruised but I keep banging. I need them to hear me. They need to know I am still here.

As my mother's hands reach for the latch to free me she bursts into flames. My father catches fire too. I can smell their burning hair, hear their primal screams as both of my parents are incinerated into piles of ash on the ground. Trails of smoke waft from their remains and in through the slanted vents of the locker. I can feel the space shrinking around me, trapping me more impossibly than before. As I am about to be crushed, I awake. The image of the flames is still there.

I am still alone in the back of the bus, bothered I've left one nightmare for another. The UT cap is again pulled low over my eyes. My arms are folded across my chest. I can feel the sweat under the brim of the cap, against the small of my back, and under my arms.

Through my drowsiness and the window, I recognize the Houston Galleria. We're heading south on what's called The Loop, passing the high-end shopping district southwest of downtown.

The traffic slows and I check my cell phone. There's a missed call. The phone's on vibrate and I haven't set the voicemail yet, so there's no message. I hit redial for the number, which has a Houston 713 area code, and wait for an answer on the other end.

"George Townsend," he answers. "Is this Jackson?"

"Yeah it's me," I speak softly, trying to remain as invisible as I can on the bus. "I'm here in Houston."

"I tried calling you again," George says. "You didn't pick up."

"New phone. I didn't know the volume was off."

"I've got a place we can talk. Where are you?"

"We're about to get off of The Loop and head back north on highway 59 toward downtown. The bus station is there."

"I know where it is," he says. "I can meet you there in ten minutes. I'll be in a black Lexus SUV."

When we pull up to the station ten minutes later, Townsend's Lexus is already there. I step from the bus and scan the parking lot for a dark sedan with tinted windows. I don't find one. I'm startled when the bus releases its air brakes. I can't believe this is my life. I take a deep breath and lower the cap on my head as I approach Townsend.

He's taller than I expected. Thinner too. He's wearing tan suit pants and a white dress shirt with French cuffs. His shoes are worn, brown leather loafers. It reminds me reporters always have horrible shoes. He has a cell phone in his left hand and offers his right as I approach him. I grip his hand with the little strength I can find and look him in the eyes, searching for signs of skepticism. He blinks and smiles.

"I'm George." He shakes my hand up and down a couple of times and lets go. "I'm glad you made it here. I'm really interested in what you have to share with me."

"I bet," I chuckle at his honesty. "Aren't you underdressed? I mean, no suit today?"

He shrugs and glances down at his clothes "I'm not on the air today. I'm part of the investigative team, so I'm not on the air every day."

"He gestures to the passenger's side of his car and turns to open the driver's door. "So," he says, "let's hit the road." He's acting as though this is a Sunday drive, like I'm not some hit man's target and he could be in danger now too. I'll let him doubt me for now. He'll find out I'm for real soon enough. I hope he doesn't run when he does, or even worse, come to the realization the instant before two bullets rip through *his* head.

I slide into the car, toss my backpack into the back of the SUV, and am hit with the smell of cigarette smoke. The air is stale and sour and I can feel it in the back of my throat. There's a half empty pack of Winston's and an open can of Dr. Pepper in the center console. Everybody drinks Dr. Pepper. It's the national drink of Texas or something.

"Who's trying to kill you?" he asks me without any hint of disbelief in his voice. It catches me off guard.

"I don't know, but it's obviously got something to do with Don Carlos Buell and Ripley."

"What's your connection to them?" "I'm not ready to talk about that yet," I say. "Let's wait until we get to where we're going."

"Okay," Townsend sounds frustrated. He has his arm around the back of my seat as he backs up, brakes, and pulls out of the parking lot and onto the street. He purses his lips as he merges into the left lane of traffic. "This seems to be a one way deal right now."

"But I do have a question for you. What can you tell me about Buell?" I ignore his complaint. "I mean, what do you know about his background?"

"What do you mean?"

"I mean, what's he into? People like him aren't wealthy because they're good people. They all have things in their past." I can feel the congestion building in my nose from the latent cigarette smoke. I sniff and wipe my nose with the back of my hand. I turn around and look out the rear window. Nobody is following us.

"I thought you worked for the Governor."

"And?" We're not getting off to a productive start.

"And," he says, "I would think you would know your opponent's baggage."

"I know spin," I admit as I check the passenger side rear view mirror. "I don't necessarily know the truth. Remember, everything I know comes from politicians. How trustworthy can that information be? I want to know what *you* know."

I don't want to tell him I'm increasingly aware I've been played somehow. I am not some trusted confidant for the Governor; I'm a tool. For a confident twenty-something with the ego I have, it's not an easy self-admission to make.

"Fair enough," he spins the steering wheel to the left. "Well, we know he's into energy. He's always worked hand in hand with fuel exploration companies and end-user energy providers. Kind of a collusion to keep everybody happy."

"How's that?"

"He invested heavily in exploitive energy. His companies backed mountaintop removal coal projects in Appalachia, and tar sands exploration in South Texas and in Western Canada, both really nasty ways to get energy out of the earth. Environmentalists hated him. They protested him and his shell companies. He made a lot of money."

"And?"

"And he suddenly pulls out of everything. Almost overnight he gets out of the earth-raping business and becomes eco-friendly."

"Why?" I knew he'd switched sides, so to speak, but never heard a rational reason why.

"The conventional wisdom is that he set his sights on public office. Since the days of 'Drill Baby Drill' ended with the 2010 BP Macondo spill in the Gulf, Buell knew he needed to be a kinder, gentler energy magnate."

"What's the *unconventional* wisdom?" I sniffle again. My throat is starting to feel scratchy. Damn smoke.

"He figured out he could get richer by conserving energy as opposed to harvesting it." "What do you mean?" We're driving next to a light rail train and heading north toward the edge of downtown. I duck as the train moves alongside us. Townsend probably notices my nervousness but doesn't comment.

"I've been working on stories about Buell for a long time now," he continues. "About two years ago he moved the vast majority of his holdings into a small Texas company called Nanergetix," Townsend slows the SUV and parallel parks in front of a large white building, a restaurant called Spaghetti Warehouse. "Nanergetix is heavily involved in vanguard, energy-related nanotechnology. Some people think they've discovered an additive that triples the efficiency of fossil fuels. I've been working on this stuff for months, but I can't get any of it nailed down."

"If that were true then it would piss off the oil companies and make the price of gasoline, oil, natural gas, and coal drop like a rock, right?"

"Exactly." Townsend puts the SUV in park and pulls the keys from the ignition. "And it would make Buell very, very wealthy."

"He's already rich."

"You shouldn't be that naïve, Jackson." He looks at me as

though I am an idiot. "People like Buell can't ever have enough money. They can't ever have enough power."

"I still don't get what that has to do with me or Ripley or Ripley's son." I unbuckle my seatbelt and turn in my seat to face the suddenly condescending reporter. He must be a liberal. Most reporters are and don't even know they're liberals. They think of themselves as open-minded and fair.

"Well, I am not sure there *is* a connec—" he stops mid-sentence. His eyes widen and he smiles broadly. His teeth are perfectly straight and too white for a smoker. He's liberal, condescending *and* vain. Perfect for television news. Just when I think it was a bad idea to connect with George Townsend, he changes my mind.

"I get it," he says. "Nanotechnology."

I don't get it. "Nanotechnology?"

"Ripley's son works at Rice University in the nano lab...the lab where they conduct more nanotechnology research than anywhere else in the world."

***

The restaurant is empty except for Townsend and me. We're sitting at a small corner table with two glasses of water and a basket of bread between us. I have my back to the wall so I can see everybody who comes and goes.

"We're going to Rice to talk to Ripley's son?" I ask. My hands are clasped in front of me on the table. I'm leaning on my elbows.

Townsend takes a piece of bread from the basket and stuffs half of it into his mouth. T.V. people eat too fast. It comes from downing lunch in a live truck between interviews or at a desk between phone calls.

"Yes," he says, "as soon as you tell me why you think you're caught up in the middle of whatever this is." He chased the mouthful of bread with a swig of water.

"Okay," I relent. It's time for me to share what I think I know. "It's because of the iPods."

Townsend, his mouth full of another wad of bread, looks puzzled. Of course he is. I'm burying the lead.

"Over the past six months, I've traveled the world delivering iPods." I take a sip of water, slip a cube of ice between my teeth, and chew as I continue to tell him about what I've done on behalf of the Governor. I can feel my hand trembling almost imperceptibly when I put the glass back on the table. Townsend doesn't see it.

"What was on the iPods?" He's entranced, as though I'm telling him the plot of some fictional political thriller.

"I don't know," I lie. Sort of. Despite what I've been telling myself, I do have a hint what was on those iPods...

***

My trip to Anchorage was the last one on the Governor's agenda. Like the other trips, it was short. When I landed at the Ted Stevens International Airport, I caught a cab to Elderberry Park. It was short ride along the shore of Cook Inlet. In the distance I could see Mt. McKinley and Mt. Foraker. It was beautiful. The sky was crayon blue and cloudless.

"That's it," the cabbie said as he pulled over on M Street in front of a brown and yellow wooden house in the center of the park. "That's the Anderson house."

I thanked him, gave him the fare, and got out of the cab. I stood on the sidewalk with my bags for a moment to stretch my right knee and to look at the Oscar Anderson House, a historic landmark built by one of the city's first settlers. The exterior of the house was yellow on its main floor. It was painted brown on both the top floor and on the exterior of the basement that extends above ground. There was a tall evergreen nestled against the left side of the house and an American flag flying on the right. I walked slowly up the cobblestone ramp to the small brown front door, a bag slung over each shoulder.

My instructions were to take the guided tour of the home. At some point during the 45-minute history lesson, my contact would find me.

I was standing on a large rug, admiring the red brick fireplace, when "Mary Brown" approached me and asked me what music I had downloaded on my iPod. Apparently, that was the cryptic, cloak and dagger clue to who she was and what she wanted.

"A little bit of everything," I answered. She nodded toward the front door and led me out of the house.

Once I clumsily slugged my bags down the hall and through the narrow front door, I saw her standing at the end of the cobblestone ramp. She was in a button down chambray shirt with dark denim jeans and a heavy brown blazer. She had her jeans tucked into knee high brown suede boots. Her blonde hair was cut short like the 1970s ice skater, Dorothy Hamill. She was attractive if a little harsh. Her features were angular, her nose long and thin.

"Let's take a walk in the park," she suggested and continued to walk ahead of me. I shifted the bags on my shoulders. She turned around and saw me struggling but didn't seem to care. She walked past a swing set and stepped on a hike/bike path that ran along the water.

After a couple of minutes on the path, she came to a small garden dotted with boulders. Brown stopped at one of them and sat, placing her palms flat on the rock and inching herself up onto it. She crossed her boots and folded her arms, waiting for me to catch up. I could imagine myself running along the path, getting in a couple of miles along the coast. What a view.

I finally caught up to her and lay down my bags on the ground next to the rock.

"This is called Hannah Cove Garden," she said. "It's a memorial to children who died young." She looked out onto the water and toward the Alaska Mountain range in the distance.

I followed her gaze. I didn't follow her point.

"Let's get to it," she said, abruptly shifting gears and pulling her focus from the mountains and back to me. "You have something for me." She was direct. No small talk with her as there was with almost everyone else I'd met and handed iPods.

I reached to unzip my bag and pull out the device. "What's the code?" The codes were always different, and I never knew what they were until the contact gave them to me.

"Spindletop," she said.

"I don't follow," I said. The iPod's UNLOCK screen showed the options were numbers only. Four digits.

"The date the Lucas Gusher at Spindletop started producing. As a Texan you should know this." Her lips curled into a wormy, toothless grin. I didn't like her.

I wracked my brain, trying to find the date among the files of useless information I'd stored in there. The date Tupac was shot: 09/09. The date Billy Corrigan announced the breakup of Smashing Pumpkins: 05/23. The fall of the Berlin Wall: 11/09. The date my parents died: 12/24.

Spindletop: I couldn't remember it.

"I can't remember that," I begrudgingly admitted. "What is it?"

"January tenth," she frowned. "It's all about Texas you know."

I'd missed the $100 question on *Who Wants To Be A Millionaire?*

I punched 0110 onto the screen's keypad and the device unlocked. I passed it to her and she flipped it over, running her thumb along the back of the device.

She began to slide down to the rock to stand, and she lost her balance. The iPod slipped from her hand, off the rock, and landed at my feet.

I held out my left hand to help her stand up and bent over to pick up the iPod with my right. It was lying face up on the ground. On the screen, it read:

CAYMAN BANK OF INTERCONTINENTAL COMMERCE

There was an account number, a bank transit code, and two sets of long numbers I assume were some other sort of bank codes. I punched the home button on the bottom of the iPod and handed it back to Ms. Brown before she could see what I'd inadvertently noticed.

She took it from me, brushed off her jeans, and returned to the bike path to walk south along the water. I took that as my clue to head back to the airport.

While waiting at the gate for my plane, I pulled out my netbook to dig a little more. I thought about what the woman had said about how everything was about Texas. If the code for her iPod was a significant date, maybe the other codes had been too.

Against what the Governor had instructed, I'd kept a list of the codes in a file on my computer. I opened the document and added 0110 to the list.

I looked at the previous seven numbers.

0302. That was the code for London. I opened a web browser,

and after agreeing to the rules for the airport's free Wi-Fi, I entered "Texas History, March 2" into a search engine.

Nine million results popped up instantly. The first: *March 2, 1836 – The date Texas declared its independence from Mexico.*

I type December 19 Texas into the search box. 1219 was the code in Venezuela. I have to scan through a few of the seven million hits before I find the significance. *December 19, 1836-The boundary of Texas established.*

I entered five more sets of numbers, each of them relevant to either Texas' rights as a Republic or significant dates in the history of Texas' role in energy production.

It was certainly clever. Did it mean something more? Why was there bank account information on the iPod? I'd heard Cayman accounts were hard to trace and easier to hide than Swiss accounts since a government crackdown in 2009.

There was something much greater at play here. Contrary to the Governor's wink of a promise, I was beginning to believe there was nothing legal about whatever it was he was perpetrating.

Until I was drugged, tortured, stalked, and nearly killed, I never thought it was much more than needlessly covert political favors exchanging hands.

I never considered my life was at stake.

***

Sitting across from Townsend, I spill my guts. Over the next half hour, between bites of buttered farfalle, I tell him about the trips, the iPods, my kidnapping, the torture, and Bobby's murder. He puts his phone on the table between us to record the conversation. I'm okay with it.

By the time I've told him everything, except for the Cayman bank information, he's staring at me slack jawed. I'm not sure why, of all things, I choose to leave out the bank. I guess I'm better off playing dumb. It's not a rational choice. I'm having trouble maintaining any sense of rationality. I think Townsend can sense it.

"I'm not sure what to say," he finally spits out. "I mean, I don't think anyone, let alone a cynical reporter, would believe anything you've told me. It's so ridiculously fantastic, I can't help but trust everything you've said."

To our right, there's a loud crash and I instinctively duck under the table. My knees bang painfully onto the black and white tile flooring. I can feel the pulse quickening in my neck and chest.

Was that a gunshot?

"It was the waiter," Townsend said, reaching down and pulling me back into my seat by my right arm. "He dropped a tray of dishes. It's okay."

As I get up I can see Bobby's face again, faded and draining color onto the floor of a gas station bathroom. It's definitely *not* okay.

I scoot in my chair and straighten myself at the table. I'm still wearing the same clothes I was in when I left Charlie's place. It seems as if that was days ago, but it's only been seven or eight hours. There's a brown spot of dried blood on my shirt next to Kinky Friedman's smiling face.

"Jackson, why would the people who kidnapped you decide to let you go and try to kill you a day later?" Townsend slides the phone toward me. "Is it possible there is more than one person or group following you?"

"What? I don't understand."

"Could it be one side, so to speak, wants to learn whatever it is you know about some grand conspiracy and the other side wants to keep you from talking?" Townsend takes another sip from his glass of water. All that's left is melted ice. He slurps it down.

I haven't thought about that possibility. Could it be I'm caught between two equally violent, desperate groups? Somehow I hold a key that both sides have a mutual interest in controlling? The look on my face must make it obvious to Townsend I hadn't considered it until he brought it up.

"It's just a theory," he says, trying to soften the blow. "I could be wrong."

"No, you're right. There has to be more to it. It doesn't make sense that the dude who tortured me would let me go free, tell me he was watching me, and shoot me in the head in a public place."

Townsend waves to the waiter and gets the check. He glances at the bill and hands the check back with a credit card.

I stop the waiter. "Let me get it." I give him a twenty, tell him to keep the change, and hand Townsend his card.

"No paper trail?" he asks.

"I wish I could say it's because I'm a generous guy," I tell him. "But I don't want any record of anything in case they somehow connect me to you."

"Whoever *they* are?" Townsend grabs the phone from the table, pushes the OFF button and slips it into his pocket as he stands.

"Right." I stand and slip my wallet back into my pocket. I've got $120 left. I grab my backpack from the floor. "Let's go find Ripley's son."

***

Rice University is on Houston's southwest side. The streets leading to the campus are lined with mature oak trees that create a natural green canopy. It's a welcome, if momentary, distraction from the task at hand.

Townsend pulls his Lexus onto the campus and past the school's football stadium. It's an old gray concrete structure that seems out of place with the school's classic university architecture.

Townsend tells me, as if to ease the palpable tension, "that's a famous stadium. Super Bowl VIII was played there. And you know JFK's famous 'Moon Speech'? He delivered it there."

I nod without saying anything. I don't have the energy for small talk.

Townsend pulls into a visitor's parking lot and finds an empty space. We get out of the SUV and I follow him across the street to a large three-story building. It's the Space Science and Technology Laboratory. The building is framed by columns around the perimeter of its first floor, creating a covered walkway. Townsend leads me to the right side of the building and into a service elevator.

The doors close and we stand silently as the elevator lurches and hums upwards. We're both looking at the yellow glow illuminate the floor numbers above the doors. 1, 2, 3. The doors slide apart and we step into the hall. Directly across from us is what's apparently called the HiPco laboratory. The door is surrounded by a series of coded locks and warning signs.

"What's that?" I ask as we walk past the lab to the left and turn the corner to the right.

"That's the lab where the researchers create nanotubes," Townsend tells me. "They use high pressure carbon dioxide and iron to spin these tiny tubes of pure carbon. They're super strong and are the building block of nanotechnology. I did a couple of stories on it."

I'm not sure I really understand it, but it sounds cool.

We keep moving along a sterile hallway lined with labs and offices. A couple of white lab coated men walk past us, but don't notice. Their heads are buried in clipboards and notes. One is eating an apple.

At the end of the hall on the left is the entrance to a suite of offices. Townsend walks through it as though he's been here before, and we wind our way to the back of the suite. Townsend finds a closed door and knocks loudly.

"This is the director's office," Townsend tells me without turning around. "I've interviewed him several times. He'll know where to find our guy." He knocks again.

The door clicks and opens inward, revealing a genial looking man with thinning gray hair and a matching beard. He's wearing blue Dockers and a short sleeve gray button down. There's a pen in his breast pocket.

"George?" His eyes search Townsend for explanation. He glances past George to me and then back to the reporter. "How are you? I'm not under investigation am I?" He chuckles.

"Of course not, Dr. Aglo." George extends his hand. "I've got a favor to ask, if that's okay."

"Anything for you." The man's expression relaxes. "You've always been such a help to us with your reporting." He slips his hand into Townsend's grip and shakes it. "It's not easy, I imagine, explaining what we do here in a couple of sound bite clips."

"Thank you," George says. "That's kind of you. I'm hoping you can help me."

"Sure," Dr. Aglo waves George into his office. I follow behind him.

"I'm a friend of George's," I tell Dr. Aglo as I move past him into the corner office. He nods and follows me into the large room.

Two of the office walls are floor to ceiling glass, with views looking out on the campus below. To the right is a wall hidden by large book shelves. Dotting the shelves are varying sizes of plastic balls. Not really balls, but spheres shaped by interconnected hexagons. Dr. Aglo directs us to sit at a conference table toward the back of the office next to a glass wall.

"What can I do?" he asks as he sits at the head of the table.

"We're looking for one of your researchers," Townsend begins. His eyes dart between Aglo and me. It's kind of uncomfortable and I wish he'd stop it. Aglo's going to catch on that something is awry.

"Okay," says Dr. Aglo. "Which one?"

"Roswell Ripley." Townsend's eyes stay on the doctor this time.

"Hmmm," Dr. Aglo tilts his head and folds his hands across his chest. He leans back in his chair. "I don't think I can help you."

"Do you know where he is?" Townsend presses.

"I haven't seen him since his father, well..." Dr. Aglo doesn't need to finish the sentence.

"He disappeared?" Townsend asks.

I'm trying to gauge the scientist's body language but I can't tell whether he *can't* help us or *won't* help us.

"I don't know," he says. "He works in a private lab on the second floor. He's funded by an anonymous donor. I don't see him very much. He sends me reports on his progress every six weeks. I'm not sure of the last time he was here."

"Don't you have electronic keypads for all the labs?" Townsend isn't letting go. "Wouldn't that tell us the last time he was here?"

"Sure," Dr. Aglo unfolds his arms and leans forward onto the table, "but, I haven't looked at it. I assume he's lying low because of the issues with his father. I can't blame him really. They do share the same name."

"Can we look in his lab?" Townsend asks without any hint of aggression. His tone has shifted. He's good at this. "It's really important we talk to him. If you're with us, I mean, that wouldn't be inappropriate would it?"

Dr. Aglo takes a deep breath and scratches the beard on his neck, considering it. He pushes back from the table and stands. He walks towards the door and waves at us to follow him. We get up, Townsend shoots me a smirk, and we walk after Dr. Aglo back down the hall to the elevator.

"What was he working on?" I ask. "Engineered nanoparticles," Dr. Aglo answers without turning around. "What science fiction might call nanobots."

"Engineered for what?" I catch up to the doctor outside the elevator.

"Energy," he says. "He is developing an additive for carbon based fuels."

We follow the doctor onto the elevator and give each other a knowing look before Aglo turns back around.

"What does the additive do?" George takes over.

"It's still in the early stages as far as I know," Aglo replies. He pushes the OPEN button on the elevator as the doors slide apart and holds it, motioning us onto the second floor. "He's trying to extend the life of those carbon fuels. The engineered nanoparticles react with the chemical composition of the fuel and allow an equivalent mass to provide greater energy. It's an octane booster, but different."

"Wait," George asks as we follow the professor down a hall similar to the one above us on the third floor. "Isn't that exactly what Nanergetix claims to be developing?"

The professor stops and spins around to face us. We almost run into him. He looks at George and then me. I can see him measuring the conversation. His mind, I imagine, is replaying it at nanoscale.

"How did you know that?" he asks George with a hint of suspicion.

"I've covered Don Carlos Buell," George answers without a pause. "He's a major investor. I thought everybody who pays attention to this stuff knew what Nanergetix was up to."

"I see," Dr. Aglo relaxes his shoulders. He studies George. The pause is uncomfortable and I slip my hands into my pockets.

"Well," he continues, hands on his hips. "I don't know what you've heard but what Dr. Ripley is working on is far more advanced than whatever Nanergetix claims to have. Of course, I can't imagine either of their work exists beyond the lab environment, but Ripley would be ahead," He says defensively.

"Could it be Nanergetix is funding his research, given you don't know the donor?"

George has balls. Big balls. Big stupid balls. We're trying to get this guy to help us and he's clearly antagonizing him.

Aglo blinks as though we've input information into his brain that causes a glitch. The data doesn't seem to compute. He tilts his head again as he did in the office.

"It's not..." he pauses again and blinks again, trying to process the query. "Well, I...I don't know. I hadn't considered that. I don't think so. My understanding from Dr. Ripley is that this is competing technology. The big challenge, of course, for both of them is developing something which can function in the toxic, high pressure chemical environment required in a combustible engine. He's so much as said that several times. He seems almost consumed with beating Nanergetix to market. I don't think so. But I cannot say with complete certainty."

Aglo turns and leads us to a laboratory at the end of the hall on the right. Its door leads to the interior of the building. He presses an identification badge to a small pad by the door. The pad beeps and a red light flashes to its left. He enters a series of numbers onto a keypad and the red light becomes a solid green. He pulls the handle on the door and swings it open into the hall.

"Let's see what we can see," he says and motions George and me into Dr. Ripley's secret lab.

***

I walk in to the constant hiss of gas running through a web of tubes overhead. They wind and twist to attach to different pieces of scientific equipment. Some of the instruments have valves wrapped in aluminum foil. There are black granite tables running the length of both sides of the room. It reminds me vaguely of high school chemistry class without the smell of formaldehyde.

The three of us spread out looking at the various work stations. None of the equipment or test tubes or Petri dishes means anything to me. I find a stack of green spiral notebooks and open the cover of the one on top. There's a page full of illegible cursive and mathematical equations. I can't decipher it or the similar notes on any of the other pages I flip through.

"Please be careful as you look through things," Dr. Aglo cautions. "And, of course, don't touch any of the equipment. All of this is very sensitive, as you might guess."

"What exactly are we looking for?" I ask, turning away from the stack of notebooks. I can't imagine Ripley left a post-it note with his location.

"Yes," adds Dr. Aglo. "What *are* we looking for?"

"I'll know it when I see it," says George. He's scanning the room, walking from work station to work station touching papers and notes. "Does Ripley have a university email address?"

"Of course," Dr. Aglo answers. "But I don't see a reason we need to access that. It's not as though this is a police investigation. The university might have a problem with giving access to that account." He leans back on one of the granite tables, his palms pressed flat against its edge.

"What about voicemail?" George persists. "Can we access that?"

"I don't think so. I don't have his pass code. And again, I don't think the university would agree to access it."

"Auto redial?" George walks over to a phone near the door of the lab.

"What do you mean?" asks Aglo.

"Do you have auto redial?"

"Yes we do," says Aglo. "But I am not sure how to access it here."

"I can," says George. "We have this same phone system at Channel 4." He turns to the phone and presses 1-1-9.

I walk over to the phone and look on the numeric display. The numbers appear one at a time: 432-426-3640.

George hits the speakerphone button and hangs up the receiver. The line rings twice and someone answers.

"McDonald Observatory Visitors Center. How may I help you?" the woman on the other end of the line asks pleasantly.

George replies, "What are your hours, ma'am?"

"We're open from ten in the morning to five-thirty in the evening every day except Thanksgiving, Christmas, and New Year's Day. We also have extended Star Party hours on some nights."

"And if I were to come visit, can you suggest where I might stay?

Is there a good hotel nearby?" George has his cell phone out and in record mode. It's on and sitting next to the speaker on the phone.

"Well," the woman pauses, "it depends. We do have some dormitory style rooms here in the Astronomers Lodge, but you'd have to be a Friend of the Observatory. Otherwise, you can stay down in Ft. Davis. There's the Butterfield Inn Cottages or—"

"Do you have any room at the Lodge?" George interrupts.

"Hang on, let me check." On the other end of the line, she's shuffling through some papers and mumbling. "Let's see," she says. "Ummm...we have a few rooms. Let me look at who's booked them. Johnson, Walker, Ripley, Franklin."

"What?" George interrupts again. "Did you say Franklin?"

"Yes," the woman says, a little off guard. "Dr. Franklin has one of the rooms. Do you know him?"

"Sure. We go way back," George fibs. "Please tell him I said hello."

"And you are?"

George ends the call and hangs up.

"Who is Franklin?" I ask.

"Not Franklin," says George. "Ripley. She said Ripley. I asked her if Franklin was staying there to make sure she was rattling off a list of guest names. Now we know where Ripley is. We have to go find him."

"That won't be easy," says Dr. Aglo. "Do you know where Ft. Davis and the observatory are?" he asks me.

"No," I admit. I should know. I don't.

"Far West Texas. It's past Marfa. I've been there. The closest commercial airport is a two and half hour drive. If you're going there, and you're in a hurry to see Dr. Ripley, you better get going."

"What's the closest airport?" George asks, slipping his phone back into his pocket.

"Midland/Odessa," Dr. Aglo says. "You could do that or El Paso."

"Sounds good," George says and starts to leave.

"Before you go..." Aglo is standing in his way at the doorway. "You never did tell me why you need him."

"Oh," George smiles. "True. Well, we think he's involved in a conspiracy that includes an assassination attempt. His research here is connected to it."

Oddly, Dr. Aglo doesn't appear surprised. He looks down at the floor before smacking his lips and exhaling. He steps aside and waves George through the doorway. I start to walk out, watching the hint of pain develop on Dr. Aglo's face. He suddenly looks much older, frailer. I imagine he's considering the possibility someone under his tutelage and guidance was deceiving him.

I'm so focused on his face, I almost miss the photograph hanging to the right of the door. I catch a glimpse of it and it stops me in my tracks.

"George," I call after the reporter who's already halfway to the elevator. "You've got to see this."

The framed photograph is from a clipped magazine article. It's a black and white portrait of a small group of people. They're assembled in an area outside the Science and Technology Building.

"Which one is Ripley?" I ask Dr. Aglo.

"That's him there," he points to the photograph. "Second row on the left."

It's not Ripley that interests me, really. It's the man next to him. I recognize him. I met him in London, at the Texas Embassy.

The man next to *him* I recognize too. We met in Caracas.

Then there's the woman sitting near the middle on the front row. She took a stroll with me in Alaska.

The man sitting next to her in the center of the picture is my boss, the Governor of Texas. I can feel my heart racing again. I'm not quite sure what this photograph means.

"Who are those people?" I ask Dr. Aglo as George walks back into the lab.

"Except for the Governor and Dr. Ripley?" he asks rhetorically.

"Yes."

"Those are energy executives. They handle new technologies for some of the largest end-to-end oil and gas companies in the world."

"Why are they in this photograph?"

"They were here for a symposium eight months ago. The Governor awarded a citation to the Institute and they all were here for that and the lectures."

"What was the symposium about?" George is the one with the

question this time.

"Emerging energy technology," Dr. Aglo says. He looks bewildered by our questions, probably wondering why we would we care about this.

"That all?" George asks.

"That, and the role of engineered nanotechnology as it might benefit the energy industry."

***

"On our way to the airport, tell me more about the people in those pictures," George says. He is pulling the SUV out of the parking lot and slipping on his seatbelt and has already shoved a thirty dollar parking ticket from the Rice University Police Department into the glove box in front of my knees.

"They're my contacts. Those people are the ones who I met with the iPods." My head is spinning trying to figure out the connections. I don't think I want to face the obvious answer.

George turns off campus and back into the shade of an oak-lined street. "They are connected to the lab and to your boss. Big Oil. Nanotechnology. Politics. The trifecta of fun."

"Yeah. I don't know I ever would have thought about nanotechnology mixing with the other two. I didn't really even know what it was until today."

"So," he says as he brakes at a stop sign. "Are you thinking the same thing I am?"

"Well, my boss is somehow involved in new energy. If Ripley really is developing a competing technology to Nanergetix, it would seem the Governor is somehow connected to the assassination attempt."

"That's what I think," George says. He accelerates and takes a swig from a warm Dr. Pepper. "The Governor and these energy people are colluding with Ripley to generate a competing technology that makes oil and gas last longer. Maybe Ripley hedges, and the Governor keeps him in line by framing his father for the assassination attempt on his political opponent. If Don Carlos Buell dies in the attempt, two birds are killed with one stone. His only political threat is gone, and the money behind Nanergetix disappears too."

"Of course," I counter, "we're making this assumption based on what Dr. Aglo told us."

"What's that?"

"You asked him if Ripley could be working *for* Nanergetix. He denied that and told us he was competing against Buell's company. We don't know that for sure."

"It makes too much sense," he says, shaking his head at me and gripping the steering wheel with both hands. "Think about it. Your boss is sending you around the world on clandestine missions to hand over iPods to a host of energy executives. You know you weren't delivering musical playlists."

I stop myself again from telling him about the bank account information loaded onto the iPod in Alaska.

"Here is connection number one: The Governor of Texas and sneaky energy executives." He presses the accelerator and changes lanes to pass a slow moving car ahead of us. "We know Ripley, the son, is working on some nanotechnology that interests the Governor and his oily friends. There's connection number two. So whatever Ripley is developing either competes with or compliments Nanergetix's neo-energy project. Nanergetix is financed by Don Carlos Buell who is trying to take your boss's job. That's connection number three."

"I agree with you, but—"

"Wait," George holds up his right hand. "Let me finish this. I'm on a roll."

"Go ahead."

"Connection number four: Buell is shot and nearly killed by Ripley's dad, a self-proclaimed secessionist who has a website proclaiming big time support for your boss. Your boss, by the way, likes to talk about secession like it's feasible. Like it's part of a political platform. Ripley says he was framed." George keeps glancing in his rear view mirror as he drives. "And he told me it was because of his son."

"Yeah," I interrupt. "For the sake of argument, don't all criminal suspects claim to be innocent?"

"Given. But there are too many connections here. It comes full circle. The Governor, Ripley, Nanergetix, Buell, oil and gas.

They're all connected somehow."

"And I'm in the middle."

"And you're in the middle," George agrees. "The question still out there is, 'Why?'. We have the who, the what, the where..."

"You mean, why am I in the middle?"

"That's part of it." George speeds up again. We're nearing highway 59. I vaguely recognize we're still in southwest Houston. "Maybe you're mixed up in this because nobody's sure exactly what you know," he continues. "Maybe they want to make sure you stay quiet about whatever it is that's going down."

"It's evident that's why I was kidnapped," I said, though I can't reconcile why I was let go or who killed Bobby.

George checks his side view mirror and changes lanes. He presses on the brake as we approach a red light. "Yeah. Why were you let go? Why did someone else, I assume, try to kill you? What was on those iPods? What is it they think you know? Does this conspiracy end with an attempted assassination? Is there more to it? Was the Buell shooting the beginning?"

I'm about to tell George about what I saw on the Alaska iPod when he jerks the SUV from the left lane and into the right. He glances in his rear view mirror and grimaces.

"This ass won't stay off my bumper," he says, slowing the SUV. I turn around to look over my left shoulder and see a car inching even with us. It's a black sedan with dark tinted windows.

"George! You've got to get us out of here. That's the car!" My heart is racing in my chest. "Those are the guys who killed my friend Bobby!"

George accelerates, speeding through a yellow light and on to a feeder road. Within a second he's merged onto the highway heading north towards downtown. He must be doing 90 miles per hour as he moves to the left and he slams on the brakes, the brakes scream, and we stop inches short of a red SUV in front of us. Traffic is at a standstill.

***

I've seen slow speed police chases on television before. I even covered one in San Antonio. Some idiot robbed a taqueria and led police through nearby neighborhoods for close to an hour before he ditched the car and surrendered. I've always wondered what must go through the mind of someone as they try to escape.

Now I am that person. I'm the fox and the dogs are giving chase. It seems surreal, being chased on the highway by two dudes who want me dead. We're traveling at something like 5 miles per hour at the most. I should be fried. Strangely, I am calm. My mind is clear. I'm focused. My heart rate has slowed.

George is doing his best to navigate between cars and five lanes of northbound traffic as the black sedan gives chase at the same speed. Every time the sedan, a Cadillac CTS, switches lanes, George forces his way over to the next lane. Horns honk at him one after the other. People must think we're trying to push our way past the logjam.

I glance behind me at the sedan. "Instead of trying to get ahead of them, why don't we fall behind them?" I suggested.

"What?"

"This traffic is so slow that if we fall behind them by a few car lengths, we'll be able to exit without them knowing, or at least without them being able to follow us."

"Good idea," he acknowledges, and checks his rear view mirror before trying to merge to the right. "We can exit up here on the ramp to downtown and take surface streets to the airport."

George moves to the far right lane, which is barely moving. The sedan tries to merge right behind us, but George slams on the brakes. It creates an opening in front of us, which the driver of the sedan lurches forward to take.

The car slowly passes on our left. Both of us watch the car as it inches ahead. Through the dark tint on the front windows, it's difficult to see into the car, but I can see there are two men, both with short, military-type haircuts. The one in the passenger seat is staring at us as they pass. He rolls down the automatic window about halfway. He's wearing sunglasses and a dark suit jacket, white shirt, no tie. He smiles at us and waves with his right hand before the window rolls up again and closes. The car merges in front of us.

"What the hell was that?" George asks. I can see the sweat forming on his brow and upper lip. He keeps wringing his hands on the steering wheel. "Who are these guys?"

"I don't know. They don't seem to care we know they're following us."

"Yeah," George says, wiping his upper lip with the back of his hand. "It's not good they let us see them."

"Why?"

"Haven't you ever watched action movies?" George glances at me as if I'm stupid. "The bad guys always kill people who've seen their faces. They don't want people to identify them. It's the kiss of death. You see their faces – you die."

"They can't kill us if they can't find us, George. Focus on losing them."

George tries to move farther behind the sedan, but they must be onto us. They stay one car in front of us as we inch closer to the exit for downtown. The sedan has no rear license plate.

"Is the exit up here?" I ask. I was on this same stretch of road in the bus a few hours ago, but I don't remember paying any attention to the exits.

"Yeah, maybe a mile," he says. "But it's on the left. If I try to merge over, they'll get back behind us. This isn't working." He looks at me, his face flushed with stress. This kind of pressure is clearly different from trying to make a deadline for a newscast. He's folding on me.

"Okay look," I say, looking behind me to the right. "There's this wide shoulder here next to us. "Why don't you get onto the shoulder and back up?"

"You mean, put the car in reverse?"

"Yeah, I'll watch out for you."

George looks in his rear view mirror before merging to the right and brakes, lurching the Lexus. He turns and puts his right arm behind my seat, shifts into reverse, and punches the accelerator. Within five seconds we're ten cars behind the sedan. Another five seconds and we're an additional ten cars back.

"That's good," I say. "Now get back onto the highway and merge all the way to the left.

George shifts back into drive and slips onto the freeway. Up ahead there's a sedan moving backwards along the shoulder. They're trying the same thing, but by the time they've made it back to where we were, George has already managed to maneuver into the far left lane and is several car lengths ahead. He's put enough distance between us and the sedan that I can't see it. George slides into the left shoulder and speeds up to 20 or 30 miles per hour as we approach the downtown exit.

He swerves back into the far left lane, cutting off an 18-wheeler that blows its horn at us. He clears the truck, and speeds down the exit ramp toward downtown.

"I'm taking Travis Street," he tells me, which is the first of three street exits off of the ramp. "I want to get off this ramp before they catch up." George steers the Lexus down the Travis Street exit and blows through a stop sign, speeding into downtown.

We merge onto Travis Street and fly through two or three intersections before George turns right onto Elgin and past Houston Community College. He almost runs over a young woman with a backpack slung over her shoulder. She's wearing ear buds and is oblivious to us until the front end of the Lexus comes within about a foot of her.

She jerks back and flips us the finger, yells something at us I am sure is laced with profanity, kicks the front of the Lexus with the sole of her sneakered foot, and finishes crossing the intersection.

George is white-knuckling the steering wheel, the color drained from his face. He needs a cigarette, I know.

He exhales and eases through the intersection. There's nobody behind us. We lost the black sedan and the assassins inside.

George speeds up again and turns north onto San Jacinto. We pass a BMW dealership and drive underneath an interstate overhead. A sign tells me it's I-45, the highway that runs from Galveston to Dallas.

We pass a large church on the left, which reminds me to pray for help.

God, please help us. Please get us out of this mess.

I think about making some sort of promise in exchange for divine intervention, but realize God knows it would be an empty offer. I haven't really kept my end of the deal with Him through most of my life. Then again, I long believed *He* failed *me* when he took my parents. I blamed Him for a long time and never really moved past agnosticism after that.

Now, in the midst of what could be the last moments of my

life, I am suddenly moved to ask for help. I'm desperate. If he's listening, he sees right through me, I'm sure.

"Praying?" George asks me.

"Uh," I am surprised by the question. "Yeah, I guess."

"Me too," he says without taking his eyes off the road. "It can't hurt."

We're driving through the intersection with Polk Street, about to pass the House of Blues ahead on the right when...

Boom! *Wham*!

My neck snaps to the left and then right. My head impacts with something, maybe the window. The SUV spins, and my whole body slams into George, who is pressed into the driver's side door. The Lexus stops when we hit a car parallel parked on the left side of the one-way street. I'm a little disoriented, but I gain focus in time to see two men walking toward the car. In the distance behind them is their black sedan, its front end smashed. They're maybe twenty-five yards from the car. I fumble with my seatbelt to unlatch it, but I can't find the button. My door is crushed.

"George! Are you okay?"

He moans and shakes his head. At least he's conscious.

"George!" I repeat. "We gotta go!"

I finally locate the button on the seatbelt and unhook myself. Scrambling into the back seat of the Lexus I stay low and manage to open the back door. I slide to the street, stumble to my feet and start running.

"Hey!" someone yells from behind me. "Hey, Quick! Stop running!"

I'm running aimlessly, not sure of where I am going. My head is pounding. My vision is a little blurry. I'm having trouble breathing as I run, but I'm not stopping.

"Quick!" It's a second voice. Both men are following me.

I turn around, continuing to run, looking over my shoulder. Both men are standing at the Lexus. I can't see George. He may still be in the car, I can't tell. One of the men, gun in hand, starts to trot toward me. I can see a crowd starting to gather near the intersection, people getting out of their cars.

I turn back around, still a little dizzy, and keep running. My legs feel heavy. I'm limping on my right leg. I can't stop. If they catch me, I am dead. I'm on a sidewalk now, running along Polk. I can feel people looking at me as I run past. My right side is starting to hurt. One of the dark suited men is jogging after me. He's not in an all-out sprint like me, but seems to be keeping pace. Maybe he doesn't want to call too much attention to himself. Ahead is the Hyatt Hotel. I dig a little deeper and run across Louisiana to the hotel entrance.

Straight ahead is a bank of glass elevators. I speed walk to the back of the atrium lobby and turn the corner to find the row of elevator doors. Still breathing hard, feeling bruised and exhausted, I press the UP button followed by the DOWN button. Whatever opens first, I'm taking.

The elevator rings and the door closest to me opens. I get in and press the button to close the door. It takes an eternity, but it shuts and I consider my options. The arrow above the door is pointing down. One button is labeled T. I don't know what that means, but I push it.

The elevator lurches downward and stops. The doors open to a sign on the wall directly opposite the elevator. HOUSTON TUNNEL SYSTEM. SOUTH LOUISIANA. There is an arrow pointing to the right directing me to the TUNNEL LOOP. I decide that's my best option. I turn right and start jogging down a long wide hallway.

I'd forgotten Houston has a massive underground tunnel system running ninety-five city blocks. It's two stories under downtown and is full of restaurants and shops. The city built it to keep downtown workers out of the heat in the scorching summer months. It was Houston's version of the heated sky bridges in downtown Des Moines or Minneapolis meant to keep workers from freezing in the winter.

The tunnel makes a hard right and a quick left. A sign on the wall reads RELIANT ENERGY PLAZA. I keep moving, not sure of where I am going. I have to keep moving.

***

I've made my way to the LOUISIANA NORTH TUNNEL despite the growing pain in my side. My headache has ballooned into a pulsing, vision-altering, migraine-like pain. I haven't seen or heard anyone following me since I dropped into the tunnel system. I can afford to find a bathroom and assess my injuries.

I am underneath the Bank of America Center when I find a men's room. I push on the door and duck inside. To my left is a wall of sinks with a full length mirror above the stainless automatic faucets. To my right are a half dozen stalls and a couple of urinals. I pick a stall toward the end of the row, close and lock the door behind me, and lean against the door.

Gingerly, I lift my Kinky shirt and look down at my right side. There's a large circular bruise at the lower edge of my ribcage that stretches a good six inches toward my stomach. There's maybe some swelling there too, but I can't really tell. I take a deep, wheezy breath. I may have a cracked rib or worse. The adrenaline that carried me here is diminishing, and the pain is intensifying. My right knee is throbbing, but there's no visible injury.

I lower my shirt and turn to open the stall door, looking to the mirror to see if there are any injuries to my face or head. The headache is a bad sign. I spin the lock on the stall just when the bathroom door bangs open.

"Quick?"

Holy crap.

It's one of the dark suited men. How the hell did he find me?

As quietly as I can, I slip off my shoes and slide them under the stall to my left. It's closer to the entrance. I place my hands on the sides of the stall and step up onto the toilet seat. This isn't going to work. I've got no other choice. I'm cornered. There's a broken handicap rail on the right side. It's about two feet long and attached to the stall by maybe one rusted screw in a stripped hole. It's not much to hold and the rail might fall if I'm not careful.

Why did I stop? Why didn't I keep running?

"Quick," the man calls again, "I know you're here. I followed the blood."

What blood?

For the first time, I see the droplets of blood on the floor. They are bright red, iridescent almost. I imagine there must be some sort of blood trail that led this psycho straight to me.

Where is the blood coming from?

My heart accelerates and the pounding in my head matches its rapid beat. I realize the blood must be coming from my head, and I must be worse off than I thought.

Bam! The first stall door slams open. I can hear his shoes squeak on the tile floor as he steps.

"Look, Quick, we don't need to play it this way. Make it easy on yourself."

I can feel the warmth of the sweat on the back of my neck and behind my ears. I try to keep my balance on the toilet seat. It's getting increasingly difficult.

Bam! The second stall door slams open.

"You can't hide from us, you know." His voice sounds strained, as though he's bending over when he talks, looking under the stall doors. "We've found you three times now."

Bam! The third door is open.

"We got you on the way from Austin. Thought we had you there." He chuckles. "Then we found you again at Rice."

Bam! The fourth door? How many stalls are there?

"And now, I've got you here," he says. His voice stretches as he bends over. He's at the stall where I put my shoes.

I've got to do something. I'm a sitting duck in here. He's gonna kill me. Sweat drips into my eyes, stinging them shut. I wipe my face on my shoulder, still pressing against the sides of the stall. Balancing myself on the toilet, I reach to unlock the latch to the stall. The door swings inward.

Bam!

The stall door next to me slams open.

"Nice trick, Quick," he chuckles. "But the shoes aren't gonna save you."

Under the stall I can see his black dress shoes. He's at my door.

"Okay," I say. I don't really have a plan. I've got to buy a little bit of time. I can see him through the crack in the door as I jump down from the toilet and grab onto the loose handicap rail.

"You've got me," I concede. "I unlocked the door for you. I'm not gonna struggle. Just don't kill me in a—"

Before I finish my sentence, the door flies open. At that instant, almost expecting it, I tighten my grip around the broken rail, pull it from the wall, and swing. Because of the awkward angle, I don't make great contact. I did get his hand. He squeals and his gun drops to the floor, sliding under the stall next to me.

The door slams open again, this time surprising me and knocking me back against the toilet. I hit my head on the back wall of the stall. It jars me for an instant and the dark suited man is on me. I try to swing at him with the rail, but I can't get any leverage. He manages to knock it from my hand and he punches me in the gut. I'm flailing, fighting against his weight without much success. He's a blur. He's strong. His hands are thick. He smells like Old Spice.

I'm gonna die in a toilet at the hands of a cheap bastard.

I get lucky. One of my kicks caught him in the gut or groin, because he falls back out of the stall and onto the floor. I scramble to my feet and grab the rail again. He's on the floor gasping for air.

I raise the aluminum rail over my head and swing down as if I'm cleaving an axe into a log. I hit him in the left knee, which he grabs, gasping for air. He sounds like a leaking tire. I swing again at the same knee, this time getting the knee and his hand.

I'm about to swing a third time when I start to lose focus. My eyes are blurring and I can't keep my balance. I almost fall back, but catch myself against the stall. I feel drunk or dehydrated. I've been both before and can't distinguish between the two.

I drop to my knees. On all fours, sweat drips from the side of my face onto the cement. Why is the sweat red? Sweat isn't red.

My head is throbbing. It's pounding. With each beat, my vision worsens.

I roll onto my side. There's a gun somewhere nearby. There's a killer on the floor next to me. I can't do anything about either one right now. I want to sleep.

I'm tired. My head hurts. It's cold. I'm facing the bathroom door, trying to keep my eyes open. Something inside me tells me if I pass out, I will die. Something is very wrong with me.

Behind me, the dark suited man moans. He's getting his breath. He'll kill me when he can crawl to that gun.

He's grunting now. I can feel him slide up against me. I'm too weak to do anything.

"You're dead, Quick," he says as he rolls over me. He's going for the gun.

I close my eyes and brace myself for the gunshot. What must have been a second feels like an eternity as time slows, almost freezing.

My pulse beats at my temple, my breath ripples the small pool of blood on the floor in front of me.

Click. The chamber. It must be the chamber. There's a small, cold cylinder pressed against my left temple.

This is where I join my parents. A calm sense of relief begins to wash over me.

One last breath. One final beat.

Pow! Pow!

Two gunshots. Or one and maybe an echo.

The weight of the dark suited man drops onto my back.

Am I alive?

"I told you you couldn't go anywhere without me knowing about it," a voice says, muffled from the ring in my ears. It's still deep and resonant. It gets louder as he approaches, familiar and frightening.

"Jackson, you really should be more careful." I don't have to open my eyes to know who it is. I smell the licorice before everything goes black.

***

The first time I was bullied, I didn't know what to think of it. It seemed to be happening in slow motion.

It was my third day in sixth grade and I was thin and wiry, small for my age. My body hadn't grown into my arms and legs or ears. I had a full length locker at the end of the hall and I hadn't memorized the combination to the lock. Most of the other kids had already retrieved their books and headed to class, and the halls were empty.

"34 right?" I remember mumbling aloud. "Or is it 34 left?"

"34, 35, 24, 37," mocked a voice behind me, followed by the laughter of two or three other people. "Baby Jacktard can't remember how to open his locker!"

I didn't turn around. I kept fumbling with the numbers and tugging on the lock. Finally it opened.

34 left!

A large hand slammed into the locker door right next to my ear.

"It is Jacktard, right?" It was Blair Loxley. He was big and strong and mean.

I turned to face him. The top of my head came to his chin. There was something nasty in his eyes, and a story there I didn't want to know.

Loxley's pimpled face was pale and his hair was shoe polish black. He was broad shouldered with a muscular thickness that belied his age. I knew he'd repeated fourth and fifth grade, and was still much larger than most of the current eighth graders.

"I asked you a question," he growled.

I glanced to his right side and saw the three other boys who'd been laughing their encouragement. I recognized one of them as a kid in my science class, but I'd never seen the other two. All three of them had their arms folded like bouncers protecting the entrance to a Sixth Street bar.

"I heard you," I said, trying not to give away any sense of fear. I imagined he was like an animal that could sense any hint of it. "I thought you were talking to one of your stooges."

I didn't really know what the word *stooge* meant, though I knew enough about Larry, Curley, and Moe to understand it wasn't a compliment.

"Stooges?" Loxley said, his tone making it apparent he'd come to the same conclusion. "You're joking right?" He turned to look at his henchmen. "He's joking right?"

They laughed and nodded. I didn't say anything, just stared into those pained eyes of his.

"I'm not joking," I said. I studied his face. I could feel my heart pounding against my chest now. I wasn't going to back down, and I was sure this would not end well. An unfamiliar, involuntary strength, was coursing through me

"Neither am I!" he grunted as he dipped his right shoulder and elbowed me in the gut.

I felt all the air leave my body and I dropped to my knees, unable to catch my breath. I gasped for air, my chest burning, tears welling in my eyes. I tried to stand, but Loxley put his hands on my shoulders and held me down. He was telling the other boys to do something, but I was too focused on trying to breathe to understand him.

Two of the boys grabbed my arms, one at each elbow, and used their free hands to twist violently against the skin on my forearms. Indian burns. *Atomic* Indian burns.

It took everything in me to keep from screaming in pain. Instead of giving in, I squeezed my eyes shut and struggled against them. It only served to make the pain worse until I blindly lifted my right leg and kicked.

I didn't connect with anything and so I kicked again. Kick. Kick. Kick. I must have seemed like an infant throwing a tantrum; eyes shut, tears streaming down my cheeks, legs flailing.

I felt another hard punch to the gut. My eyes popped open and I felt drool trailing from the corner of my mouth. I was out of air.

"Don't do it again, Jacktard," hissed Loxley. "Don't resist me. Take what's coming to you and shut up. If you tell anyone about this, the next time will be worse."

He shoved his palm against my forehead, slamming it against my locker, then he led the two henchmen away.

I sunk to the floor quietly. My arms were on fire, my breath was slow to come back.

I was determined to get even.

PART II
NOT EVERYTHING IS
BIGGER IN TEXAS

"Future years will never know the seething hell and the black infernal background, the countless minor scenes and interiors of the secession war; and it is best they should not. The real war will never get in the books"
--WALT WHITMAN

CHAPTER 4

"Jaaaacksonnnn?" The voice is muted but soft and sweet in my left ear. "Jaaaaacksonnnn, baaaaabyyyy? Cannn yoooo heeeearrrr meeeee?"

It's Charlie. Her voice is breaking through the fog.

My eyes are closed and heavy. I can feel her hands wrapped around the fingers on my left hand, feel the slight squeeze.

"Jaaacksonnn?" she whispers. "He's waking up." She must be talking to someone else now.

I'm trying to open my eyes, trying to move and wake up.

Where am I?

"He should be waking up soon," says another woman's voice. This one is gruffer, masculine in tone. "The sedative doesn't last long."

Sedative?

I'm trying to move but can't. I'm paralyzed.

Am I paralyzed?

A distant beeping noise gets louder and faster.

"Hear the heart monitor?" It's the man-woman voice again. "He's waking up and his heart rate is quickening. He can probably hear us talking about him."

"Should I keep talking to him?" Charlie asks, squeezing my hand again.

"Sure."

"Jackson, baby," she says, her voice soft again and closer to my ear, "you're safe. You're okay. You're here in the hospital with me.

Everything is going to be fine."

Hospital? Hospital?

It all rushes back: the gun shot, the fight in the bathroom, the tunnel, the crash, Bobby's blood, The Saint, the iPods...

The beeping, which had slowed, is again loud and fast. There's an involuntary twitch in my left arm.

"Jackson, open your eyes. Try to open them a little," Charlie says.

My eyes feel like they're glued shut. Slowly, and with considerable effort, I'm able to open them. At first all I can see is white. As my pupils shrink, I can make out the fuzzy shape of Charlie sitting at my bedside. Apparently my head is turned to left, and she's been talking to me in my right ear. I'm totally disoriented.

"Oh, Jackson, I was so scared." She leans in and kisses my cheek. "They told me you were here, and I rushed to get here."

I try to speak, but my mouth is dry and my lips seem cauterized. Against the scratch in my throat I whisper, "How did you find out?"

"How did I find out what?"

My focus is improving and I can see the furrow in her brow. Her red hair is pulled back in a ponytail and there are thick smudges of black under her eyes. Her nose is red.

"That I was here?"

"They said they found my number in your phone. You'd texted me or something. They called the last number dialed."

She's right. I did text her from the bus.

"How did I get here?" I lick my top lip slowly. My mouth is dry.

"Somebody dropped you off," Charlie says. She reaches for a Styrofoam cup on the bedside table, dips a plastic spoon into it and shovels out some ice chips, which she scoops into my mouth. "This'll help."

I guess the look on my face betrays my confusion, because she continues to explain.

"Some guy pulled up into the ambulance bay right behind the emergency room entrance, found a wheelchair and put you in it. He wheeled you up to the nurses' station and left. He didn't say anything, just left you there with your head bleeding." She scoops another spoonful of ice into my mouth.

"The doctors told me you had two bad cuts to the back of your head. They removed a couple of pieces of glass too. They said it looked like you'd been in a car crash. You also had a concussion."

"I *was* in a car crash." I clear my throat. "It was downtown."

"Is that why the cop is here?" She looks past me toward what I guess is the hallway outside my room. I hadn't looked that way yet.

Cop?

"He's been outside your room for an hour or two now," she speaks softly again. "The doctors won't let him in the room yet. They said he wants to talk to you."

I twist myself to the right and shift my weight to the right side of my body. I'm tangled a little bit in the IV line that disappears into my right hand, but I manage.

Through the door to my room, I can see the hustle of the emergency nurses and doctors across the hallway. Sitting in a chair to the left of my door is who I suppose is the police officer. He's wearing a white shirt with a blue blazer, gray pants, and a burgundy colored tie loosely knotted around his neck. He looks fit and his dark hair is combed back and gelled flat against his head.

"He's not in a uniform," I say without turning back to Charlie.

"I know. Someone must have died in that car crash, Jackson."

"What?" I spin around and feel the pinch of the needle in my hand.

She takes my left hand again. "He told me he was a homicide detective and..." she pauses, as though she's finding it difficult to share bad news, "he said he needs to talk to you when you're up to it. Were you driving, Jackson?"

Charlie's eyes glass over and well up. A thick tear runs down her face and detours at her lips.

"Oh God, Jackson," she sighs. "Were you driving a car that killed someone?"

I shake my head. I'm still fuzzy about many things going on around me, but I wasn't driving. The cops should know that too.

"I wasn't driving."

Charlie wipes the mascara from under her eyes with the backs of her index fingers and puffs out her cheeks to exhale. She seems spent but she's still beautiful.

"I've got to clean up," she says. She stands and fans her face with her hands. "I am a mess!" She leans down to kiss my forehead. "I'll be back in a minute."

I roll back, still twisted in the IV line, to watch her leave. My eyes are fixed on her skinny jeans until she stops to talk to the officer in the chair. She says something, looks back at me and smiles, and disappears down the hall.

The officer stands, brushes off the arms of his blazer, and walks to the doorway of my room.

"Ah'm Detective Crockett," he says, leaning in against the door jamb. He has a deep southern twang. "Your girlfriend here says you're feelin' better. Maybe we could talk?"

"Sure," I tell him. What other choice do I have? "Is George okay?"

"Who's George?" he asks. "I'm here to talk to ya 'bout Bobby."

The beeping from the heart monitor gets louder and repeats faster. It's an unintentional lie detector. The detective notices and tilts his head. His right hand has a red and yellow tattoo. There is something inked on his fingers too.

"Hmmph," he grunts and slips his hands into his pants pockets. "Sumpin' got ya nervous, Mr. Quick?"

"Do I need a lawyer?" I don't think I want to tell this guy anything.

"I dunno," he says, taking a step into the room. "Do ya?" He takes another step toward my bed when he's interrupted.

"Excuse me," says a tall woman with broad shoulders and a surgical cap on her head who pushes past the detective and stands between him and me. "You can't be in here." I recognize the baritone. It's the man-woman. "I've already told you this," she says as her words push Crockett back out of the room. "He hasn't been awake for ten minutes. I need to check his vitals. He's had injuries to his head."

"The girlfriend gave me permission," he says, maybe a little bit intimidated by the doctor. "So I figgered..."

"You *figgered* wrong," she mocks him. "Now go!" She waves him back to his chair. "If you bother him again until I give you permission, you'll be out of my hospital."

The cop backs up to his chair and sits down. He brushes off his jacket sleeves and crosses his legs. He pulls out a cell phone and starts dialing.

The man-woman turns her full attention to me and grabs a clipboard from the end of the bed. "I'm Doctor Graff," she says, "and you are...Jackson Quick?"

I nod.

"You have had a nasty day, Mr. Quick," she tells me. "A concussion. At least one. You've got a couple of deep lacerations to the scalp at the base of your skull. We pulled some glass fragments from your head. They looked like tinted window glass, probably from a car. Blood work shows no alcohol in your system, or any other drugs. You did lose a fair amount of blood and were dehydrated when you got here."

I just look at her.

"So," she says, "your prognosis is good. We stitched you up with a half dozen dissolving sutures. You might need a little Tylenol or something for the next couple of days, but other than that..."

"I can go?"

She shrugs her massive shoulders and folds her arms across her chest, pressing the clipboard flat against herself. "I guess so. It'll be a few hours. We need to do some paperwork and such, but you should be out of here by later this morning."

"Morning?" I ask. "When did I get here?"

"Middle of the night," she says. "Six or seven hours ago. Someone just dropped you off. We thought you were homeless at first, then we found your wallet in your front pocket, and your phone."

I roll back onto my left side. For some reason, it's more comfortable.

"How do you want me to handle this cop out here?" Doctor Graff walks around to the left side of the bed, sitting in Charlie's chair. "Want me to stall him? I mean, I know I should be helpful to the police. Lord knows, I don't know you from Adam. But that cop gives me the creeps. He's way pushier than most who come in here."

"Where is here?" I ask. I still don't know where exactly I am.

"Memorial Hermann Texas Medical Center. Busiest trauma room in the country," she smiles, unconsciously pulling back those shoulders with pride. "What do you want me to do?"

"Have you seen his badge?" I asked. "What police department is he with?"

"You know," she says, considering the question, "I don't know. Let me check." She gets up from the chair, still holding the clipboard and walks back across the room to the hallway. I can't see into the hall.

Charlie is standing in the doorway, her hands in her pockets. Her hair is out of its ponytail and softly frames her face. She smiles at me and walks to the right side of my bed, next to the IV machine. She sits on the edge of the bed and puts her hand on the white sheet covering my legs.

"You okay?" I ask. My voice still doesn't sound normal. It's raspy.

"Am *I* okay?" She laughs and tosses her head back. "You're in a horrible crash, the police want to talk to you, and you ask if *I'm* okay."

Doctor Graff appears in the room behind Charlie. "Mr. Quick, it looks like you'll get out of here a little sooner than I thought."

"Why?"

"Well," she says, "when I asked the cop which agency he works for and to show me a badge, he up and left."

I look at Charlie and back at the doctor in confusion.

"He didn't want to answer me," Doctor Graff said. "Maybe he wasn't really a cop."

"I don't get it." I look at Charlie again. "I thought he talked to you, Charlie?"

"He did," she says. "He told me he worked for homicide."

"He didn't tell you *where* he works?"

"No."

My attention returns to the doctor. "Your hospital let him in here without knowing who he is?" My voice cracks.

Doctor Graff arches her back in indignation, her voice deepens. "We let *you* in here without knowing who you are. We're a hospital, not a secure government facility. We didn't let him get close to you."

Close enough.

Whoever he is, he knows about Bobby. He knew where to find me. I am not safe. Charlie is not safe.

"Charlie," I put my hand on her leg. "We have got to get out of here and disappear."

***

I'm at the back entrance of the hospital, sitting in a wheelchair and waiting for Charlie to pull her car around when I see "Detective Crockett" standing at the opposite end of the parking lot. He's leaning against a wall, smoking a cigarette. At first I don't think he notices me, but he tosses the butt to the sidewalk, grinds it into the cement, and starts walking toward me.

I can't wait for Charlie. I stand up and push back from the wheelchair.

"Sir," says the nurse behind me, "you'll need to stay in the chair until your ride pulls up."

I ignore her and spin to walk away from the hospital and Crockett.

"Sir!"

I'm too focused on where I need to go to answer her. I need to get away from this guy, whoever he is.

I reach the end of the parking lot where it meets the street and turn left. My legs feel lighter than I would have expected. I guess being rehydrated has helped.

"Jackson!" he's calling after me. I don't turn around, but I can hear the stress in his voice. He's jogging, breathing heavily. "I need to... talk. To. You! You. Need. To. Stop."

I start to jog to the next intersection, which meets at the front entrance to the hospital. It's Fannin Street, a main street that runs through the medical center, I remember. The traffic is heavy with early morning commuters.

"Jackson!" He's running now. Maybe only ten yards behind me. He's fast.

I pick up my pace and begin to run as Charlie drives past me in her silver Jetta. I try not to look at her, but I can sense she sees me and is confused. Her brakes screech on the pavement.

"Jackson! What are you doing?"

I don't turn around. Can't she see I'm being chased? Is she blind? I raise my hand to wave at her as I keep running and round the corner onto Fannin. I turn left in front of the hospital and notice the light rail train approaching in the distance. It's coming toward me. Across the street, where the tracks run, there's a train platform.

Oblivious to the traffic, I sprint across two lanes to the platform just as the train passes in front of me, separating me from Crockett. The doors open and I slip into the rail car to find a seat. There are maybe a half dozen people on the train, and several of them appear homeless. I find a rear-facing seat in the front of the car.

I slip into the molded plastic seat, which reminds me of a McDonalds' booth, winded from the brief run and try to catch my breath. There's blood on my Kinky shirt. I would have thought the hospital would wash my clothes.

The Metro light rail trains run essentially north and south. The large, color-coded map on the wall of the train car shows a northbound stop at Rice University, which I consider, but decide to skip. A couple of stops away is a transfer station to buses. That's a possibility, as is the one in the middle of downtown.

What am I doing? I can't keep running aimlessly. They'll find me again. I have got to get to Ripley in West Texas.

I pull my cell phone out of my front pocket and thumb through the menu until I find my missed calls. I toggle to George's number and hit send. It rings twice.

"George Townsend."

"George? Is that you?"

"Is this Jackson?"

"Yeah, it's me. Dude, I can't believe you answered your phone. I thought you were hurt or dead!"

"Yeah," he sighs, "almost." He sounds tired. "I got bruised up pretty badly in the crash, but I'm okay. Where are you? "

"On my way to find Ripley. Where are you?"

"I'm at home. The station gave me the day off."

"I don't get it," I tell him. "Don't you want to finish this?"

"I *am* finished, Jackson," he says. "I don't think..."

"Don't think what?" I snap, irritated.

"I don't think I can help you anymore."

"What? Why not?" I lurch forward as the train stops at a platform. A few people get off, several more get on.

"This is too heavy for me, man." I can hear him suck on a cigarette and exhale. "This is life and death. I almost got killed."

"I *told* you this was life and death." I'm trying hard to keep my voice down but it's difficult. I'm pissed off. "You *knew* that. I told you my friend got killed. I told you I was kidnapped and tortured. There are big things happening here."

"Too big," he says. He doesn't sound like the same ambitious reporter he was yesterday.

"They got to you didn't they? Somebody scared you into backing off. Was it the other guy in the dark suit? The professor at Rice? Buell?"

"Buell?" he scoffs. "You're being paranoid."

"Paranoid?" I laugh. "It's not paranoia when you're *really* being followed and men are *really* trying to kill you, George."

He says nothing, sucks in another drag.

"We have to meet." Something's not adding up and I can't tell what it is over the phone.

Silence.

"George?"

"Okay," he reluctantly agrees. "George Bush Monument. It's a public park. You know where it is?"

"No."

"It's across the street from the main post office on the corner of Franklin and Bagby. Meet me there in a half hour."

I flip the phone closed and slip it into my pocket. The train is slowing again. Another stop. No one gets off, but a couple of people get on.

The map on the wall of the car tells me I should take the train to Preston, get off there, and walk four or five blocks west to Bagby. I can find the monument from there. I'm focused on the map when a man sits down next to me. I don't recognize him until he speaks.

"Jackson," he says. "You are always on the run, aren't you?" I smell the licorice on his breath. It reminds me of pain and I unconsciously rub my wrist.

I start to get up but he firmly grabs my forearm and urges me to sit. I comply.

"You should sit with me," he hisses. "You owe me one."

His eyes are black and lifeless. It's as though the iris bleeds into the pupils, making his eyes look permanently dilated. There are deep creases at his temples and thick swells of skin underneath his lower lids. He is older than I imagined. His hair is white, not gray, though his eyebrows are still black. He's clean shaven and his angular jaw protrudes forward. His skin is ruddy and folded. He is a large man who appears uncomfortable in his expensive clothing. He clears his throat.

"I saved your life, good boy."

"Saved it?" My voice raises an octave and only the squeeze of his paw on my arm lowers the volume to a whisper. "You put me here. I am running because of you, you sadistic piece of—"

"Right," he says. "This is my fault. It is so typical of your generation to blame others for problems of their own making." He releases his grip on my arm, closes his eyes, and sighs, adjusting the red silk cravat at his neck

"What do you want from me? What do those other dudes want from me?"

"Those other dudes," he chuckles. "That's why you owe me, Jackson." For a split second, there's life in his eyes. "You need to trust what I am about to tell you." His stare lasts a second longer than is comfortable and I glance away. "You are well aware your life is at risk here. This, Jackson, is much bigger than you."

"I know," I say, still avoiding eye contact.

"Do you know what is on those iPods you delivered?" His grip tightens, but loosens when I squirm.

"I told you I don't," I remind him. "You need to trust what *I'm* telling *you*."

The train lurches to a stop and more people get off.

"We know," he whispers close to my ear. "You synched an iPod to a computer before you delivered it to the contact in Tulsa."

Tulsa was my final delivery. It happened a week ago, or two weeks ago. I've lost track of my days. It was just a couple of days before the psycho sitting next to me managed to drug me and torture me. My pulse is quickening, sweat forming on my lip.

"Is that why you took me?" I ask. "Trying to find out what I knew?"

He doesn't respond.

"Look," I try to assure him. "I never hooked up any of the

iPods to any computers."

"So," his lips stretch into a smile, two worms simultaneously inching themselves across his cheeks. "You admit you know about the iPods. That is most assuredly progress, Jackson."

"Progress," I shoot back, "would be *you* telling *me* what all of this has to do with Don Carlos Buell."

"That is complicated."

"Really?" My sardonic response surprises even me. The fear I felt the moment he sat down next to me has given way to a resigned confidence. I've got nothing to lose.

"You don't need to know more than you already do until the timing is right," he says. "What you *do* need to know, is that you cannot trust anyone involved with this."

"Yeah," I laugh. "Like that isn't first the most trite spy novel, movie thriller line ever, and second, you told me to trust *you.*"

"Look, I'm telling you to let this play out to what I imagine is its logical conclusion. Be careful. You're traveling west?"

"How do you know that?"

"I told you I know everything you're doing," he reminds me. "Go where you need to go and do what you need to do to figure this out. They're more afraid of what you know than I am and I can only do so much to help."

"Why do you want to help me?" I ask him. "You tortured me for days. You could have killed me."

"I didn't," he says, the thin smile worming across his face again.

"So?"

"So," he says as the train slows again. "That means I don't want you dead."

"Whose side are you on?" I watch him stand to get off the train. As much as he makes my skin crawl, I don't want him to leave. "What is happening?"

"You're doing my work for me, Jackson," he says. "Right now, I'm on your side."

"But..." I stand and start to follow him. I'm too slow. The door shuts and the train pulls away from the platform. The Saint is gone.

They're afraid of what *I* know, he said.

What do I know?

Next to me in the molded plastic seat is a newspaper. The Saint left it. It's turned to an article about the Governor's race: *Buell Picks Up Steam, Sympathy After Shooting*

A shot in the arm, so to speak. The bulk of the piece explores the latest polling:

"Our internal numbers," according to a source within the Buell campaign, "are showing large jumps in groups most likely to vote. They're also indicating to us that, while the Governor's ridiculous secession message is resonating with fringe-thinking Texans, it's not as strong as his (Buell's) likeability and his revolutionary thinking on a future for the energy industry. He knows this could usher in a new kind of energy dominance, the way Texas took the lead in wind power years ago."

The source spoke to the Chronicle on the condition of anonymity, because the source is not authorized to speak on behalf of the campaign.

The campaign did point to the widely released polling averages on the website Real Clear Politics. Those numbers reveal a startling nine point swing in Buell's favor since the attempted assassination in Houston less than a week ago.

"Swings like this are not unprecedented," said longtime University of Houston political science professor and pollster Bob Murray. "They generally indicate previously undecided voters have made up their minds. We're not talking about many voters flipping their votes from one candidate to the other."

Buell's lead is outside the margin of error for each of the polls used in the RCP.com index. It is not the kind of momentum the current Governor's campaign expected to have at this point in the election cycle.

"We're aware of the apparent shift in sentiment after the unfortunate attempt on our opponent's life," said campaign spokesperson M. Wiley Helms. "We also believe Texas voters are smart enough to vote with their heads and not their hearts. Sound economics, staying on the path of making Texas stronger, and a realistic vision for our collective future as Texans, is what we think guides every voter's decision come election day. People can feel sorry for a candidate without having to vote for him."

So Buell is seeing a bump from the shooting. He's benefitting from almost getting killed. It's similar to the movie *Bob Roberts*, where an upstart senate candidate sails to an unlikely victory after being shot and supposedly paralyzed.

He benefits. *I'm* on the run.

Why did The Saint want me to see this? It's no coincidence. Maybe he's trying to tell me something about the shooting without really telling me.

I've got to get to West Texas.

***

The George Bush Monument is on the west bank of Buffalo Bayou, the stream of brown water that runs through the city and empties into the Houston Ship Channel and Galveston Bay. The monument is on an elevated hill near Bagby and Franklin Streets, hidden from the streets by oaks and pines. I've been to Houston countless times and never seen it before.

At the center of the monument is an eight-foot tall bronze sculpture of the forty-first president. He's wearing a two-button suit and has his right hand in his pants pocket. His right knee is bent and there's a Mona Lisa smile on his face. It's impressive up close.

Surrounding the statue is a semicircular wall depicting the four stages of the president's life, highlighting various events from his birth to the inauguration of his son, George W. Bush, as forty-third President of the United States. I'm reading some of the bullet points when I feel a hand on my shoulder.

I spin around, swinging my arm at whoever it is behind me.

"Hey," George Townsend says, "it's me." He backs a couple of steps away from me.

"Sorry," I say. "You shouldn't sneak up on me."

"Okay," he says. "I don't want to call much attention to us so I didn't call out your name."

I look around to see if there are any obvious snoops nearby. I don't see anything.

"Look," George says. He steps closer to me and lowers his voice. "Whoever this is wants you dead."

"And? Tell me something I don't know. Is *that* your breaking news?"

George frowns. "I don't need the attitude. You dragged me into this."

"Sorry," I apologize. I take a deep breath to reset. "Let's start over."

"Okay," George looks over his shoulder and inches towards me. He's whispering. "The plates on the car that crashed into us came back to a private security company. My assignment desk looked into it."

"And..."

"And," he pauses for effect as if he's announcing the lowest vote getter on *American Idol*, "they do a lot of work for Don Carlos Buell."

"I knew it."

"They also do a lot of work for the Governor," he adds. I'm not sure what to make of it. ""I didn't see that coming. I mean, what does that *mean*?"

"It means, powerful people, regardless of who they are, don't want you around anymore."

"Okay." I nod, trying to process this new information. "Okay."

"Okay, what?" George looks over his shoulder again, clearly nervous.

"This doesn't change anything. We still need to get to West Texas and talk to Ripley. We still need to know what this is about. Are you in?"

"I don't know..." he backs away a step.

"Is work the problem? Do they need you at the station?"

"No. They gave me a couple of days off because of the accident. And I don't have anything on air until next week anyhow."

"George, if I'm in danger, you are too. You have to figure out what's going on here too."

George looks at me and down at his feet. He shifts his weight and covers his face with his hands. He lets out a sigh and a frustrated grunt.

"What?"

"Okay," he relents. "But we can't fly there together. We need to travel separately."

"Whatever you say." I don't care how we get to West Texas as long as he goes with me.

"I'll fly out of Hobby on Southwest," he informs me. "There's a flight that leaves in two hours. You take United out of Intercontinental. It leaves in two and a half hours, but we'll get in about the same time. I'll meet you at the Dollar Car Rental counter."

"What city?"

"Midland. And, by the way, I've got your backpack. You left it in my car when we wrecked. I'll get it to you at the airport in Midland."

"I thought you were backing out? Why would you already know about flights and rental cars if you were going to back out?"

"I'm a reporter," he says. "I cover my bases. I didn't know what I was going to say when I got here. I didn't know what I was going to do, but I needed to be prepared in the event the story got the better of me."

I smile at him. He knew what he was doing all along.

George turns to leave the park and I pull my cell phone out of my pocket.

"I'll see you there."

I wave at him and dial Charlie to tell her I need a ride to the airport.

***

"You've completely lost it," Charlie says as I buckle into the passenger seat of her Jetta. "I don't understand what this is about. People are chasing you? You're going to go where?"

"I can't really explain. I don't want you getting into any trouble."

"Are you sure your head injuries aren't more serious than the doctor let on?" She glances in the rear view mirror before looking at me. "I mean, seriously Jackson, you're scaring me."

I take a deep breath and put my left hand on her thigh, turning my body toward hers. I can only imagine how confusing and frightening this must be for her.

She's a smart woman with experience in political circles, but she has no experience with espionage or treason or whatever my cloak and dagger life has instantaneously become.

I can only imagine what's running through her head. She must be terrified. I mean, she's outwardly tough, she can hold her own in a bar or on the floor of the State House, but this is totally different.

Time for the truth. At least a little of it. Maybe that will help ease her mind a little bit.

"Look, this is real," I explain. "I've somehow mixed myself up in something bigger than I knew, and now it's all coming home to roost."

We pass the intersection for the north loop. Charlie's in the fast lane, pushing 75 miles per hour.

"What do you mean?" she asks without looking at me, her eyes narrowed and lips pursed.

"I was doing some favors for some people, political fav—"

"What people?" She cuts me off and steers into an interior lane. The car in front of us in the fast lane is moving at a considerably slower speed. Charlie passes him on the right and shifts back to the left, picking up speed again.

"I can't get into that. If I tell you too much, I'll put you in danger."

"You've already put me in danger, Jackson. I mean, you asked me to drive you here to Houston this morning." She glances into the rear view mirror again. "Wasn't that putting me in danger?"

She has a point. I'd risked her life the second I knocked on the door of her apartment after my kidnapping. I was being selfish, true, but I'd wanted to see her. Asking her to drive me here to Houston was another selfish move. In retrospect, it was dangerous too. It certainly was for Bobby. Now, to have her drive me to the airport, I'm endangering her again.

Thinking of others, since my parents' deaths, has not been my strong suit. My world revolves around me, and that revolution is clearly spinning out of control. I have to think about others losing their balance while I try to maintain mine.

"You're right," I concede. "I'm really sorry." She's cruising at close to 80 miles per hour. To the right of the freeway is Gallery Furniture, its big LED sign proclaiming delivery TODAY!!! It stands apart from the seemingly endless blur of strip malls, power lines, and car dealerships that line Houston's roads.

She's clearly irritated with me. "You need to tell me everything. Start with where you're flying."

"West Texas."

"More specific," she says, pushing the accelerator to move past a lumbering 18-wheeler.

"Odessa."

"Why?" Charlie checks her rear view again, looks past me, and slides over two lanes to the right. We're getting close to the beltway and the exit for the airport.

"There's someone there who can help me."

"Who?" Charlie spins the wheel to the right as she decelerates into the exit lane. She glances at me only momentarily. She's focused and deadly serious. There is no hint of expression her face. This is not a side of my girlfriend I've seen. Somehow she flipped a switch.

"Doesn't matter." "The hell it doesn't," she says and fingers her turn signal to indicate we're exiting to the north beltway eastbound. Once she's headed east, she glares at me. "You dragged me into this. I deserve answers."

I'm not sure where the switch flipped, but Charlie went from concerned, to agitated, to angry in the span of a few lane changes.

"I'll call you when I get there," I say vaguely, trying to avoid the question. "That way you know I'm okay. It'll be fine."

"I don't think so," she says. She yanks the wheel to the right, cutting off a small pickup truck, and exits onto the feeder road.

"What are you doing?" I ask, bracing myself against the dashboard to avoid falling into her lap.

Charlie doesn't answer me. Instead, she pulls over into the parking lot of a gas station, squeals into a parking space, and turns off the engine. She unlatches her seatbelt and turns in her seat to look at me.

"Look, I don't mean to snap at you." She reaches for my hand. "I am really worried. I don't understand why you can't tell me what is happening to you. Maybe I can help. We're supposed to be a couple, you know."

"I get it, but your Jekyll and Hyde routine is freaking *me* out a little bit."

"What is that supposed to mean?" She pulls her hand away.

"Just that. You were a little intense there a minute ago. Going all, 'I don't think so!' and 'The hell it doesn't!'" I mimic her serious face and wait for her reaction.

Her face relaxes into a smile. She giggles.

"It's the adrenaline," she says. "It got the better of me. I'm scared."

"I know." I take her hand this time. "It'll be okay. I've got to figure this out, then we can go back to normal." I'm not sure I believe what I'm telling her. I hope she does.

"Promise?"

I nod and lean in to kiss her gently on her lips. She puts her hand on the back of my head and runs her fingers up my hair before I pull back.

"I've got to go to the bathroom. I'm gonna run in here since we've stopped."

I turn to pull on the door handle and step out of the car. She laughs and I turn back to look at her checking herself in the mirror.

"Good idea," she says. "It's a long drive from Odessa to the observatory."

"I bet it is," I laugh and stand to shut the car door.

An electronic chime rings when I slide through the gas station door. At the back of the small building and, past the beer cooler, there's the bathroom door, marked with a plastic sign that reads, 'Customers Only.'

Once in the bathroom, I flip on the light and turn to the toilet.

There's blood everywhere. On the walls. On the floor. On my hands. I close my eyes and open them again. The blood is gone. The sight of Bobby, dead in my arms, is not. I take a deep breath and turn to lock the door when it hits me: *It's a long drive from Odessa to the observatory.*

CHAPTER 5

I didn't tell Charlie I was headed to the Ft. Davis Mountains and the McDonald Observatory.

The mirror above the small porcelain sink has a crack in the glass running almost straight down the center of my face. Still, the sallow tone of my skin is evident along with the faint pattern of an ashen beard on my chin and jaw. My eyes are swollen and the dark circles underneath them more closely resemble bruises.

How could she know?

My hands spin the hot and cold taps and the water creaks into the basin. I pump some orange liquid soap from the dispenser and rub in into my palms. There's a slight grit in the soap, an exfoliant maybe.

The water, still cold, feels good splashed onto my face. I have to admit I was hoping for something more baptismal than refreshing.

There is no hiding from what I now know is true. I am a patsy.

The Governor played me. My girlfriend played me. I am alone, besides a reluctant reporter, in getting myself out of this.

How could she know?

I didn't tell her, she doesn't know George, and even Ripley doesn't know we're headed for him.

I reach into my pocket and pull out my cell phone, dialing information for Rice University. The operator connects me.

"The Richard E. Smalley Institute for Nanoscale Science and Technology at Rice University. How may I help you?"

"Dr. Aglo, please."

"Just a moment," her voice is replaced by silence, a series of clicks, and more silence.

"Dr. Aglo here," the scientist's voice is familiar. "Who is this?"

"This is Jackson Quick. We met yesterday. I think it was yesterday. I was with the reporter George Townsend."

"I know who you are." His tone has changed. He doesn't sound happy to hear from me.

"Have you told anyone about our visit, sir?"

Silence.

"Sir?" I ask again.

"Yes."

"Who?"

A pause. I wait.

"I don't know," he says finally. "They were not kind. Threatening really. Asking about you and what you wanted with me."

"What did you say?"

"To be perfectly honest with you," he huffs, "I don't like being in the middle of this. I was doing a favor for a friend in letting George and you into Dr. Ripley's lab. I didn't have any idea you would cause me this kind of trouble."

"I understand. I didn't think I'd cause you trouble either. Someone was following me and I didn't know it. Can you tell me what the people looked like and what they asked you specifically?"

"I really don't—" he stops mid-sentence. There's worry in his silence. "I don't know how much I should say. I don't know what they know. They could be listening to this conversation. They were very persuasive about why I should cooperate with *them*. " "Was there a woman?"

"I'm a scientist," he pleads. "I deal with a world on a much smaller scale than the one into which you've apparently fallen. These are dangerous people, I believe."

"Was there a woman?" I persist.

"I'm sorry," he says. There's an audible tremble in his voice. "I can't say anymore. Please don't contact me again."

There's a click and the line goes dead. His refusal to respond answers my question.

I shove the phone back into my pocket and there's a sharp pain in my side. My ribs are bruised or fractured. I never found out before I left the hospital. My head still hurts.

The bathroom feels much smaller than when I stepped into it. The crack in the glass appears wider. My face is more gray than pale now. My Kinky T-shirt is stained brown with Bobby's blood. I'm not sure what to do.

Think, Jackson, think...

Slowly, still having to go to the bathroom, but knowing I've got urgent issues, I unlock the door and step out into the convenience store. Charlie's car is parked against the building. She can't see me. Given how long I've been in here, I figure she's getting impatient. Or suspicious.

Or both.

At the front of the store, behind the counter, are a couple of clerks talking to one another. The door to the right of the store chimes open. A short, well-dressed man walks in with a Bluetooth earpiece in his left ear. He's wearing dark pants, a white shirt, and a dark tie. He looks like a driver.

A chauffeur!

I step over to him on the candy aisle. He's choosing between an Almond Joy and a Snickers when he notices I'm standing a little too close for his liking.

"Can I help you?" He turns to face me and takes a simultaneous step back.

"I hope so. You're a driver, right?"

"Yes."

"I need a ride to the airport. Do you have a fare with you right now or could you take me?"

"He flips his wrist to look at his watch. "I think I could. What terminal?"

"I'm flying United Express."

"Okay. Cash?"

"Yeah."

"Let me get these candy bars and we can go." He points toward the door opposite Charlie's car. "You can wait over there by the black Lincoln."

I thank him and slide out the door to his car, which is still running. The windows are tinted what I imagine is as dark as the law will allow. I try the rear driver's side door and find it unlocked. I get in and pull my wallet from my back pocket. There's one hundred and twenty dollars inside, more than enough to get me to the airport.

The driver pushes through the door of the convenience store and plops into his seat a few moments later. He glances at me in his rearview mirror without saying anything. His right hand slips the car into reverse, then into drive, and we pull past the gas pumps, past Charlie sitting in her car, and out onto the feeder road.

As we pull away, I see Charlie get out of her car, tucking a handgun into her pants at the small of her back. I guess we're officially broken up.

***

She knows where I'm going. Not good.

I can't go to Midland.

What do I do?

My mind is racing to the point that all I can think about is how my mind is racing. I need to focus.

The driver slows at a stop light before the entrance to the beltway. To the right is Rick's Cabaret, the strip club where Anna Nicole Smith got her start. To the left, on the other side of the beltway, is an Amegy bank. My bank.

Perfect.

"Can we make a couple of stops before hitting the airport?" I ask the driver.

He glances at me in the rearview mirror and sighs.

"Please?" I ask. "I'll pay cash and I'll tip really well."

"I really don't have much extra time. I've got a pickup in The Woodlands in ninety minutes."

"No problem." I point across the freeway to the bank. "I need to go there first."

The driver looks over his left shoulder to merge into the turn lane before the light turns green. He steers the car onto Imperial Valley, crosses under the beltway, and swings into the bank's nearly empty parking lot next to a small Hyatt hotel. I thank him and run into the bank where I find a single teller behind the desk.

The woman looks to be around thirty maybe, and her brown roots need coloring to match the strawberry blonde covering the rest of her head.

"May I help you?" she asks.

"Yes please." I hand her my driver's license. "I need to withdraw six thousand dollars please."

The woman's eyes widen. She looks at my license and then at me. I approximate the smile on the card and she smiles back before placing the ID on the keyboard of her computer.

Without looking up from the monitor in front of her she says, "I need to check your account Mr..."

"Quick."

"Yes," she says. "Quick."

A second teller has appeared to help with the drive through lane, dressed similarly to the first one. It's funny the things I notice.

"Is there a problem?" I ask the strawberry blonde.

"No sir," she says. "It's a large amount. I need to check on a couple of things."

Her fingers type away. I'm beginning to sweat, beads forming at my temples.

"Just a moment," she says. She turns to the other teller, whispers something, and hurriedly walks through a door at the end of the counter. I'm guessing it's a manager's office or something.

I dig into my front pocket and pull out my cell phone to check the time. This is taking too long, but I need the money. It's the only way my plan will work. I can't use ATMs, I can't use my debit card. Cash is my only option to avoid Charlie and whoever else it is who wants me dead.

The teller emerges from behind the door with a tall, thin man. He's in a short-sleeved pale blue dress shirt with a dark blue tie and pants tightly buckled at his waist. His hair is thinning, but he's done a respectable job of camouflaging it with creative combing. He's a modern version of Ichabod Crane, holding a slip of paper in his hand as he approaches me from the other side of the counter.

"Mr. Quick? Becky here tells me you'd like to make a large withdrawal from your account."

"Becky is right," I smile at the ineffectual teller. "Six thousand dollars."

"Yes," he says, sliding the piece of paper onto the counter in front of me. "That's what Becky indicated."

"Is there a problem?"

"Oh no," he furrows his brow. "There's no problem, sir, but for withdrawals of that size, we typically need to go through a few extra steps."

"What extra steps?"

"Well," he pulls a pen from his shirt pocket and uses it as a pointer on the slip of paper in front of me, "I'll need you to fill out this withdrawal slip first."

I take his pen to begin filling out the form.

"Now may I ask, if a cashier's check will be sufficient for your needs?"

"No," I say without looking up from the form, "it will not. I'd like cash. It doesn't matter if it's twenties, fifties, or hundred dollar bills. I don't want a check."

"I see." He slips into Becky's spot at the computer and begins typing. Becky's looking at my shirt. She looks away when my eyes briefly meet hers.

I get it. My shirt has blood on it, my face is bruised, and I have bandages on both arms from the IVs at the hospital. Here I come, death warmed over, looking for six grand in cash. No wonder they're skittish.

"Look," I say, trying to ease the unspoken tension, "I was in a car accident. Totaled my car. I got released from the ER, where they didn't bother to wash my clothes, and I need to get another car."

Ichabod Crane stares at me blankly.

"I'm in sales," I lie. "I can't be without a car. I don't want to waste money on a rental while I sort through the insurance mess, so I'm buying a used car. A two-year old Camry. I like to pay cash because I get a better deal at the lot. I'd go home and change, but the meter on the Town Car is running."

"I understand, Mr. Quick," says Ichabod. "I don't need an explanation. It's your money."

I lean on the desk and slide the withdrawal slip back to him. "I know I look like crap, I know it's a lot of money, and you're protecting my account. I appreciate that."

I don't know whether he buys what I'm selling or not. I don't care. I need this expedited.

"I'll be back in a moment," he says. He takes the slip from the counter and retreats back to his office. After a lot longer than a moment, he returns with a white envelope.

"Let me count this for you," he says. He opens the envelope and thumbs through a stack of fifties and hundreds, counting out loud.

"...fifty-eight fifty, fifty-nine, fifty-nine fifty, six thousand." He organizes the stack and shoves it back into the thick envelope, which he lays on the counter in front of me.

"Thank you." I pull the envelope off of the counter. It's surprisingly heavy.

"Do you need a balance?"

"No, thank you." I turn to leave. "I'm good."

***

"You've got thirty minutes," the driver announces as he pulls into a parking spot on the east side of Greenspoint Mall. He'd cut across Benmar Drive to what was effectively the backside of the mall.

Greenspoint, which is framed to the west by I-45 and to the south by the north beltway, was not in a great part of town. The mall is known by police and reporters as "Gunspoint" after a sheriff's deputy was kidnapped from the mall parking lot and later killed. That had happened in 1991 and the mall was never the same. It always looked half-abandoned when I would drive by it, and I had never once thought of shopping here until now.

I tell the driver, "Be back in twenty-five."

I hop out of the car, feel a slight ache at my bruised ribs, and jog through the entrance to the left of the movie theatre. Once inside, I spot a mall directory and scan for the stores I need. The first stop is Radio Shack. I need a new phone.

"I need a Smartphone," I tell the first customer service rep I see. "Something that lets me download apps, surf the net, that kind of thing."

Ten minutes later I've got a new phone, a new number, a new

email account.

"It'll be a few minutes for me to set up the phone for you and activate the account," the rep tells me as she sets the phone, charger, and Bluetooth headset on the counter by her register.

"That's fine," I say. "I've only got a few minutes and I need to grab some other stuff. Can I pay for it now and pick it up in ten?"

"Sure," she tells me. "Not a problem. That'll be three hundred dollars, plus the tax."

I point to a pair of sunglasses in the display case next to her. "What are those?"

"Oh," she lights up. "Those are the super cool POV ACG-20 3 megapixel Action Video Camera Sunglasses."

"What do they do?" I ask, half knowing the answer. She pulls them from the case and hands them to me. I put them on. They're comfortable.

"They can record up to two hours of video. They have a rechargeable battery. You can download the video to your computer with a USB connection."

"I'll take them," I put them back on the counter next to the phone. If there's a connection that can make them download video into my phone, I want that too.

"The glasses are one fifty," she says. "There is a connector we have in stock. It's probably around fifty dollars."

I hand her six one hundred dollar bills and tell her she can keep the change if she's ready with the phone when I get back.

Next door to the Radio Shack is a Champs Sporting Goods store. I immediately pull an extra-large white and red University of Houston T-shirt from a hanger on the wall inside the doorway. It's an extra large. I find a blue and gray Texans' hoodie and some matching fleece sweatpants. With those tucked under my arm, I grab a pair of gray basketball shorts from a display table and pile it on the checkout counter.

"I need some shoes," I tell the kid behind the counter. "Size eleven please. I don't care what brand. Nike's fine. Adidas. Whatever."

"How much do you want to spend?" he asks, standing up from the small stool on which he was sitting, texting on his iPhone.

"Doesn't matter," I say.

"Okay." He smiles and disappears behind a curtain leading to the back of the store. In three minutes he's back with three boxes. Two of them are Nike and one is Under Armour.

"I'll take them."

"All of them?" He looks surprised. "Don't you want to try them on?"

"No," I say. "I'm good. How much?"

He takes a small electronic scanner and beeps the prices into the register. $279.58 appears on the green LED register display facing me. He scans the clothing and a small black backpack I toss on the counter. $394.53. I thumb out four one hundred dollar bills.

"Keep the change."

I pull the boxes off the counter. I can't hear what he's saying to me as I bolt out of the store and back into the Radio Shack. I've got five minutes and five thousand dollars in my pocket.

"I'm back," I say to the rep at Radio Shack as I stride toward the counter.

"It's all ready to go," she tells me, swinging her body from behind the counter and walking toward me with a small plastic bag in one hand and the phone in the other.

I thank her, grab the bag and the phone. I pull all three pairs of shoes from their boxes and stuff everything but the phone into my new backpack.

"Do you need me to get those?" The rep gestures to the three shoe boxes I dropped to the floor. Before I can say anything she's already bent down to pick them up.

"Thanks," I say. "I'm in a hurry." I sling the backpack over my left shoulder and turn to leave.

"I can tell," she looks up at me as she gathers the boxes. "Be careful."

Be careful.

"Too late," I snicker. "*Way* too late."

***

"I'm not meeting you in Midland," I tell George. "It's not safe."

"What do you mean?" he asks. I can hear the public address speaker in the background. He must be at Hobby airport.

"Charlie, my girlfriend, is one of them." I'm standing in a bathroom stall inside Terminal B at Bush Intercontinental Airport trying to speak softly. "She knows I'm going there. I mean, *was* going there."

"What are you going to do? I mean, I'm boarding the plane in, like, five minutes."

"I'm flying to El Paso."

"El Paso? Why?"

"Dr. Aglo mentioned Midland or El Paso were good airports to get to the observatory," I remind him. "I am on a US Airways flight. I need you to do me a favor before I land."

"What?" He's irritated. I can tell.

"I need you to reserve a car for me with your credit card. I can't use mine."

"Okay," he sounds relieved the favor is no more dangerous than a rental car deposit. "Leave it in your name?"

"Leave it for Jackson Ellsworth." I unzip the backpack full of clothing I have hanging on the back of the stall door.

"Ellsworth?"

"It's my middle name. It's on my driver's license. Don't leave it in my last name. They'll find me. Use Advantage Rent a Car." I give him the phone number.

"Okay. Anything else?"

"Yeah," I rip the tag off of the new T shirt, "I have a new phone number. After I hang up with you, this phone goes in the trash. I called Charlie with it. She's been trying to call me. I don't know if she can track me. I've got to ditch it."

"Good idea," he says. He tells me he's got the new number, he'll arrange for my car, and he'll talk to me once I've landed in El Paso.

I hang up and toss the phone into the toilet, then pull the Kinky T-shirt over my head and toss it onto the floor along with my shoes and pants. I've spent a lot of time in public bathrooms these last two days; none of it good and none of it to actually go to the bathroom.

It feels good to slip on a clean shirt and shorts. I pick a pair of black and white Nike shoes from the bag and lace them up. They're a little tight, but they'll be fine.

I make sure my wallet and cash envelope are in the backpack before I zip it closed and put it over my left shoulder. It's considerably lighter now, loaded with two pairs of shoes, the hoodie, the sweatpants, and the small Radio Shack bag. I put the new Smartphone into the backpack's outer pocket and exit the stall.

My flight boards in a half hour, and I still have to switch terminals, buy a ticket, and get through security. Right now, more than making my flight, I am concerned with avoiding Charlie.

The realization our relationship is a lie, or *was* a lie, is disorienting. I'm not sure how to process it, really. I loved her. I thought she loved me. Until a couple of hours ago, I imagined the two of us together for the rest of our lives. Marriage, kids, family, the whole bit.

Family. My Achilles heel.

Years of therapy have made me incredibly self-aware. They've blinded me too. I want so badly to have what I lost when my parents died, I'm not discerning enough to distinguish reality from desire.

When the desire involves a lifetime with a smart, engaging, gorgeous woman, I should know better than to ever think it involves reality.

My reality is that I need to catch a flight, get to Ripley, and figure out why I am a target. I take the elevator to the lowest level in the terminal to catch the intra-terminal train.

The train looks more like a people mover from Disney World. That's because it *is* from Disney World. I read once the same engineering firm that created the people mover in Tomorrowland designed the intra-terminal train. Bizarre.

I hop on the train and sit in a rear facing seat with my backpack in my lap. The train lumbers into motion and begins its jerky trek through the bowels of the airport. Next to the train is a carpeted walkway. A few people are speed walking from one terminal to another; others are clearly airport employees who are exercising during a break.

The first stop is the Marriott Hotel. I pull out my new smartphone and look for a signal. I have one, but it's weak. There's really nobody to call anyhow. George is on his flight by now.

A recorded voice announces our arrival at the hotel and the train stops. The doors slide open. Through the glass window in the back of my small train car, I can see a couple getting into the car behind mine. They're lugging two huge suitcases and have trouble arranging themselves.

Terminal C is next. That's the busiest part of the airport, since United runs every gate. I turn off my phone and slide it back into the outside pocket of the backpack.

"Now approaching Terminal C," says the recorded, non-regional, pleasant sounding woman's voice over the train's speaker system. "Please gather your belongings and exit carefully."

I lean back and close my eyes while the doors slide open. The adrenaline that's kept me moving is draining its way out of my system. People shuffle on and off of the train in the other cars. It's two more stops until I get off at Terminal A.

"Now departing for Terminals D and E," says the recorded voice. "Departing Terminal C." I can hear the train rumble to life as we jerk toward the next stop.

"You don't know whachur doin'," says a voice close to me. "You're clueless."

I sit up and open my eyes. There's a man sitting in the seat across from me. He's wearing a cheap looking blue blazer with a burgundy tie, gray pants, and a pair of brown leather boots. His hair is gelled flat against his muscular head and his teeth are clenching a toothpick.

He looks familiar.

"Excuse me?"

"Ah said," his southern drawl is distractingly thick, "yew don't know whachur doin'. You're all mixed up in a big thang that's got yew runnin' scared. You think you can figgur it out." I don't say anything. I'm trying to place his face and his accent.

"Butcha caynt." He leans back against the plastic seat and crosses his legs. His blazer drops open against the seat and I can see a handgun holstered against his left side. "Deep down," he says with a smirk, glancing momentarily at the gun he knows I've spotted, "yew know you're in over your head."

"Who are you?" I ask, tightening my grip on my backpack.

"Detective Crockett," he spits out his name like a wad of

tobacco. "We met at the hospital. You bolted on me." He says *you* like he's referring to a sheep.

"What do you want, *Detective?*" My inflection makes it clear we *both* know he's not a cop. The train jerks around a tight corner on the tracks.

"I guess that kinda depends on what *you* want, Jackson."

"I want to know why you're interested in me. I want to know why my friend Bobby is dead. I want to know what *you* want from *me.*"

He pulls the toothpick from his teeth and leans forward, his palms flat against the edge of the plastic seat. On his right hand is a military insignia, maybe the Marines. On his pinkie and middle finger are numbers or letters – either fives or Ss. On his ring finger there's a straight line or slash, and on his trigger finger, leading from the back of his hand to his middle knuckle, the letters B-O-O-M. He sees me looking at the ink and smirks, pinching the toothpick tighter between his pursed lips.

"I want you to git off of this train and skip wherever it is you think you're goin'," he spins the toothpick along his teeth. "Cause that ain't gonna happen."

"And if I don't?"

"Right," he laughs. "We're gonna git off together here at the next stop. You are gonna come with me. Maybe, once you do that, you'll get some of the other answers you want. Got it?"

I don't respond. Or move.

"Now approaching Terminals D and E," says the recording. "Please gather your belongings and exit carefully."

Detective Crockett stands with the help of a chrome pole in the middle of the car. He holds the toothpick back loosely in the center of his lips like a cigarette, motioning with his hand for me to stand. The train is still moving.

I slowly stand up, holding the backpack in front me, and move toward the doors to face the glass. I can feel him move up behind me on my left. He's shorter than I am but he's more muscular.

"Awright," he tells me, "when this train stops, you're gonna walk to the left."

"What?" I ask him as the train shudders to a stop.

He starts to repeat himself, but as he opens his mouth to speak,

I swing to my left and throw an elbow to his face. I hit his mouth, shoving the toothpick past his teeth.

He grunts and staggers back into the chrome pole, grabbing his throat with his tattooed hand and pitifully reaching for me with the other. I can see his eyes bulging with shock and blood pouring from his mouth.

The doors slide open and I turn to run. Instead of turning left, I bolt to the right. There's a twinge in my right knee. If I can get to Terminal A and past security before he can find me, I'll be okay. He can't get through the TSA checkpoint with his gun.

***

"That'll be three hundred and seventy-nine dollars, Mr. Quick," the US Airways desk agent says. "And I'll need to see your identification."

"It'll be cash," I tell her, handing her eight fifty dollar bills. Ridiculous for a one-way ticket. "Here's my driver's license." She takes the money and my ID. "You're sure you don't need a return ticket?" She glances at the picture on the ID and at me before handing it back.

"No thanks. Not sure when I'm coming back yet."

She hands me my change and my boarding pass. "Have a safe flight, Mr. Quick. You'll be boarding at gate A18. Security is to the left and down the short hallway."

After thanking her, I turn and scan the crowds. There's no sign of Detective Toothpick. Still, I walk over to a row of seats near a Starbucks and drop my backpack onto one of the chairs. I unzip the large compartment, grab the hoodie, and pull it on over my T-shirt.

Across the terminal lobby, I spot a news stand and walk quickly over to the shop. There's a tan colored "Houston-Space City" baseball cap on a mirrored rack next to the magnets and snow globes. I grab it, yank off the tag, put the cap on my head, and get in line at the register.

There are two people in front of me. The man working the cash register is painfully slow. I slip the cap lower across my brow and work the bill with my thumbs, trying to curve the fit. It's not fitting like Bobby's worn UT cap, which I must have lost in the car accident.

From beneath the stubborn bill, my eyes scan the crowds. Everyone in a black top is suspect. I don't see the detective or Charlie. It hits me. I'm stupid for only now piecing this together.

Charlie knew where I was going. She had to know I was at Rice. The black suits knew I was at Rice. Charlie and the black suits could be on the same team.

Charlie and the detective were both at the hospital. He shows up at the airport after I shake Charlie. The detective could be one of the black suits.

But if they're all working together, why did the black suits want me dead while Charlie didn't try to kill me?

The detective could have killed me. He didn't. Maybe Charlie and the detective are on one team and the black suits are on another.

Are some of them working for Buell? Are some on the Governor's payroll? Where does The Saint fit in to all of this? Whose side is he backing?

My head starts to throb again. Maybe I wasn't stupid for not thinking of all of these possibilities before. I reach the front of the line and spot a small bottle of Tylenol on the counter. I slide it over in front of the cashier and plop the hat tag onto the counter.

"This and the hat," I point to the cap on my head. "How much?"

"Twenty-three dollars even," the cashier says, punching the buttons on the register without looking at me. I hand him a fifty, pocket the change, and start to trudge toward security.

Then I see her.

Charlie!

She's standing directly between me and the wide hallway dividing the ticketing terminal from the security checkpoint and the gates. Her hair is pulled back in a long ponytail and she's wearing sunglasses. It's her. Tall. Auburn hair. Kick-ass body. Definitely her.

She clearly hasn't seen me yet, but there's no way for me to move past her without being noticed.

I turn around and step back to the news stand. If I stand just right, I can see her in the mirrored rack that holds a couple of Space City hats. She's looking at every man passing her on his way to security. She glances at her phone. I'm easily fifty yards from her. She doesn't see me.

A tall man on his cell phone is standing directly behind me. "I don't know," he says to whoever is on the other end. "I guess I'll check with baggage downstairs."

Bingo.

"Excuse me," I say to the clerk behind the register. "Are you able to page people from your phone?"

"What do you mean?"

"Like a loudspeaker page. You know, from the airport. I'm trying to locate someone."

"Oh, yes. We can do that. Who are you looking for?" He picks up the receiver to the cordless phone on the counter and pushes a couple of numbers.

"I need to meet Ms. Corday in Terminal B baggage claim."

He raises the phone to his ear, tells the operator, or whoever, what to announce, and hangs up. "Thanks." I turn back to the mirrored rack and hear the announcement over the airport's public address system.

"Ms. Corday, please meet your party at the Terminal B baggage claim," it's a pleasant female voice. "Ms. Corday, your party is waiting for you at the Terminal B baggage claim."

My view in the mirror is unobstructed, so I can see Charlie clearly staffing her post. At first, she doesn't seem to hear the announcement. She tilts her head, squints, and checks her phone again. She punches something into the screen and puts the device to her ear.

She starts walking purposefully toward the center of the terminal and a bank of elevators, still talking to someone on the phone. Her free hand is flailing. She's clearly irritated. When she reaches the elevator doors and presses a button, I turn toward security with my head down, and walk quickly to the checkpoint. Despite the temptation, I don't turn back to look at her.

By the time I've cleared security, my head feels better. Once I've boarded the plane, my pulse has slowed.

I'm in seat thirteen A. It's a small aircraft and seats maybe seventy people. Thankfully I'm in the emergency exit row. I've got a little extra legroom but my side is uncomfortable in the tight seat. There are two flight attendants helping the other passengers with their bags and the flight seems full.

I lean forward and pull out the emergency information card. The plane is a Bombardier CRJ700. I don't know why I do it, but I always like to check the emergency card and learn the type of plane. Not that it'll make any difference if we crash.

A woman slides into 13B next to me. She smiles at me and slips her small purse under the seat in front of her. I smile back and shift my weight to the left, against the interior wall of the plane.

"Ladies and gentlemen," a deep male voice fills the cabin through the intercom, "welcome aboard flight 2551 to El Paso, Texas. We appreciate you choosing US Airways for your travel plans today. Our trip will take approximately one hour and nineteen minutes. We'll be cruising at 515 miles per hour and should have you to the gate a couple of minutes early."

I tune out the rest of his message and close my eyes.

CHAPTER 6

I remember being in a rhythm. In my head and on the track.

Breathe. Stride. Step. Stride. Step. Breathe.

The air was cool and damp, filling my lungs through my nose as I ran. Each breath out through my mouth was warm and puffed little clouds of fog as I chugged along the asphalt. It felt good. The burn in my legs was invigorating. My quads felt muscular and lean as they helped propel me forward.

Breathe. Stride. Step. Stride. Step. Breathe.

In through the nose. Out through the mouth. A small puff of air against the cool of the early evening. Chug. Chug. Chug.

I was on the junior high track, running my eleventh of twelve planned laps on the inside lane. I was running three miles after school, a good way to clear my mind and take a mental break before homework. All the organized teams were gone for the afternoon, so I was alone, with a mini-walkman strapped to my arm and Carl Carlton singing into my earphones. I was in an early 1980s funk phase.

Breathe. Stride. Step. Stride. Step. Breathe.

I was watching another puff of air dissolve in front of my nose, and totally into the music, when Blair Loxley appeared out of nowhere, tackling me onto the grass infield.

The hulk had been harassing me on and off for weeks. Since the locker incident, he'd found opportune moments to punch or trip me out of the sight of any adults. I'd punched back a couple of times, but for the most part I'd tried to avoid him. Either he found me easy pickings or a challenge.

Regardless, he was on top of me, straddling my hips as I tried to wriggle free. He was too strong and his first punch caught me in the right shoulder below my neck. The second hit was to my left jaw. My headphones were tangled around my neck, ripped from their connection to the mini-walkman still strapped to my thin bicep.

The third blow was to my ribs with his right elbow. I was taking a beating while he held me in place with his weight and left forearm.

"Take what's coming to you," he grumbled as I struggled against him. "Take what's coming to you, Jacktard."

I could hear crying, a foreign whining that sounded like a small child. It must have been me. There wasn't anyone else around.

I was already winded from the more than two and half mile run. Once I'd taken his first salvo, I managed enough strength to knee him in the groin.

He grunted and grabbed himself, momentarily losing his hold of me. I used that split second to roll away from him and scramble to my feet.

I backed away from him and turned to run, but the adrenaline knocked me off balance and I fell to the ground, my chin sliding on the damp St. Augustine grass. By the time I'd managed to get to my feet again, he had me in a bear hug and lifted me off the ground before throwing me down.

My foot slammed awkwardly onto the ground, twisting my ankle and knee. Something popped and I felt a bolt of pain shoot from my knee to my foot as I fell awkwardly to the side. I let out a bizarre wail. The pain was like breaking glass.

Through the tears in my eyes I could see Loxley standing over me, his fists still clenched. His knuckles were white. I remember the anger in those knuckles. In those angry eyes, I saw something new. There was fear.

He knew he'd gone too far. Pushing me against a locker and punching my gut was one thing. Attacking me on the track and tearing the anterior cruciate ligament in my right knee was something else.

"You're the one who's gonna take what's coming to you now!" I screamed at him through tears and spit. "You're in for it now. I'm gonna kill you!"

Loxley took in the words without saying anything. He kept glancing at my knee. The bully refocused his gaze, narrowed his eyes, and spit on me.

"Whatever, Jacktard!" He sneered, turned, and walked away. No explanation. No apology.

I stayed on the ground for what must have been a half hour before a school maintenance worker found me and helped me from the field in a golf cart.

I never told my parents how it had happened. They believed it was an accident that happened during my run.

I never wanted to involve them or allow them to worry about me. I wanted to handle my own problems, to fix them by myself.

I missed the next three weeks of school. After surgery, crutches, and six months of rehabilitation, I was back on the track. It was slow at first, but I made a full recovery. At least my knee did. It occasionally ached from prolonged sitting or an awkward turn. It wasn't bad. Not nearly as bad as what happened the next and last time Loxley and I got together.

***

"I've turned on the seat belt sign," the captain alerts the cabin as we begin our descent into El Paso. "Please remain in your seats with those belts fastened until we've arrived at the gate and come to a complete stop. Thanks again for choosing US Airways."

Through the emergency exit window, there's a bright sky over West Texas and northern Mexico. The ground below slowly rises to meet our plane, and I focus on the veiny fingers of creeks and rivers almost dry in the tan hills west of the city. It's barren almost; a wasteland. It's like humanity has died and left behind an earth ready to rejuvenate itself. The world is free of consumption, ambition, and conspiracy.

We've descended a few hundred feet and rush past the neighborhoods that bridge the mountains from the runway.

I scan the small homes lining the blacktop streets. Most of the houses or trailers are on dirt lots without sodded yards. They look dry, save the occasional dot of green brush. It's a big sandbox. I imagine the lives inside those houses and, right now, in this moment, I envy them.

They have a home. They have a family. They know their place in the world for better and worse. They're not running for their lives. They're living them.

Me? I don't know what's next.

I don't know what I'll find in the mountains. Even if I get the answers I need, will it be enough to stop the people trying to catch me or kill me?

My stomach drops when the landing gear hits the runway. The wheels screech and the airplane bounces into the air before settling again onto the ground, whining to a slower speed.

"Welcome to El Paso, Texas," says the captain, then he announces the local time. "We hope you have a wonderful time here in the Sun City or wherever your travels take you."

Wherever is right.

***

"I just landed."

I've got my newest phone to my right ear and the backpack slung onto both shoulders as I make my way through the El Paso International Airport.

"It's about time," George says, sounding exasperated. "I've been waiting for your call for an hour now."

"Where are you?"

"I'm on I-20 near Monahans," he says. "I gotta tell you. There's somebody following me."

"What do you mean?"

"Hang on," he says. "I'm lighting another cigarette."

I can hear the click of his lighter and the sizzle of the end of the cigarette. He must be holding the phone close to his mouth.

"Isn't your rental car nonsmoking?" I ask. Ahead, there's the sign for the counters and an escalator to the lower floor of the terminal.

"Yeah," he says and blows out the first puff of what I envision as a nasty cloud of smoke. "Like that's the worst of my problems right now. I need the cigarette more than I need to worry about a smoking fee."

"Understood."

"So, back to me being followed," he continues. "I get off of the plane and I'm looking around to make sure I don't see anyone suspicious or anything. After you told me about switching your phone again, I got a little freaked."

I step off of the escalator, turn left, and see a Starbucks ahead of me on the left. That'll be my next stop. I need some caffeine to get me out of this "my life sucks and I'd rather be living in a dirt bowl next to an airport than be me" funk.

"I don't see anyone. So I get my rental car, walk out to the lot, and grab my car," he pauses and puffs. "No problem, right?"

"Right..."

"Then I'm on I-20 near Odessa when this black SUV speeds past me and exits on this loop that goes around the city. I notice it because the driver's going so fast."

I'm in line at Starbucks. The prices are even more outrageous in an airport.

"Well, that loop, 338, crosses I-20 twice," George is speaking faster now. "Right when I pass it the second time, you know the western part of that loop?, the same SUV gets back on the highway right behind me."

"How do you know it was the same SUV?"

I'm not surprised he's being followed. The fact that they'd use a black SUV is weird. Isn't there a less obvious car? The bad guys in movies are *always* in black SUVs.

"I'm positive."

"How do you know?"

"Because it has New Mexico license plates."

"And?"

"New Mexico plates are bright blue with yellow lettering," he says in a tone that indicates how stupid he thinks I am. "They're not hard to spot. It's the same vehicle, Jackson."

"Where are they now?"

"Two or three car lengths back." He takes another drag. "There's a minivan between us. They're there. I don't know how to shake them. I can't let them follow me all the way to the observatory. We're screwed."

"We're not screwed," I try to reassure him. "Hang on. I'll call you back in a minute."

"I'd like a venti Americano with room for cream, please." Espresso with a little milk will wake me up. I pay for the overpriced coffee, give the barista my name and slide over to the end of the counter.

I open the internet application on my phone. Opening a search window and keyboard I type in MONAHANS TEXAS.

Up pops a list of nearly two million results. I click on one of them linking to the visitor's guide. The screen clears and refreshes with a list of restaurants. There's a pull down menu for shopping. I activate that link. Most of the shopping is on either South Stockton or Sealy. I close the application and redial George.

"Yeah," he answers on the first ring.

"Have you passed Monahans yet?"

"Not yet. Why?"

"Exit there and look for either Stockton or Sealy Streets."

"Why?"

"There are a fair number of stores there. Those look like relatively busy streets. You might be able to find a way to shake the SUV." I grab the Americano off the counter and move it over to the condiment table and pop off the lid.

"Okay," he says. "I should be exiting in a couple of minutes. "I'll call you back once I do. How's the car?"

"Haven't gotten it yet." I stir in sweetener and some nonfat milk. "Should be on the road in about fifteen minutes though."

"Talk to you soon." He hangs up without waiting for a response.

I stir in sweetener and some nonfat milk, take a sip of the coffee, and start walking to get my car. The first counter is a combination of Hertz and Advantage. When I step up, the clerk greets me with a big smile and a West Texas drawl.

"How may I help you?"

I slip off my backpack to grab my wallet. "I have a car reserved for Jackson Ellsworth."

"Okay, sir..." She starts clicking away on her computer. "I see your reservation. There is already a credit card attached. I need your driver's license please."

I pull out the license and hand it to her.

"Let's see," she takes the license and glances at it. "This says your last name is Quick and not Ellsworth."

I reach across the counter and point to the license. "Ellsworth is my middle name, see? Sometimes that happens. People hear 'Quick' and think it's not part of my name."

She smiles. "Makes sense. No problem, Mr. Quick. Have you outta here in a jiffy! Would you like a GPS?"

"Sure. Please add it to the card." George's card.

"I have you in a midsize vehicle," she adds while looking at the computer screen. "Will that be okay?"

"Any chance you have a big SUV? In black?"

"Let me check," she punches a few keys. "Yes, we do. It has satellite radio."

***

The music on the radio has a catchy beat. I take a sip of the twenty ounce coffee and, for a minute, I'm on a mindless road trip in West Texas.

I'm on I-10 heading east, driving parallel to the Texas-Mexico border. At times, I'm just a few hundred feet from Mexico. I wonder if I'd be safer there, trying to survive the drug cartels.

"That was Dion's 'Donna The Prima Donna'," the deejay chimes in at the end of the song. "A big hit for the crooner after he went solo. It reached number six on the charts in late 1963."

The deejay is about to introduce the next song when the radio goes silent and my phone rings over the speakers. I press the answer button on the right side of the steering wheel.

"Hey, George."

"I lost 'em," he proclaims. "I really lost 'em!"

"Where are you?"

The GPS stuck to the dash tells me I'm cruising at 78 miles per hour. I should be at the observatory in a little more than two and a half hours.

"Monahans. Where you told me to go."

"Why do you think you lost them?" I grab the coffee for another swig.

"Well," he pauses, "here's the thing. I took the exit for

Monahans at the last second and looked for the streets you mentioned. This is not a big town. They didn't follow me. They didn't take the exit. I've been sitting in front of this restaurant, 'El Chapito', on South Stockton for twenty minutes and I haven't seen them. I lost them."

"Perfect. Get back on the interstate and drive the speed limit all the way to the observatory. Let me know when you get there."

"All right," he says, sounding relieved. "I'll call you when I get there."

"Sounds good."

I hang up without telling him what he doesn't want to hear. He didn't lose the tail. They already know where he's going. They have to know. The black suit who nearly killed me in the tunnel said they'd followed us to Rice. Dr. Aglo told me he was being harassed. They didn't lose George. They're letting him think they did.

Given how skittish George has been since the car accident, I don't need him worrying more than he already is.

I hope they don't get to him before I do...

I pick up my phone from the passenger seat and call him back.

"Hello?" George picks up on the second ring. "Jackson?"

"Yeah. Hey listen, on second thought, I don't want you to get up to the observatory before me. We should arrive together."

"Okaaaay," he says apprehensively. He knows there's something I'm not telling him.

"It's safer if we go there together. We don't know what kind of guy Ripley is. He's been under stress. He could be armed for his own protection. We know his dad likes guns, right?"

"Yeah," says George. "Okay. Where do you want to meet?"

"I-20 and I-10 meet at Texas highway 118. That's where we both turn off to head to the observatory. From there it's about a forty-five minute drive. When you get there, or near there, and find a good meeting place, call me."

"All right," George hangs up and the radio turns on again.

"Thanks for listening to the Oldies Hour on 1150 AM," says the deejay. "Now it's time for talk. Stay tuned for the latest headlines and your phone calls on KHRO 1150 El Paso."

I check the GPS. At my current speed, I should meet George in about an hour and a half.

***

"The Governor, in the days leading up to a critical debate, is now trailing in the polls to energy gazillionaire Don Carlos Buell, and that is really touching a nerve here," the talk show host elaborates. "You've got tens of thousands of Texans who like the idea of secession. They're sick of the way the federal government sticks its filthy little nose into everything we do. Tax here, fee there, and so on."

I'm about an hour from meeting George and the conversation on the radio is piquing my interest. Apparently the Governor gave another speech at which he hinted at the need for Texas to consider seceding.

"Let me take a call here from Mark Helms," the host says. "Mark, you're on the air with Curt, KHRO 1150 El Paso."

"Yeah, Curt, love your show. I'm gonna tell you why secession would work. Then I'm gonna explain why it wouldn't."

"Go for it, Mark," says Curt. "Enlighten us all."

"Okay, Curt, here's why we could do it," Mark says seriously. "We lead the country in cattle. We have more of them and we export a ton of them. We keep all that cattle to ourselves and we're in good shape, especially since we got more ranches and farms too. We're major cotton producers."

"So agriculturally we're okay?" Curt asks.

"Yep. We have our own power system. Our electric grid is independent of everyone else. That's huge."

"Given," Curt concedes.

"We have access to the Gulf. We are not landlocked. That's big. There are big ports in Houston and Corpus Christi. With the Panama Canal expanding, we could be huge trade partners for the Chinese."

"Good points, Mark."

"Thank you," Mark says. "I'm not done yet. We've got NASA and a ton of aerospace companies. Dell and Hewlett Packard have a lot of people in Texas. Technology-wise we don't need the rest of the country."

"Not sure I agree," argues Curt. "There's this place in northern California called Silicon Valley and in North Carolina there's the Research Triangle Park. Those two places alone are significant technological engines for this country. Plus, much of the research NASA conducts is outside of Texas. The Jet Propulsion Laboratory is in California, for example. So as good as your agriculture, grid, and trade points were, this one falls short for me."

"Yeah," counters Mark. "Well, what about oil? We've got the majority of the refineries in the country. The petrochemical industry survives because of Texas. Think of all the things we get from that. There are plastics, medicine, glue, ink, soap. I mean the list is endless. Even the Astroturf on our high school football fields is made from that stuff. We've really got our own economy down here. It's better than everyone else's."

"That, of course, is the elephant in the room," admits Curt. "The energy industry is where most experts would argue Texas is most valuable to the United States and, as a result, has the gun to the head of the federal government."

"I don't know," says Mark. "That's why I'll tell you there are some real obstacles too."

"You did say you had some reasons secession couldn't work," prods Curt.

"I didn't say it *couldn't* work," Mark corrects the host and I turn up the volume a notch. "I said it *wouldn't*."

"Okay," says Curt with a touch of irritation in his voice. "Why *wouldn't* it work?"

"Money," says Mark. "Plain and simple. It's too expensive. You've got to come up with so much cash to pay for a military, border protection, roads, farm subsidies, welfare, social security—"

"Hold on a minute, Mark," interrupts the host. "You're advocating social welfare programs? That's part of what has gotten us into a financial crisis. You'd want to continue it with farm subsidies and welfare?"

"Yes and no," Mark clarifies. "We would have to provide a backstop of some kind. We can't go cold turkey. That'd be stupid. We'd have to structure a system from the ground up, which empowers people. It doesn't have to be a crutch like what we have now. It could be better."

"Not sure about that, Mark." I can hear Curt shaking his head through the radio. "I do agree the economics are prohibitive. Let's get a better handle with an expert. Right after the break, we'll talk to an expert from the South Texas College of Law about the reality and the fiction of secession."

Some music, BTO's 'Taking Care of Business', starts playing and there's my boss' voice. It's the Governor in what I imagine is a stump speech, appealing to his base.

"We are The Republic of Texas. We are not like every other state," the Governor chuckles in a self-deprecating way I've heard so many times before. "We fought for our independence too!" he says, voice beginning to soar. "At Goliad! At The Alamo! At San Jacinto!" The crowd roars.

"I might be a farm boy from Hempstead and I might have a little ole degree in business from Texas Tech, but I know liberty," another chuckle. "*I* know how we should be living as red blooded Texans. *This* is not it. We are not a 'fly over' state as the media elite would have the rest of the country believe. We are not suckling on Washington's teat."

The music amplifies and a commercial starts. I'm about five miles from Van Horn. The GPS tells me I've got about forty minutes until I meet George.

CHAPTER 7

The Governor's speech on the radio reminds me of a conversation we had not long after the Alaska drop off. We were sitting across from each other on bar stools outside of Home Slice Pizza in Austin. Two state troopers sat at the table next to ours, sharing a large extra cheese.

The Governor folded his thin slice of white clam pizza and turned it sideways to take a bite. With one cheek stuffed full he pointed to the plate in the middle of the table.

"You gonna have a garlic knot?" He winked when he pointed. It was an instruction as much as a question. "They're delicious."

I took one, dipping it the marinara sauce before taking a bite. I'd already finished my slice of pepperoni. The Governor was on his third piece of the white clam specialty. He loved Home Slice and its thin, greasy New York style pizza.

"You know," he said, wiping his chin with the back of his left hand, "this is about the only thing worth importing from the East Coast." He swallowed and took a swig from a Mexican Coke made with real cane sugar.

"They got it all wrong over there, Jackson." He picked up a napkin and wiped his upper lip. He was still holding the slice in his right hand.

"Sir?"

"They think we're all tumbleweeds and oil fields here. Oh, and refineries. They imagine pipes and filthy air everywhere. We ain't Calcutta."

"Calcutta?" I turn the cap on my bottled water to chase down the garlic and take a sip.

"It's an example, Jackson," he waves his hands in explanation. "You know, a filthy city. When Sarah Palin left Fox, we lost the only sensible voice on the East Coast. She's been here to Texas. She knows we're more than that. I mean, *really*, son," he leaned on the table with both of his elbows, looking at me intently, "we are *so* taken for granted here. We could survive."

The last syllable dragged with his drawl and he nodded at his own sentiment, staring past me into the distance. He looked for a moment like a dog whose attention was grabbed by a squirrel.

"Survive, sir?"

"Go it on our own," he said, his eyes refocusing on mine. "*Secession.* We could leave the other forty-nine and be good. It just takes money."

"I'm not sure I'm following the logic, Governor. There were eighty-thousand signatures on the White House petition to secede after President Obama was reelected. That went nowhere."

"That was hooey anyhow, Jackson," he says. "Eighty-thousand is less than a percent of the Texas population. That's nothing. Asking the White House to approve secession? That's like a slave asking his master for permission to go free. You don't do that. You run away first and have it set up so you can't get put back into the chains."

He shifts in his seat and goes on. "See, I've given this some thought... " The creases in his brow relax when he smiles broadly. "If you talk to some financial gurus, they'll tell you we can't survive without the billions the federal government gives us. That isn't true. We put more money into the system than we get out of it. That's fact. I mean, we send close to three hundred billion dollars in various taxes to the feds. We'd keep that money here."

"What about defending ourselves?" I ask. "Don't we need the military?

"No," he shakes his head. "We'd build our own. The average military expenditure for countries across the globe is about four to five percent of their gross domestic product. If we spent that here in Texas, we'd be one of the best defended nations on Earth."

"What about banking and currency?"

"We could stay on the dollar in the short term. Other countries are on the dollar. Until we can figure out what our trade position is in the world, we'll be able to use the dollar."

"You make it sound so simple." I'd never thought he was serious.

"All it takes is the startup capital," he admits, leaning back in his chair. "We need a few billion to get going."

"Is that all?" I roll my eyes, forgetting for a split second with whom I am talking.

"Really, Jackson?" The Governor seems as shocked as I am embarrassed. "Your sarcasm is not becoming."

"I'm sorry, Governor, I—"

"Don't worry about it," he says, interrupting me. He pinches the bridge of his nose and chuckles. "Even I know it sounds crazy sometimes."

***

My hands on the wheel, I glance past the edges of the highway to the brown landscape that frames the road. Every few hundred yards there are black pump jacks. Some of them are still, resting from their endless task. Others are busy pecking down and up, spinning the siphon that draws the oil from old wells which have long since lost their pressure.

The windows to the SUV are up, but I can imagine their rusty whine as they suck the black goo from deep inside the earth. Pumping. Spinning. Whining. Always staying in one place. With a purpose.

Unlike me.

I've never settled anywhere. I've always been in flight; from my past, from my present, from myself. Until a couple of days ago, the chase was always figurative. Now, speeding toward a nano-scientist in the mountains of West Texas, it's freaking literal.

The radio is still on, callers droning on about secession and nullification and the Supreme Court. I'm somewhat tuned out, thinking about what all of this means.

I think back to the iPod in Alaska and the account number that flashed on the screen.

An account number.

Obviously there's a money transfer involved. Either the Governor is giving or receiving. My guess would be receiving.

Receiving lots of money.

There's the photograph on the wall of Ripley's office at Rice. My contacts, all in one place, meeting with a man who's working on enhancing energy efficiency. I recall what George said to me in Houston, right after we left Rice: "*The Governor and these energy people are colluding with Ripley to generate a competing technology that makes oil and gas last longer. Maybe Ripley hedges, and so the Governor keeps him in line by framing his father for the assassination attempt on his political opponent. If Don Carlos Buell dies in the attempt, two birds are killed with one stone. His only political threat is gone, and the money behind Nanergetix disappears too. Your boss, by the way, likes to talk about secession like it's feasible. Like it's part of a political platform.*"

There's a cluster of pump jacks to the right side of the highway, all of them pumping in unison.

The Governor is using oil companies to fund secession.

It makes sense. The oil companies love Texas. They're all based here. The Governor has made sure the business climate suits them, while Washington continues to threaten taking away tax breaks. The loss of those incentives alone would cost the big five energy companies more than two and a half billion dollars every year. If their taxes went up, the losses would be even greater.

Imagine what those oil companies could stand to gain by operating in the New Republic of Texas? They help fund his operation secretly with what he, himself, called starter capital.

As a further reward, he helps them gain access to Ripley's cutting edge technology. Everybody gets rich and the Governor gets his new country. He has the votes in both sides of the state legislature to declare independence.

A perfect plan.

Ripley gets nervous about the secret arrangement and the Governor plays hardball. As George suggested, he knocks Buell out of the way, while at the same time putting pressure on the young Ripley by framing the old man.

Where do Charlie, the black suits, the detective, and The Saint fit into this? If The Saint is on the opposite side of Charlie and the detective, and he killed a black suit to save me, is he really on my side as he claims?

Whose side am I on?

***

The Chevron station in Salt Flat, Texas is a good meeting place, north of I-10 at the intersection with Highway 118. I pull into the parking lot next to a faded blue Ford F-250. I check the rear the side view mirrors before turning off the ignition, grabbing my phone and backpack, and stepping out into the dry heat of West Texas.

I can taste the dust in the air, and I lick my lips and duck into the small convenience store. A bell chimes, announcing my entrance. To the left there's an eyeball security camera above the register counter. The clerk, sitting on a wooden bar stool, looks up from his issue of *Hot Rod Magazine* and nods a greeting. There's music playing on the single speaker radio next to the register. Johnny Cash.

I return the nod, slug the backpack onto my right shoulder and walk back to the floor-to-ceiling cooler along the back wall of the store. The aging, corrugated shelves are only sparsely populated with snacks, toiletries, motor oil, and fuel additives.

I reach for the cooler handle and hear Waylon Jennings' scratchy voice on the radio. Maybe the song's a duet.

Diet Dr. Pepper is on the bottom shelf so I reach down to grab a couple of bottles. I'm thirsty from the dry air and I need the caffeine. On my way to the counter I snag a pack of peppermint gum and place it on the counter with the sodas.

We shall all sing Hallelujah, I'm American by birth and southern by the grace of God.

Definitely a duet.

"Johnny Cash?" I ask the clerk, who's gotten up from the stool to ring me up.

"Man in black," he says. "Nobody better." He keys the prices into the register.

"How much?"

"Four fifty," he says. "Need a bag?"

"No thanks." I hand him a twenty. "Sorry I don't have anything smaller."

"Not a problem."

I gather up the drinks and gum and turn to leave when the door chimes. It's a familiar face. He's smoking another cigarette.

"George," I smile at the rumpled sight of him. "What took you so long? You should have beaten me here."

"I kept taking exit ramps to avoid being followed," he says, glancing at the clerk as he does.

"Hey," I turn to the clerk. "Do you mind if my friend here leaves his car for a little while? We're gonna ride together up to the observatory."

"How long?" The clerk's returned to his stool, the magazine open on his lap.

"I dunno... It's getting late, so maybe first thing tomorrow morning?"

The clerk moves his eyes between the two of us. He looks down at the magazine and flips a page.

"What do you think?" I take a step toward the counter. "Less than twenty-four hours?"

"I'll give you twenty bucks," offers George.

"Fifty," the clerk counters without looking up. He flips another page.

"C'mon," I plead. "You don't want us going down the road feeling bad do you?"

The clerk looks up from his magazine and smiles at me. "Okay. Twenty."

"Deal," I slip the cash onto the counter.

"You can pull it around back. There's a covered spot back there." He points in the direction of the back of the store.

George leads me out into the parking lot and walks to his rental and opens the driver's side door. "What was that about?"

"He's a Johnny Cash fan."

"So?"

"'Going Down the Road Feeling Bad' is a Cash song."

George rolls his eyes as he slides into his car. "I thought I caught a weird vibe in there."

"See you around back." I shut the door. We've got a lot to talk about on the short ride ahead.

***

Highway 118 heads south but it feels like we're driving north, and it narrows as we climb into the Ft. Davis Mountains. The landscape quickly dissolves into an endless parade of mesquite and yaupon. The sun is setting to our right, casting long shadows on the brush.

"How long now?" George is reflexively tapping his heel on the floorboard, his knee bouncing up and down.

I glance down at the GPS. "Twenty minutes maybe. I hope we're there by dark."

"I made some calls," George says, turning toward me but still fidgeting in his seat. When he speaks I can smell the smoke on his breath.

"Okay," I shrug.

"I got the license plate for the black SUV that was following me," George tells me. "The one with the New Mexico plates."

"You're burying the lead," I tell the television news reporter.

"The plates come back to a company called NewMex Holdings. It's out of Taos County, right along the Texas border, near Cannon Air Force Base. It's a small area, only a couple thousand people live there. From what I could find out, there's a post office box there. No real address or anything."

"A dead end, then?" I take a gulp of diet Dr. Pepper.

"Hardly." George is still bouncing his knee. He keeps licking his lips. He must need a cigarette. "I had my investigative producer look up some stuff for me. He found NewMex is owned by a Dallas company called F. Pickle Security Consultants. That's the same company I mentioned back in Houston. They owned the car that crashed into us. They also do work for the Governor. FPSC has fifteen of these shell holding companies in its name. It looks like they're all used for buying vehicles and holding leases on various properties."

"Who is FPSC? I mean *Pickle* is a weird name." I thumb the sweat on the side of the soda bottle and take another sip. "What do they have to do with any of this? Are they contracted spooks or something?" I chuckle at my own suggestion, but when I turn to look at George I can see he's not laughing and his leg has stopped thumping.

Without thinking, I jerk the steering wheel to the right and speed onto the narrow shoulder of the road. The SUV pitches to the right more than I expect and I pull back to the left and brake. Dust engulfs the SUV as we sit there, staring at each other in silence.

I push the hazards on and hear the faint click of the red warning button flash on and off. "I need a second."

"Since you're sitting here," George says, "I might as well continue."

"All right." I put the soda bottle in the center console and replace the cap. I'm not thirsty anymore.

"F. Pickle Security Consultants is a company founded by, run by, and full of former CIA, NSA, and FBI agents. They took their knowledge, skills, and clandestine experience and went into the private sector. The company is about 25 years old. They're the ones that supposedly helped Enron in its overseas dealings in the late 1990s – intelligence gathering, relationship building, cash handlers. When Enron went belly-up, it almost took Pickle with it. The company, though, sustained enough other lucrative contracts to survive."

"The thing is," George waves the back of his hand at the dashboard, signaling for me to start driving again, "nobody knows exactly who their current clients are. If it hadn't been for the Enron debacle, nobody on the outside would ever have known about them at all."

I slide back on the highway and press heavily on the accelerator to climb the incline leading us further into the Ft. Davis Mountains.

"How do you know all of this?"

"Like I said, my investigative producer helped me. He worked for CNN until they blew apart their investigative documentary unit in 2012. He's *really* connected and knows stuff most people don't *want* to know. He was from Houston, wanted to come home. It worked out." George shakes his head to reclaim his thoughts. "I digress. Here's where it comes back to us. It tells me I didn't *really* lose those guys following me here. They're somewhere. They're watching us."

The road forks to the right at sign for Highway 166. I stay to the left on 118.

"The last time a car followed us was when we got into the wreck, right?"

"Right," I say.

"It was after we left Rice..." George pauses. He's stringing me along.

"Just tell me, dude." I press the accelerator out of frustration more than necessity. The engine resists for a moment before complying.

"Okay. I got a parking ticket at Rice. We weren't there that long. I figured if I got a ticket, and the guys in that black car were following us, they probably got one too. At least, if they got out of the car to find out what we learned inside the lab, it was a possibility. Then I thought that couldn't be, because they were following us on 59. I guess they have two cars tailing us. They are professionals right?"

I nod.

George rubs his thighs with both hands. There's a sweat stain on each leg from his palms. "So, I know a cop over at Rice. I gave him a call and asked him to run all the tickets within an hour of when I got mine. He found one in the same lot, across from the nano lab, about thirty minutes after mine. The car was registered to Black Bayou Holdings, which if you can't already figure out, is a subsidiary of Pickle."

"That still doesn't tell us who they're working for, does it?" I'm trying to split my attention between the road, which is now starting to wind, and George, who looks like he's about to explode.

"It wouldn't," he admits, "except Black Bayou Holdings is in Houston. Guess who is listed as one of its corporate officers with the Texas Secretary of State?"

"Who?"

"The Vice President in charge of strategic acquisitions for Aleutian Energy Providers."

"Who is he?"

"She," George smiles, his lips quivering. "You've met her. In Alaska."

***

The landscape rushing by the SUV is less mesquite and more piñon pine and juniper. The thermometer beneath the speedometer reads five degrees cooler than it did when we turned onto 118. I run over a dead rattlesnake; I'm not the first, or second, to have done so.

The road veers east and curves in an S before heading south and east again. We're getting close. We might beat the sunset.

"Mary Brown," I say for the third time, remembering her lack of warmth more than the chill of Anchorage. "The one with the Dorothy Hamill haircut. She's funding the black suits?"

"Not exactly," George says. "She's on two teams. On the surface, she's the go-between. She communicates to Black Bayou, or Pickle, whatever it is Aleutian needs. She takes the intelligence Pickle gathers and alerts those who need to know at Aleutian."

"Why would she be so clumsy to have public records connecting her to both companies?"

"It's not that clumsy," George has resumed thumping his knee intermittently. I don't think he's aware of it. "I mean, how many people are going to cross-reference an Alaskan oil company vice president with some small holding company in Houston?"

"Somebody did."

"Yeah," he admits. "She's been doing both jobs for at least the last five years. This is nothing new. She's been operating in both capacities long enough, that this is a perpetual mode of operation. I bet, if I'd had time, my producer would have found more of your contacts involved in similar arrangements. This is something big that's been brewing for a while."

"So it's the oil companies that wanted me dead to start with. They're the ones who killed Bobby. They're the ones who followed us to Rice and slammed into us downtown. They're the ones who nearly killed me in the tunnel bathroom."

"What?!?" George's jaw drops and his face draws a new shade of sallow. "What are you talking about?"

"I thought you knew? After the wreck I ran into the tunnels. I stopped in a bathroom to check my injuries when one of the black suits cornered me."

George is still slack jawed. He says nothing.

"I fought back against him, but I was losing too much blood," I swallow against my throat. "I got weak. The guy was about to kill me when..."

"When what?" George is riveted. His leg is in overdrive, up and down like a juiced pump jack.

"I don't know really." I shake my head. "Somebody came in and killed him."

"Who?" Up and down. Up and down. Up and down. It's beginning to drive me nuts.

"It was The Saint."

"The Saint?"

"The guy who kidnapped me."

"Holy crap." George grabs his heads with both hands. His eyebrows are pulled back tighter than Joan Rivers'. "I can't believe this crap. I can't believe this." George is starting to hyperventilate. So much for faking compassion.

"Look," I say in a soft but firm voice. "Calm down, George. This is good."

"How is it good?" He balls his hands into fists alongside his head, grabbing clumps of hair. "How is any of this good? I knew I shouldn't have come. No story is worth this. None."

"George," I repeat.

"I've won three Lone Star Emmys!" He holds up three fingers without completely letting go of his head. "Three! None of them put my life in danger. Even my Headliner Award. Nobody died. Nobody!"

George keeps ranting about awards and death. I tune him out long enough to notice a large deer off to the left side of the road, easily six points, with thick shoulders and a large white area on its neck. Its large ears make it look like a donkey with antlers.

***

The Governor took me deer hunting once. We were sitting in a couple of highchairs in the back of a Chevy Silverado at dawn. He handed me a cup of hot coffee and a gun.

"The coffee's Venezuelan," he nodded at the Styrofoam cup.

"The rifle's a Ruger M77 Hawkeye All Weather Bolt Action. It's .308. Nice trigger action. She shoots true."

"Thanks for the coffee," I told him. We both smiled.

An hour later we were both cold despite the coffee. Then we saw the first buck. The Governor's eyes widened.

"My oh my," he whispered, motioning for me to shoulder the rifle. "See the white spots on the back?"

I nodded and slowly positioned the Ruger against my right shoulder.

"That's a fallow," he said, binoculars still to his eyes. "It's a trophy, Jackson. A real find." He motioned for me to take a shot.

The deer was a good fifty yards from us in a small clearing. It was stopped broadside. I kept both eyes open and spotted the deer through the scope. The Ruger's butt was tight against my shoulder when I slowly, deliberately pulled the trigger.

One shot cracked through the chill. The deer fell.

"Jackson!" The Governor slapped me on the back a little harder than I'd have liked. "Right in the kill zone. In the shoulder, behind the heart and lungs. Beautiful! You say you've never fired a weapon?"

"No sir."

"You're a natural."

My stomach turned when he said it. I didn't fire the weapon again that day.

***

George is finally beginning to calm himself as we drive past the Chihuahua Desert Research Station a couple of minutes from the McDonald Observatory Visitor's Center.

I look at him for a moment to catch his attention fully. "It's good we are beginning to figure out the sides here. The guy who kidnapped me doesn't want me dead. Charlie doesn't want me dead. They both had opportunities and didn't kill me."

"Okay," he says. His leg jitters have stopped.

"The one guy I'm not sure about is that fake detective with the Marines tattoo. I don't know for sure if he's with Charlie or on his own."

"Does it matter?" George asks. "He's against *us*."

***

The Frank N. Bash Visitors Center is an adobe colored stucco building that sits low between the mountains that frame it. In the distance atop Mount Locke, barely visible against the dark skies post-sunset, are a pair of large white domes. They have the appearance of grain silos, but they are powerful telescopes. They're the centerpiece of the McDonald Observatory.

George and I walk up the circle drive to the entrance, hoping it's open. The lights are on inside, and to our surprise, the doors are unlocked.

"Welcome to the McDonald Observatory," greets a cheerful, round woman upon our entrance. "How may I help you? Are you here for the Star Party?"

"Yes ma'am," I answer without thinking. "Do we need reservations?"

"I don't think so," she looks at a piece of paper in front of her. "We're light on attendance tonight."

"What's a Star Party?" George whispers out of the corner of his mouth.

"I don't know," I whisper back. "Maybe it'll help us find Ripley."

The woman looks up as we approach her and she smiles. Her full cheeks are rouge red and her white shoulder-length hair is parted down the middle. She's wearing a cardigan buttoned only at the top and horn-rimmed reading glasses on her disproportionately small nose.

"You're in!" she says. "Now, it's right here at the Gale Telescope Park behind this building. It lasts a couple of hours. Since it's clear tonight, it should be fun viewing. Now, that'll be twenty-four dollars."

"What about the telescopes up the hill?" George asks and hands the woman the cash. She takes the money with one hand while pushing her glasses up her nose with the other. "Those are available on Special Viewing Nights. Those *do* require reservations. Would you like to make one for another night?"

"No thanks," I answer. "What about your lodging?"

"If you are here for a Special Viewing Night or are a friend of the observatory, then yes. We do have a couple of rooms available. I happened to check with Nancy up at the lodge because we had a cancellation. Are you supporters of the observatory?" She smiles with her lips pressed together. Her eyeglasses slide down her nose again.

"We'd like to be," I offer. "What sort of donation would make us the kinds of friends who could stay at the lodge tonight?"

"Hmmm," she squints at George and at me. "It's a little unusual, you know. Typically we don't do this sort of thing, but we do have the room..."

"We're happy to pay the rack rate," George hopes to seal the deal. "In cash."

"If you can both donate fifty dollars, you'll be a friend at the Stargazer level," she counters. "It's our lowest level. It comes with complimentary Star Party passes, but since I already sold you those, I can't cut you a discount. You could both have a room for eighty-eight dollars for tonight. There's no rack rate. We're not a hotel, sweetie."

"Sounds good," I tell her. We both give her our names and the cash for the membership and the room.

"Now," she tells us as we start to leave, "when you head up to the lodge, you'll need to check yourself in. Give it about thirty minutes. I'll call up to Nancy. She'll put your keys out in the great room. Sign in at the clipboard, take your key, and find your room. There's snacks in the refrigerator and out on the tables. Breakfast is self-serve tomorrow morning."

We both thank her and head back to the SUV.

"You heard her say there's a clipboard for check-in?" I say to George as we step out of the visitors' center and into the cool West Texas night. The temperature has dropped in the few minutes we were inside.

"Yep," George says. "Means we can find which room Ripley is hiding in."

"Yeah," I say, popping the remote locks on the SUV and getting in. "It also means those black suits could find us."

***

The clipboard was on a small folding table at one corner of what the woman at the visitors' center called the great room. There were eight other names on the list, none of them Ripley's.

"Let's figure out these names," I suggest. "G. Edwards, M. Harrold, F. Jackson, S. Blackmon, A. Johnson, J. Palance, P. Walker, Franklin."

"When I called from the lab," George reminds me, "the woman said there was a Ripley registered here. Maybe he's not here."

"He's here. Where else would he go?"

"If we led the spooks here," George suggests, tapping me on my shoulder, "maybe they got him."

"Could be." I study the names. "When you talked to the woman on the phone, she read a handful of names to you. Ripley was one. What were the others? Are they on this list?"

George steps up to the table and leans over the clipboard. He runs his finger down the list of names and back up again. He points to Franklin.

"I remember that one." He points to Walker, "That one too."

"Ripley..." I mumble. "Ripley...." I flip the pages on the clipboard back and forth, noticing Ripley's name was there the previous two nights. He was in different rooms each night. Franklin, Walker, and Johnson were in the same rooms. There were no other guests. I flip back to tonight's sign-in.

"Believe it or not," George chuckles.

I figure it out.

"Room eight," I tell him. "J. Palance."

"What?" George looks at the name on the sign in sheet. "How do you know that?"

"Sign in and get your key." I scribble a pseudonym and take the key to room six. George does the same and picks room twelve.

The long hall to our left is dotted with numbered doors on either side of it, odd on the left, even on the right. The hallway is dark, so it's not easy to read the numbers.

"Here it is," I announce just above a whisper. "This is the one."

"How do you know?"

"I thought it might be J. Palance," I explain as we stand outside the door of room eight. "Because Jack Palance was the host of the *Ripley's Believe It Or Not!* Television show in the 1980s. Pretty clever. I looked at the handwriting for Ripley and Palance. They matched."

"How would you know about that show? Aren't you a little young for that?"

"Reruns. Sci-fi channel." I knock on the door and hold up a finger to my lips, suggesting George simmer down. "I had time on my hands as a kid."

There's a shuffling in the room and a mattress creaks. Someone's getting off the bed to come to the door.

"Hello?" says a meek voice from inside the room. "Who is it?"

"We're here to help you, Mr. Ripley."

"My name is Palance."

George shoots me a look.

"Jack is it?" I ask.

"Uh," there's a pause. "Who is this?"

"I know you are hiding here. I am too. We are running from the same people."

The floor creaks from inside the room.

"My name is Jackson Quick. I am an aide to the Governor. I did stuff for him that got me into trouble. I'm on the run like you."

"I'm George Townsend. I'm a reporter from channel four in Houston. I interviewed your dad. He told me you were the key to whatever this thing is, that if we found you, you could help him."

Nothing.

"Let us prove it to you," I suggest. "I'm going to slip my license under the door. George is going to do the same. Then you know it's us. We're not here to hurt you. We're not with the guys in the dark suits."

"Why would you say that?"

"Say what?"

"The guys in the dark suits."

"Have you seen them?" George asks.

"They killed my friend," I offer. "They nearly killed me. We know who they are."

George bends down on a knee and slides his license under the narrow gap between the floor and the bottom of the door. I follow his lead and do the same.

"You see the licenses?" George steps back from the door. "We're telling the truth."

There's a click at the door and the sound of what's probably the sliding chain of the door lock and the handle spins.

"Don't come in yet!" Visible through the small opening is the thick barrel of a gun. A pistol probably. George and I raise our hands in surrender and the door opens a bit wider.

Peering from behind the door – and the pistol – is the younger Roswell Ripley. The nanoscientist. He doesn't resemble the man in the photograph on the wall in his lab. His cheeks are drawn and almost translucent. He looks ill. His brow looks glued into permanent concern, his bloodshot eyes sad but alert. They dash between George and me, matching our faces to those on the licenses. He exhales and his shoulders slump. The tension in his face eases.

He uses the revolver to wave us into his room. We slip inside and he quickly shuts the door before sliding a chair against it and up under the door knob.

"Nice gun," George hasn't taken his eyes off of it.

"Yeah," Ripley glances down at it, "it's my dad's. A Smith & Wesson Governor. I've got it loaded with shotshell. You know, in case..." He walks over to a small chest of drawers, clicks the safety with his thumb and carefully puts the gun on top with the barrel facing the wall. The gun *protecting* him from my boss is called the Governor.

The room is small but clean. There's the chest, an unmade queen-sized bed and a small desk. The desk chair is the one propped against the door.

"You can sit on the bed," Ripley offers. "Why are you here? How did you find me?"

"Your dad told me to find you," George says. "I kinda blew him off at first, thinking he was nuts. You know, everybody's a conspiracy theorist when they get in trouble."

"Right." Ripley walks over to the desk and leans against it. "I get it."

"Jackson here calls me looking for help, and we start talking, trying to piece things together. That leads us to Dr. Aglo at your lab."

"You talked to Dr. Aglo? You've been to my lab?" Ripley folds his arms and stands. The questions sounded more like accusations.

"We wanted to find you," I say. "George knew Dr. Aglo. We reached out to him. He showed us your lab. We were looking for clues as to where you might be."

"What in my lab told you I was here?"

"Auto redial," George answered. "The last number you dialed from the lab was the visitors' center here. We figured you might be hiding out here."

Ripley sits on the edge of the desk, relaxing the tension in his body. "Why are you here?"

"I need your help." I stand up from the bed and take a step toward Ripley. "What you know could save my life."

"The same might hold for you," he says. "You might be able to save mine."

CHAPTER 8

Ripley is pacing back and forth, arms folded. "There is no real definition for what I do. The feds have many definitions for it. It's a taxonomy for a kind of research at the nanoscale."

"Which is?" I ask.

"Picture it like this," he stops for a moment and holds his thumb and index finger up as though he's pinching something. "This is a millimeter. It's tiny, but not really. A nanometer is one million times smaller than a millimeter. Rationally manipulating or designing a material to perform a function at that scale is essentially nanoscience."

"Like the carbon fibers they're building at Rice," George offers. "Enough of those nanoparticles strung together make a really strong fiber. A fiber you could use for a bullet proof vest or a more conductive power line."

"Exactly," Ripley says without any hint of surprise. He's focused. He's lecturing. "Now there are endless possibilities for this kind of work. Take the medical arena..." He's pacing again in the small space between the door and desk. "You can take a nanoparticle that identifies, targets, and eliminates certain kinds of cells. You can use magnetic nanoparticles, injected into the blood stream, that help clarify imaging."

"Like an MRI?" George is the good student; the attentive one at the front of the class.

"Yes," Ripley acknowledges without pause. "Some of those medical advances are being used by the energy industry for subterranean mapping. The easier it is to see, the greater the chance there is of accurately predicting the presence of oil or natural gas."

"There are other industrial uses," he adds with a tilt of his head, as though he is considering the alternatives. "Say, for example, the ability to inject a nanoparticle into household paint which helps it resist water penetration a touch better than before. These are all within the juxtaposed enormity of nanoscience."

"I thought nanoscience was some magical new deal that sent little robots into tiny places to fight, or fix, or change stuff," I admit with an embarrassed laugh. "I had no idea."

"Most people don't," said Ripley. "It's really not as romantic or as exciting as people think. We haven't even figured out how to create those 'nanobots' in such a way that they can perform under the heat, pressure, or chemical environment that exists ten thousand feet below the earth. I mean, we can make them, but they don't move. We can't get them to move."

"Is that what you're working on?" I ask. "Is that what all of this is about?"

"No," Ripley laughs as though the idea is ludicrous. "First of all, when I say 'we', I mean the nanoscience community. I'm not personally working on that part of the equation."

"Then what are you working on?" George asks. "How would it be so important, or controversial, your dad gets framed for an attempted assassination?"

"How would it endanger our lives?" I chime in. That's what I want to know. What really has us holed up in a small lodge in the middle of nowhere?

"It's a long story," Ripley says. He leans against the desk again.

George crosses his legs at the ankles, folds his arms, and settles in. "We're not going anywhere. We came here to get answers."

Ripley's eyes dart around the room as if he's searching for the words. "It's complicated," he says finally.

"That's fine," George says. "Wait. I've got to record this."

"What?" Ripley waves his hands in front of him. "No. I'm not okay with that."

George stands and pulls out a small video recorder from his back pocket. It's like a flipcam or something. "You want us to save you? Then this is your ticket. It's a bargaining chip."

"It's also evidence," Ripley's voice is as a loud as a whisper can be without being a yell. "I'm not about to self-incriminate!"

"Calm down, Dr. Ripley," I step between George and the scientist. "Nobody's asking you to do that. It's insurance. Okay?"

"What do you mean by insurance?"

"What if something happens to you?"

He tilts his head, his eyes aim at the floor. He's considering it.

"Better yet," I raise my finger, "what if something happened to me or to George? There's got to be some proof of what going's on, of what you're involved in. I mean, if someone's willing to frame your dad and force you into hiding, don't you need an insurance policy?"

Ripley bites his lower lip, his eyes still fixed down and to the left until he blinks himself out of his thoughts. "Fine. Record it."

My phone rings.

George and I exchange looks. We're the only ones with this number.

It's an unknown number.

The Saint.

***

"What do you want?"

I step into the hallway outside of Ripley's room. It is dark and empty, and there's a slight echo.

"I know it's you."

"Very good, Jackson. You're getting there, good man. You're getting there."

"How did you get this number?"

"Bribery works wonders," he says. "Especially with a minimum wage electronics store clerk. I could have offered the girl a large cheese pizza and it would have worked."

"What do you want?" I repeat.

"How's the West Texas air? A bit dry?"

"I don't have time for this." I lean against the wall next to Ripley's door and look left, then right. I'm alone.

"You *are* aware you're not alone."

153

The hallway is still empty. "We know about Pickle and NewMex and Aleutian Oil."

"Pickle," The Saint laughs. "It's such a funny little name. Given your circumstance, quite appropriate don't you think?"

"The suits that killed Bobby and tried to kill me are somehow connected to Aleutian Oil. They're here somewhere. They're following us."

"I knew you were a smart one, Jackson. Good man. You're with the good doctor now?"

"I thought you knew everything? Why are you asking?"

"My suggestion would be you separate yourself from him." No laughter.

"What do you mean?"

"The men from Pickle want you dead. Of that, I'm certain. They would likely prefer Dr. Ripley meet an untimely end as well." The Saint clears his throat and takes a sip of something. The sound of ice against glass clinks through the connection. "You've made it easy for them. You've led them straight to him."

"They don't know he's here."

"You found him didn't you?"

"Yes, but—"

"Jackson, my good man," he interrupts, "you're smart. I assume George Townsend the reporter is smart. You're learning the game, but don't think for a moment that men with the kind of experience they employ at F. Pickle aren't light years ahead of you at every turn."

"Why haven't they gotten us already?"

"They're watching you, Jackson. They're waiting. It is much easier for them to get three of you at once, than it would be to hit you individually."

"What about Charlie?"

"What about her?"

"Is she on their side?"

"She's on someone's side, Jackson. It's not yours. Who she is and what it is she wants I don't quite yet know."

"What do *you* want?"

"You need to survive, Jackson," his voice deepens. "You are more important now than you were when you delivered the first

iPod to London. You're less of a pawn and more of a knight."
Backhanded compliments? "I underestimated you in that bar. I saw a weak, needy, restless orphan willing to do anything for a father-figure and a pair of long legs."

He pauses, clearly baiting me.

"I see much me in you. Your drive. Your persistence. Your ability to survive. Your raw intelligence. Oh, and your ability to keep secrets."

"Whatever." He disgusts me. I'm nothing like him.

"I do what needs to be done, Jackson." The hallway is still empty. "Do what needs to be done," he tells me. "We'll both get the answers we need. You have to separate yourself from Ripley. I'm telling you it's imperative."

The phone goes silent and I slip back into Ripley's room. If The Saint is right, we don't have much time.

***

"The science is simple in theory," Ripley starts, talking directly into the camera.

"Look at my shoulder," George instructs. "Don't look directly into the camera. It looks better when you aren't staring into the lens."

Ripley complies and starts again. "The science is simple in theory. To increase the fuel efficiency of a gallon of gasoline, you need to, in effect, amplify its octane. Fuel efficiency, in and of itself, is essentially thermal energy, right? If you take the potential energy you have in a drop of gasoline and you convert it to kinetic energy, you're creating fuel efficiency. The better the conversion, so to speak, the better the efficiency."

"How do you make it better?" George was holding the flip cam out in front of him, looking at the image of Ripley in the small LCD screen on the back of the camera.

"There are a number of ways to do that," Ripley exhales, as though he's irritated with a child's repeated questioning. "You can increase the efficiency of the fuel itself. This is represented by its heat value, among other things. You can better the efficiency of the combustible engine, which goes to the processing of that heat and the conversion to kinetic energy. You can improve the aerodynamic properties of the vehicle; design and weight. All of those efforts improve the efficiency."

"What is it you're working on right now?" George widens the picture, zooming out.

"To explain that, I have to tell you what Nanergetix is doing."

"So do that." George zooms in again, awaiting the answer.

"Nanergetix is using nanoparticles to affect the potential energy in the fuel itself. There is only so much automobile manufacturers can do to improve engine efficiency and reduce aerodynamic drag."

"What do you mean?"

"Well, it's all well and good the Obama administration set these astronomical fuel standards in 2012. They've given auto makers until 2025 to make cars and small trucks run at essentially fifty-four miles per gallon. That's a stretch. While the automakers are on board, publicly, the oil industry is fuming."

George looks up from the LCD. "Could you explain?"

"Let me back up." Ripley leans back against the desk and sighs. "Nanergetix is helping the auto industry, okay? Much of the funding for their work doesn't come out of Don Carlos Buell's pockets. It comes from the automakers. Detroit threw a lot of money at him when he decided to go green. The oil industry felt betrayed. He wouldn't take their cash. He doesn't need it. He's on some mission."

"And?"

"Nanergetix is essentially trying to use engineered nanoparticles to increase the convertible energy of every drop of oil. They add the particle in the refining process and it helps the gasoline stretch farther than it would otherwise."

"By making gasoline go farther, we'd need less of it?"

"Exactly. Can you imagine the profit for a company that does that? If the government requires all petrochemical refineries to use that technology? We're talking billions upon billions of dollars in perpetuity."

"Buell is not popular with the oil companies?"

"Not at all," Ripley says. "He's persona-non-grata, which is why I believe it was the oil companies that wanted him dead. Without his vision, Nanergetix is nothing."

"If he's governor," I interject, "he's in a better position to control the legislation governing the industry."

"Yes." Ripley glances at me before returning his attention to George's shoulder. "Nanergetix is getting increasingly close. Right now their efforts work only in a lab environment. They're having trouble with the particles adhering beyond certain temperatures, but they're close."

"How do you know this?" I ask.

"Nanoscience is a very small community. When everything is under a microscope, it's very hard to hide."

"You're making some assumptions based on hearsay," George states. He sounds like a lawyer.

"Maybe," Ripley acknowledges. "But the rumors are persistent enough they're believable."

"You're trying to mimic what Nanergetix is doing and beat them to the marketplace?" George asks. "That way the oil companies can control it?"

"Quite the opposite," Ripley says, closing his eyes. "I'm being paid to stop it."

***

The shades are pulled against the single-paned windows of the lodge. The wind outside is howling with such intensity it sounds as though the glass might shatter at any second. The night winds in the Ft. Davis Mountains are fierce.

With only the lamps beside the bed and on the desk lighting the room, and George with his small flip cam aimed at Ripley, it's as though I'm in an Oren Peli film. All we need is a poltergeist attacking us to complete the effect, though the kind of stuff the scientist is explaining seems unreal enough.

"Nano markers are little invisible serial numbers," he explains. "We insert these markers into anything commercial – make-up, processed leather goods, food, pharmaceuticals, refined oil, etc."

"Why would you do that?" George asks.

"The market would let you know what you're buying is the real deal. It prevents the sale of counterfeit...anything, really. If I tested a batch of Prozac I knew had this marker in it, and the marker doesn't pop up, it's clear the medicine didn't come from Eli Lilly. Or say, for instance, I bought barrels of what I thought was oil from Saudi Arabia, but the marker indicated it was from West Africa, then we have a problem. It's protection for the manufacturers and the consumers."

"At the same time," Ripley continues. "If you could mimic the marker of the original product, and attach it to the counterfeit—"

"An untraceable black market," I say. I get it.

"Yes," nods Ripley. "Or a fuel that doesn't really go as far as you think it should. Reducing the efficiency of gasoline by an almost imperceptible amount changes the balance sheets by billions of dollars over time."

"So you're trying to copy the marker in Nanergetix improved gasoline." George gets it too. "By doing that, the oil companies can pretend they're refining the oil using the new nanoparticles, but they're really not."

"Yes."

"The oil companies are paying you to do this?" I ask.

"Sort of," Ripley replied. "They're funding the project," he says, still looking at George's shoulder. "But they're not alone. Your boss is involved. He's the one who first approached me, who misled me about what I would be doing."

My boss. The oil companies. The iPods. The money. It's adding up.

"What did you think you were doing?" George asked him.

"Well," Ripley glances into the lens before averting his eyes again. "I *thought* I was working on creating a marker that would identify products refined in Texas. It would help with business and taxes and other stuff I don't really remember. The idea, as the Governor sold it, was to help Texas define itself from the rest of the industry."

"Then you found out what you were *really* working on?" My question.

Ripley nods. "I started asking too many questions. I was warned against it. I couldn't help myself. I threatened to quit, to go public."

"Buell gets shot, your dad gets framed, and you disappear," George again.

"Yes."

We stand in the dim light quietly for what seems like forever, the wind threatening to crash through the windows. None of us, I guess, know what to say next.

George hits the stop button on the flip cam and lowers it to his side. He sidesteps to the chest of drawers and leans against it.

Ripley folds his arms, closes his eyes, and tilts his head back toward the ceiling. He exhales deeply.

I sit on the bed trying to quickly process what we've learned. It's a lot to take in.

"You think the same people who want me dead also want you erased from existence?" I don't look at Ripley when I finally speak, but he knows I'm talking to him.

"I guess. I don't know. I mean, clearly the Governor is not happy with me. Apparently the oil companies don't like me. If, as you think, they've hired some undercover agents to kill you, what would stop them from wanting to do the same thing to me?"

"It doesn't make sense that they'd want you dead," I say. "You're *their* key to beating Buell. You are the one working on their project. If they kill you, they're back to square one. They wouldn't do that."

"Then different people want us dead?" Ripley stands up from the desk. "Somebody wants you dead and some other faction wants to kill me? That doesn't make sense either."

"What's our next move?" George pipes in. "We can debate who wants who dead all night, but we've got to come up with a plan. We have to get out of here. We need to get back to Houston to the newsroom. We can protect both of you from there. At least until we sort the rest of it out."

At his core, George is trying to figure out how to break this twisted story, but he is right. We have to get somewhere safe.

***

It is nearly dawn and the sun is about to come up. Ripley is standing at the window. We each slept for about an hour, in shifts. George is the one resting now.

"It's time to go," I say. "Do you have a car here?"

"Yes. It's outside the lodge. What's your plan?"

"We've gotten some sleep," I said, knowing it wasn't nearly enough. "I imagine whoever is waiting on us did too. The best bet is to split up and meet back in Houston. You can't hide out here forever."

"Not now that you've led them to me." His back is still to me, but the anger dripping from his words is hitting me in the face. "I'm going to die here for something I *wouldn't* do. My father will die in prison for something he *didn't* do."

I rub the exhaustion from my eyes. "We'll make it out of here if we're smart. I'll take your car and you go with George. If you're with him, you might be better off. Maybe."

"Maybe," he snorts, laughing at the absurdity of it. "I deal in absolutes, Jackson. I'm a scientist. I see it or I don't. I can find it or I can't. I'll survive or I won't. There's very little room for maybe."

"You believe in theory. *Theoretically* you can survive this if we get you to George's newsroom. They've got security there. They'll protect you until all of this gets sorted out."

"What do you propose exactly?" Ripley said. There's a soft red glow warming the side his face from the sun peeking over the mountains.

"You and George fly out of El Paso. Same flight. Maybe you fly to Austin and drive from there. Maybe you go straight to Houston. That's up to George. Once he lets his station know what's going on they'll be able to help."

"Then?"

"You get to the station and wait for me. We can regroup from there."

"What if we don't make it?"

"I thought you dealt in absolutes?" "Theoretically." He turns toward me. His eyebrows are still bunched together. His lower lip is pouting, revealing a slight under bite. At least he's looking at me.

"Then we'll have to assume we'll make it," I effect a smile I imagine is hardly convincing.

George stands from the bed and stretches languorously. "You know reporters can't assume. We get in trouble for that."

"I'm not a reporter," says Ripley. "Let's get this over with."

George rolls his eyes, fixes his shirt and belt, and walks to the small bathroom. Ripley moves to the dresser and picks up the gun. He opens the cylinder and closes it.

"Loaded still?" I ask.

"Yes." He checks the safety. "Shotshell. Six of them."

"You said that when we first got here," I said, remembering what he'd told us after pointing the gun at us through the door. "You mean ammo like a shotgun?"

Ripley nods. "I'm not a good shot. With the shotshell, I don't have to be particularly accurate. That is, as long as I'm close enough. It's not really meant for distance shooting. Are you good with a gun?"

"I dunno," my shoulders shrug almost involuntarily. "I don't shoot much."

"Much?" Ripley's brow arches with interest. He's still holding the gun, waving it toward the door without much thought.

"Well, I have fired a gun. A rifle. Some other stuff. I wouldn't say I'm a good shot or anything. I try to stay away from them."

"Why?" Ripley places the pistol on the chest of drawers, spins the barrel toward the wall and turns his attention back to me.

"Just do," I mumble. "Look, we've got to get going. Now is as good a time as any. The faster we get to an airport, the more flight options we have to get out of here."

"I'm ready," Ripley sighs. He's probably trying to convince himself of it.

George appears from the bathroom. "So am I." His hair is slicked back, his face is pink, and his eyes bloodshot. He looks like hell. "Let's do this."

I sling my backpack over my right shoulder. "George, you should go with Dr. Ripley in his car. I'll take mine. We can switch at the gas station."

"What do you mean switch?" Ripley asks.

"We left my rental at a gas station about forty-five minutes from here," George tells him. "I guess if we're getting tailed, we could switch it up and confuse them?"

"That is the dumbest thing I've ever heard," Ripley says, a vein in his forehead exposing itself. He's clearly about to explode. "You two have no clue what you're doing."

"Well, I wouldn't say—" George tries to interject.

"No, really," Ripley says in a strained whisper, trying not to raise his voice, "you two are absolute morons. You find your way to me, you bring with you trained killers, you've got no weapons, you've got no plan - my life is not a game."

"I think you're—"

"What would make either of you think this could work?" His forehead vein is purple and thick. "You are clearly out of your league. Now you want to 'switch cars'? You want to 'maybe take a plane into a different airport' to avoid these professional head hunters? How can you be so naïve? Neither of you *look* like idiots, but you must be."

"You're right," I admit.

Ripley, his chest heaving from the adrenaline of his rant, looks bewildered.

"What?" George looks at me with confusion and maybe some hurt.

"We're idiots," I repeat. "I mean, we really *don't* have a plan. We don't know what we're doing. We're no match for professional killers or whatever. We didn't think this through. The truth is, *our* lives are in danger too. Something bad is happening. Too many people are keeping secrets. It could be your nanocrap, it could be something we haven't thought about. I still don't know."

"Yes, clearly y—" Ripley starts.

I raise my hand at the scientist to stop him. "My turn. You had yours."

Ripley glares at me.

"So what if we brought the heat with us?" I propose. "What were you going to do? Hide out here forever? If *we* so easily found you, do you really think professional killers would've taken much longer? Then you'd be alone. Now at least, you've got some help. We do have a plan. We want to get all of us to the safety of George's newsroom. Nothing's going to happen to us there, if we can make it."

"I feel like a trapped rat."

"A lab rat?" George asks snidely.

I look at George with a glance that tells him to ease up on the sarcasm. "You can blame us all you want. You can call us idiots or whatever. The bottom line is, we're all still alive. We need each other. What do you want to do? It's your call, Doc."

Ripley looks at the floor and then at me, a hint of what I imagine is guilt in his eyes, before he glances at George and the floor again. He leans over at his waist, hands on his knees, and begins to sob. It's an ugly cry, the kind no man wants to witness of another. I can't blame him. He *is* a lab rat. He's a nerd. He's not equipped to deal with this.

I'm not equipped to deal with this either.

George looks at me and starts to reach for Ripley, to comfort him. He stops short and we stand there, the scientist crying himself dry.

There's a knock at the door that stops the sobbing. Still bent over, Ripley looks at the door and stands erect to look at us. He grabs the gun from the chest of drawers and uses the back of his sleeve to wipe his nose and eyes free of snot and saline.

There's more banging on the door, this time louder and more insistent.

"Who is it?" he asks, trying to sound composed.

"I need to speak with you," says a voice through the door. It's a woman. She sounds scared.

***

Ripley inches to the right side of the room's door. "Who is it?" he repeats, more urgently this time.

"Nancy," the voice says shaky. "I'm the, uh, caretaker here."

"What do you want?" Ripley has positioned himself with his back to the wall, his right arm up with the gun pointed toward the door. His hand is shaking.

"I need to speak with you about your room," she says. "Could you, uh, open the door please, Mr. Palance?"

Ripley looks at me for an answer. I shake my head. Not a good idea.

"I'm not feeling well," Ripley says, his eyes still fixed on me. "Is there a problem?"

"Well, sir," more hesitancy, "w-we're overbooked. I need to speak with you about your room for tonight."

"It's a little early for that, isn't it?" Ripley glances at the red numbers on clock next to the bed. 6:05AM. "I mean it's—"

The door explodes, knocking Ripley backward against the wall. George shrinks behind the chest of drawers at the entrance to the bathroom. I fall back onto the bed as Ripley's gun spins in the air and lands next to my head.

I grab the gun and slide off the bed on the far side of the door. I'm inches from the window.

From behind the bed, another explosion. It's clearly a gunshot. A blast, maybe, from a large caliber weapon. To my left, splintered wood flies past. Lying flat on the ground and looking underneath the bed to the doorway, I can see a body. It may be Ripley. I can't tell.

Another blast. I quickly look above the bed.

The door is unhinged and shattered. At the threshold is a man with dark hair and sunglasses. His lips are pursed. A small shotgun of some kind is at his waist, aiming toward the chest of drawers.

Without ducking, I check the safety, pull the hammer, and aim.

One shot at his head. A dark spot spreads above the lenses of those glasses. The man with the gun stumbles for a moment and falls.

From behind him, the flash and pop of another gun, a handgun. I drop to the floor and try to aim the Governor toward the door. There's a body in the way. That won't work.

Bang! Bang!

What's left of the shattered door splinters into the air. I can smell the pine.

On my stomach, I inch to the end of the bed. I can see George. He's tucked in a ball, his hands covering his ears, his eyes closed.

I've got to get us out of here.

From my position on the floor, I push up to my knees with my left hand. My right is already aiming the pistol at the door. I pull the trigger twice, feeling it resist the second pull.

By the time I focus on the man in the doorway, he already has a bullet hole in his right knee and in his stomach. He's still standing.

A third pull on the trigger and he falls on top of the first shooter. There's sawdust dancing in the sunlight beaming through the window. For an instant there's complete silence, apart from the slight ringing in my ears.

Ripley screams. "We're gonna die!" He's still pressed against the wall, at the corner of the room next to the bed. "We're gonna die!"

"Shut up!" I snap at him and, using the bed, pull myself onto both feet. "Do you have more bullets?"

"What?" He looks at me with his eyes wide.

"Bullets," I repeat. "Where are they? I've got one left. I need five. "Give me the shotshell this time."

"What?" He's squinting now. Maybe he can't hear me from the gunfire?

"You said there was shotshell in this gun. It's loaded with regular bullets!"

"Uh, yeah," Ripley blinks. "In the top dresser drawer." He points toward the chest of drawers but doesn't move.

"George, get the ammo out of the drawer."

Shoving the desk aside, I step to the window and release the latches on either side of the double paned glass. The window slides open and I lean outside. The drop is straight down, maybe 40 feet. We're on the edge of a sheer, rocky plateau with nowhere to go.

"That's not going to work," I mumble and turn back to the room. "We're going to get out the way we came in and we need to hope there's nobody waiting for us."

"They might already be on their way," George offers along with a handful of shotshell. "We need to go now, don't we?"

I take the bullets and load them into the five empty chambers of the revolver without looking at him or saying anything. I spin the weapon closed, re-shoulder my backpack, and start for the door.

Past the bed, there's a woman's body on the floor. It's Nancy or whoever was claiming to be Nancy. There's blood soaking her back and puddling underneath her. Looking down, I notice blood and a tear in my pants along my shin. That first blast must have hurled something into me. It's either shrapnel or wood. I don't want to look at it.

I've seen too much blood.

CHAPTER 9

George is armed with the small shotgun belonging to the dead man with sunglasses. Ripley is carrying The Governor again. I'm holding a nine millimeter semiautomatic. After shoveling the dead assassins out of the doorway, taking their weapons, their wallets, a buck knife, and a set of keys, we make our way toward the entrance of the lodge. All three of us are breathing heavily. We probably look ridiculous, a scientist, a reporter, and a political hack acting like special operations.

"Do you think that was all of them?" Ripley manages between breaths. "Are we in the clear?"

"No telling," answers George. "That might have been the first wave."

"Great," Ripley inhales and sighs. "I told you this plan wasn't worth a piece of—"

"Shut up," I bark. "We're alive."

Ripley's right. This plan is no plan at all. We're clueless. We're probably walking into a trap of some kind. We've got no choice. This is our only way out.

"How did you do that?" Ripley asks, his tone softer.

"Do what?" I ask, turning around. I can see the Nike covered feet of the man with sunglasses.

"Kill those men?"

I spin back around to catch Ripley's pained expression, "I don't know. I didn't think about it."

"I mean," Ripley whispers, "you killed two men. Just like that."

"Like I said, I didn't think." I keep walking. "Survival instinct, I guess."

I don't know whether it's survival instinct or just instinct. Maybe I'm death's minion. For years I've been avoiding facing it. Now it's staring me in the face.

The gun felt good in my hand, familiar. It belonged there. I didn't feel a thing when I saw either man die. No remorse. No guilt. No anything. I just stepped over the bodies

"Right in the *head*," Ripley says. "Right in the head!" He starts moving again.

"Enough, okay?" George snaps. "He saved our lives right?"

"Sorry," Ripley says. "I just...I suppose I..."

I lead the three of us into the kitchen, where we first checked in to the lodge, and then carefully out the door into the daylight. It's better not to think about what I've done.

We stay along the side of the building, protected somewhat from the open terrain as we move toward the cars. The air is dry and cool from the dawn. There's a slight wind swirling around us that sends a shudder down my spine. My eyes are on the horizon, my mind somewhere else completely until Ripley voices the bad news.

"Our tires are blown." He's the first to notice it. We inch closer. All four tires on both vehicles are flat. "What do we do now?"

I scan the area. The parking lot, the sloping mountain behind us, and the winding, narrow road below us. That's when I see it.

"We take a new ride." I grab my old backpack from the SUV, empty its contents into my new pack, and leave the empty bag on the ground. "There's a car about fifty yards downhill from here. We have the keys."

Quickly, we edge our way down the road to a beige four-door Crown Victoria. I push the unlock button and the remote and the door click in unison.

"We might get out of here," Ripley says optimistically as he slides into the back seat of the Ford.

"Maybe," says George. "We've got a long way to go to get to Houston."

I walk around to the back of the car and pop the trunk. It's empty aside from a spare tire and a small black leather briefcase. I drop my backpack and pull out the briefcase.

I slam shut the trunk just as Ripley gets exactly what he's been trying to avoid.

***

The bullet hit him in the left side of the head. He must have been turned toward the driver's side. The shot sliced through the rear windshield within an instant of me closing the trunk.

Ripley is slumped on the rear bench seat of the sedan, eyes fixed open. He looks like a marionette cut from its strings and dropped to the ground.

The world slows around me and I turn to my right, looking down the mountain. I catch a quick flash of something straight downhill about two hundred yards and the sound of a loud engine turning over.

George panics next to me, his back pressed against the passenger door in terror. I jump into the driver's seat, toss the briefcase at him, and spin the car around.

"Seatbelt," I tell George without looking away from the road ahead. There's a wake of dust trailing from whoever shot Ripley.

The same road we'd carefully driven up the mountain, we're now traveling down at a dangerous speed. The rear tires lose their grip on the asphalt with each spin of the steering wheel. Twice I almost lose control and tumble off the road, but we're closing in. Maybe one hundred yards to go.

"Open the briefcase," I tell him. It doesn't sound like my voice. It's too calm, too in control. "Find out what's inside it."

"I can't," he says, fumbling with the twin locks on the front of the case. "It's locked."

"Use the buck knife."

"Ripley had it."

"Get it from him!" I jerk the wheel to the right and decelerate enough to avoid colliding with thick brush on the shoulder of the road. "It's gotta be back there."

George hesitates before climbing past me and between the front seats. He's grunting and breathing heavily. "Got it!"

He slides back into his seat. The knife is bloody, as are

George's hands. He slides the knife into the case and starts prying it back and forth, up and down.

The dust up ahead is getting closer; one hundred yards now. I jerk the wheel to the left and brake to regain control as the tires squeal in resistance.

"I can't open it," George says. "I can't do this now." He tosses the case and the knife onto the floorboard in front of him and finally buckles his belt.

"Check the glove box. Maybe there's something in there."

"What are you looking for?" George asks, pulling open the box. "There's a map and an owner's manual."

"I don't know," I admit. "Anything." The car accelerates under the weight of my right foot on the pedal. With each swerve, Ripley's body slides across the back seat, banging against the back of my seat. The dust is closer. Maybe fifty yards. We swing another corner.

"What is *that*?" George asks, his right hand bracing him against the dash. "It's look like we caught up with them!"

Up ahead there's a black sedan upside down against an embankment on the inside of a sharp turn. The wheels are still spinning. There's an arm sticking out through the driver's window. About ten feet from the car, toward the outer edge of the curve, is a long rifle of some kind.

A rifle for a sniper?

I slam on my brakes and the Ford fishtails to a stop. We're about twenty feet from the wreck. This *is* the car we were chasing.

"Stay in the car," I tell George and grab the nine millimeter from under the driver's seat. There's a cloud of dust emanating from the wreck, the tires spinning and whining. The driver's foot still must be on the accelerator. I point the gun at the car and walk toward the arm lying lifelessly on the ground.

When I get to within a couple of feet, I kneel down and peek into the car. The airbag is blown, so I can't see the driver. The arm definitely belongs to a man. I nudge it with the gun. Nothing.

There's a moan from inside the vehicle. The passenger's side.

Getting back on my feet, I sidestep to the other side of the car. There's glass everywhere, the windows crushed from the weight of the car. Another moan.

I point the gun at the window as I kneel down. It's only when I see the passenger that my hand starts shaking. I take a deep breath and try to steady my aim. It's not easy.

The passenger is bruised and bloodied, white bone sticking through the right forearm from a compound fracture, but I know who it is.

"Charlie?"

***

I was eight years old when my father first let me handle a weapon. He was an expert sharpshooter and was on the college rifle team at N.C. State. There were trophies in his office. He had a framed target on the wall behind his desk, and a bowl on his desk filled with spent brass bullet casings. I remember him digging into the bowl, grabbing a handful, and letting them clang back into the bowl. It was stress relief, I guess.

"A gun is not a toy," he'd reminded me repeatedly. "It is a tool for sport and for self-defense. Violence is never a way to solve problems. Never."

The day we first went to the range, I felt like I was a member of some special club.

The range was outside, with about twenty firing positions. It was cool outside. The air smelled like burning charcoal and the leaves on the ground were every color but green. We were the only ones there, my dad and me. Two men with a gun.

He handed me a pair of headphones and helped me put them over my ears. He checked that they fit snugly and signaled for me to slide them off and around my neck. He pulled out a pair for himself and did the same.

From a vinyl bag, he pulled out the rifle. It was beautiful.

"This is a Henry lever action .22, son," he said, holding the weapon by its smooth walnut stock. "It's like a cowboy rifle. My dad gave it to me. Someday, I'll give it to you. It's light. Weighs maybe five pounds unloaded. You'll be able to handle it."

My dad pulled the hammer with his thumb and fingered the trigger back. He lowered the hammer and rechecked the trigger. It was locked. "I'm gonna show you how to safely load this rifle, okay?"

I nod. I couldn't take my eyes off the gun.

My gun!

"This is what's called the tube..." My dad spun the end of the black cylinder underneath the barrel to the left and pulled out a gold looking tube. "Back here is the loading port." He pointed to an oval hole on the bottom side of the long cylinder. He picked up a bullet and dropped it in to the magazine.

"This rifle holds about fifteen bullets, give or take. Don't overload it." He picked up the gold colored tube and slid it back into the cylinder. "Now this has a spring in it," he warned. "When you push this back into the rifle, don't let go of it." He twisted the tube back to the right and it locked in place.

"Okay," he said, pointing the muzzle down the range toward a target. "You're loaded and ready to go. Remember – with a loaded weapon, you never point it at anyone. It's always away from people."

I nodded eagerly and licked my lips. I couldn't wait.

"Now I'm going to fire off these bullets. I want you to watch what I do," my dad said as he tucked the weapon under his arm, with it pointed down range, and put on his headphones. "Then you're going to load it and get your turn to shoot."

My dad turned to the side and shouldered the rifle. He pressed the butt against his right shoulder. "You always want the weapon tight against your shoulder," he said without taking his eyes off the target, "otherwise it'll kick back and hurt you."

Holding the forestock with his left hand, he took his right hand, trigger finger extended, and pulled on the lever. It clicked when it loaded the bullet and clicked again when he pulled it back. He tilted his head to the right and fired. A brass casing popped out of the right side of the barrel.

For the next thirty-seconds he repeated the action over and over again.

Pull. Click. Fire. Pull. Click. Fire.

When he'd emptied the rifle, he slipped it under his arm, locked the trigger, and pulled his headphones down around his neck.

"Let's go check it," he smiled and waved me to the other end of the range, where his target hung against a large bale of hay. I tailed behind my dad, three quick strides for every one of his, excited to see how well he'd done.

"See?" he said, drawing an invisible circle around the fifteen holes in the thin paper. "A tight pattern there above the bullseye. No matter where you hit, you want a tight pattern. That means all the holes are close together."

He rubbed my head with his left hand. "Now it's your turn."

I walked as fast as I could back to the firing position. My dad attached a new target and followed me. I could barely contain myself.

He held the gun while I unscrewed the magazine tube and loaded fifteen bullets. My little hands trembled from the excitement of it. I had trouble forcing the spring-loaded tube back into position, so my dad helped me turn it and lock it.

He handed me the weapon much as a drill sergeant returns a rifle to a soldier during inspection. He smiled and winked, proud of me before I ever fired a shot.

I took the rifle and, in one motion, slipped my left hand under the forestock while raising the butt to my shoulder. With my trigger finger extended, I grabbed the lever. The metal was cold.

Pull forward. Click. Pull back. Click.

I bent my finger to the trigger and tilted my head to aim through the site.

Pow!

My dad stood silently watching as I slowly repeated the motion again.

Pow!

With each successive shot, I moved more quickly to the next until I was out of ammunition. My dad was still smiling.

I started to run to check my target.

"Ah-Ah!" Dad stopped me. "No running. You need to lock the trigger."

I pulled the hammer, the trigger, and released the hammer again.

"Good," he said, reaching for the weapon. "Now go check it."

I walked like a kid rushing to the high board at the community pool. My dad was right behind me. Neither of us expected what we found on the recycled paper target.

"Holy crap!" my dad said. "Can that be right?" He pulled the target from the hay bale and looked at it more closely.

I'd seen the target, but didn't know why he was confused.

"This pattern is tighter than mine. I mean, you've got all fifteen shots left of center. Unbelievable!"

"I didn't hit the bullseye," I said.

"Doesn't matter. You're within an inch of it. Your consistency is uncanny. I told you pattern is what matters. Your aim was true every time."

"It's good?"

"It's better than good, Jackson! You're a natural."

***

"Ripley's ours," Charlie mumbles. Her head is resting on my legs after I've managed to pull her through the broken passenger window of the car. Her right arm is broken. That's clear from the bone sticking through the skin. Her left foot is probably broken too. It's twisted at an odd angle. Her color is fading. Not good.

"He *was* ours," she says, her voice strained. I take her head in my hands and try to get her to focus on my face. "He was working for us."

"What do you mean?" Charlie! What do you mean?"

Her eyes float past mine and return. Her lips are purple, blue almost. She licks them and sighs. A raspy sigh.

"He worked for us," she coughs. "He was helping us. He...flaked. He was a risk."

"Who is *us*?"

I thumb away a tear from her left cheek. Her skin is cold.

"You weren't what they said," she smiles. "You're tougher than they said." Her voice is almost inaudible. I lean over, closer to her broken body as she whispered. "They thought you were weak."

"Who is *they*?"

"The plan won't work will it?" she says, looking past me and into the sky. Is she delirious? "The plan is bad, sir. Ripley won't play along. Framing his dad won't help. Shooting you didn't help. Quick isn't what we thought he was. It's all bad. I didn't do this right. Both sides went bad..."

She mumbles something unintelligible and giggles. Blood leaks from the corner of her mouth and trails down her cheek onto my leg. She coughs and more blood bubbles up. Charlie is dying.

"Is that your girlfriend?" George is standing behind me, shooting video right over my shoulder.

I nod.

She says something else about Buell, me, my boss. I can't understand any of it. Her body shudders against mine and relaxes. There's a final nauseating gurgle before her eyes widen.

Charlie is gone. Limp. Lifeless. Dead.

I take my fingers and close her eyes before sliding her torso off of my legs.

"Did you roll on all of that?" I ask George.

"Yes, but I don't know how much of what she said was audible."

I slide myself back from her body and lean over to look inside the car. The driver is still lying there. On his right hand is a tattoo of the emblem for the U.S. Marine Corps.

It's Crockett, the fake detective.

He's dead too.

Crockett and Charlie? Together?

There was that look they gave each other at the hospital. Crockett fit the description of the "douche Jean Claude Van Damme" with whom Bobby said she left the bar on the night I got drugged. To my left, there's the long rifle on the road.

They were a team. A sniper team.

On the ceiling of the back seat is what looks like a large duffle bag. I reach through the broken window and pull it over the headrest. It's heavy, but I manage to sling it out of the car.

I push myself to my feet, grab the bag, and trudge back to the Crown Victoria and pop the trunk. I toss in the bag and walk over to the rifle. It looks like it's okay, the safety's on. It finds a home in the trunk too.

"Let's go," I motion to George as I get into the driver's seat and drop my handgun into the center console. He's videotaping the scene. The wreck. The blood. My dead ex-girlfriend.

We're halfway to the highway before either of us says anything.

"Did you know she was a..."

"Sniper?" I ask. "No."

"She kept saying *us* and *they*."

"I know." I wipe my forehead with the back of my hand. I'm sweating.

"She was talking about Nanergetix," George says. "And Buell."

"Where do you get that from?"

"She said it."

"I didn't hear that."

"Right before I asked you if she was your girlfriend," he says. "She was mumbling, but I heard her say Buell. She said Naner-something. Had to be Nanergetix. I'll know for sure, hopefully when I listen to the tape back in the newsroom. If it turned out, I mean. Buell's company, that's who she was working for. That's who Ripley was working for."

"You think?"

"Dude," he says, his voice elevated, "it's clear. Ripley wasn't really working for the Governor. Neither was your girlfriend. They were both double-agents."

"Double agents?" I laugh at him. Ridiculous.

"Not real double agents," he corrects himself, "you know what I mean. Ripley wasn't really trying to imitate the nano-marker as he claimed. He was faking it. Somebody caught on to him, and Buell couldn't take the chance of being connected to him, so he had him killed."

"And Charlie?"

"She was spying on you," he said. "She was working for Buell all along. You were her, I dunno, mark? "

I laugh and look over at George. He's not laughing.

I slam on the brakes and the Crown Victoria screams to a stop in the middle of the road.

"I'm not thinking clearly," I say. I step out of the car to open the rear driver's side door. "Not clearly at all."

I yank Ripley's heavy body from the back seat and drop it to the pavement. His head slams to the ground with a sickening crack.

George is turned around, looking over the front seat. "What are you *doing?*" He looks terrified.

"I made a mistake," I say to him. "I put the weapon that killed Ripley in our car with his body. Not smart. Gotta get rid of both."

"Aren't we going to be worse off by dumping a body and a gun in the middle of the road?" George has gotten out of the car and is standing along the passenger's side now.

"We can't be worse off. I don't want a dead body or Charlie's rifle in the car. We don't have time to drag her off of the road."

"Look," George moves toward me at the rear of the car, "you're a little stressed right now. Your girlfriend—"

"Ex," I correct him. "Ex-girlfriend."

"Okay, ex-girlfriend," he says. "She's dead. She probably isn't who you thought she was. Our lives are still in danger, and we're only now beginning to piece together all of this cloak and dagger stuff. It's a lot to absorb. Let me drive."

I don't know how George is keeping it together, when he's been the nervous, ill-equipped one all along. He's right. I need a second to think.

I slide into the passenger's seat and pull out my phone. There's a good signal.

George straps his seatbelt, starts the car and puts it in gear. We've got some time before we hit the highway. Maybe twenty minutes.

I type Charlie's name into the browser on the phone. There are a few hundred results. Her Facebook page and Twitter account pop up. There's a web article about her being hired by the Governor to work on his staff. Not much else.

"What are you doing?" George asks.

"Looking for Charlie on the internet."

"What do you mean?"

I scroll down the list of links including her name. "You said she's not who I thought she was. I'm looking to see if there's something about her I missed."

"You typed in her name?"

"Yes. Nothing unusual."

"What name did you enter?"

"Charlie Corday."

"Is that her full name?" George checks the rearview mirror. "Have you entered her full name?"

"Charlotte Corday?" I tell him. "No."

I type in Charlotte Corday and up pops more than four hundred thousand links. There's a Wikipedia article and images of a woman named Marie-Anne Charlotte de Corday d'Armont. I scroll through the list of links: Charlotte Corday, assassin; Charlotte Corday, killer and royalist sympathizer; Charlotte Corday, executed for killing French revolutionary leader. I click one of the pages:

Charlotte Corday stabbed to death Jean Paul Marat, an outspoken leader of the French revolutionary movement. She assassinated him in his bath and calmly waited for the authorities to arrest her. She was executed four days later.

"This is too much of a coincidence..."

"What?" George leans over, trying to look at my phone.

"Charlotte Corday was an eighteenth century assassin. She was an assassin like Charlie."

"That's not her real name," George says, half asking a question, half stating what is likely fact.

"Probably not," I tell him. "How did I not see this?"

I click on another link and my screen fills with Jacques Louis-David's apparently famous painting of Corday killing Marat. She's tall and slender, beautiful and deadly. Just like Charlie.

Marat never saw it coming. Corday led him to believe she was switching sides and would give him valuable information. Instead, she stabbed him in the chest. How appropriate "Charlie" should choose her name.

"Who was she?"

"Good question." I turn off the phone. "We need to go to Austin to find out."

"We need to get to the newsroom," George protests, "not Austin."

"Before we go to Houston we need to find out who Charlie is. Or was. I bet the answers are in her apartment. I've got a key."

"Why does it matter who she was? We've got to get to a place where we're safe, where we have time to finish piecing this together."

"Let's split up," I suggest. "You go to Houston. Get to the newsroom and start using your resources there. I'll get to Austin and figure out what I can learn there. How does that work? We can't put this together without knowing everything."

George says nothing. He glances at the rearview mirror and accelerates.

"I still don't know how the energy companies, Buell, and those iPods all fit together." I tilt the air vent toward me. It's warm in the car. "Why is everyone getting killed? Why didn't Charlie kill *me*? Where do the Pickle guys fit into this?"

"You can ask them," George says, glancing in the rearview mirror again and gripping the steering wheel more tightly.

"What?"

"They're behind us."

Following us, not even a car length back, is a large black SUV. Two men are in the front seat. One of them, the passenger, is armed.

PART III
DON'T MESS WITH TEXAS

"All new states are invested, more or less, by a class of noisy, second-rate men who are always in favor of rash and extreme measures, but Texas was absolutely overrun by such men."

---GENERAL SAM HOUSTON,
FIRST PRESIDENT AND GOVERNOR OF TEXAS

CHAPTER 10

My life has devolved into a Jason Bourne movie, but the bullets are real. There aren't stunt men or actors chasing me. They're Pickle people bent on killing me and George.

"This is bad. These are the guys who were following you yesterday aren't they?"

"Yep," he says. "Yellow and blue plates." George steers out of a curve and accelerates. The black SUV is within inches of our rear bumper. We've got to do something to shake it.

"Keep it steady," I advise, grabbing the 9 mm from the center console and climbing into the back seat. I slip on the bloody leather and tumble onto the floor, still holding the gun.

"Be careful!" George yells. "You could have shot me."

I inch my way into the passenger's back seat and stay low. "Let me know when you're about to make a sharp right turn."

Still crouched in the seat, I find the rectangular button on the left side of the gun behind the trigger. A light thumb press drops the clip into my left hand. There are two rounds left.

"Left curve!" George yells.

I slide the clip back into the gun and push it up with my palm. It clicks into place as the car lurches to the left and my weight pulls me to the right against the door.

I grab a seat belt shoulder strap and yank it until it locks, hen wrap it around my right ankle. A tug tells me it should hold.

"Right coming up!"

I turn to the rear of the car and, completely twisted in the seatbelt, reach to my left and pull on the door handle. The door opens wildly and almost slams shut, but I jam my shoulder into it and lean out of the car. My face is maybe six inches from the blacktop. I grip the gun with both hands and extend myself as far as I can, the door beating against my arm and shoulder.

We haven't hit the turn yet, so I can't see anything but the back of the Ford and the tire spinning against the road.

My body slides away from the open door, but the seatbelt holds me in place. The front of the black SUV slides into view. I extend my arms and pull the trigger. Nothing.

The safety's on!

I thumb the safety off and quickly aim again at the car trailing us.

Pow! I hit the lower edge of the front passenger's side door. A miss.

The SUV slides back to the right and out of view.

"Another right!" George yells. The SUV moves back into position. I aim again. I've got one bullet. My right finger presses the trigger and pulls.

Pow!

Almost immediately the SUV swerves when its right front tire explodes and disintegrates in a series of loud thumps.

Hit.

I pull myself back into the Ford and yank the door shut. Still caught in the seatbelt, I pull myself up to look out of the rear windshield. The SUV wobbles and the driver overcorrects to the left. He drives up the edge of an embankment and the engine whines as the SUV flips onto its side and slides, still following us, for a good fifty yards.

"You got 'em!" George is watching in the rear view mirror. He sounds giddy. "Should we stop?"

"Hell no," I tell him, untangling myself from the belt and climbing into the front seat. I'm covered in Ripley's blood. "We need to keep going."

"Don't we need to know more about those guys?"

"We are out of ammunition. The gun is empty, and they're armed. We don't need to know more about *them*. You already know who they are."

"Maybe they have documents or information that'll help."

I pull the front belt across my lap and snap it. "We're good. What we need is to connect the dots we haven't drawn together yet. That's Charlie, the Governor, Buell. The oil companies themselves. Those guys are working for the oil companies."

"You said we needed to piece together 'Pickle guys'. Remember?" George stops the car, pulling onto a narrow shoulder.

"Yeah, I did say that." He's right. They may know something.

George looks at me like he's waiting for me to change my mind.

"Fine. Let me check the back for a weapon."

"I've got Ripley's gun." George pulls it out from underneath the driver's seat. I hadn't seen him put it there. "It's got six rounds in it, that shotshell stuff he was talking about."

"It's good from close range," I tell him, taking the revolver from him. "But we need more." I unlatch the seatbelt and get out of the car. The air is warmer, thicker. There's more green along the side of the road. We must be close to the highway. The sound of the trunk popping open scares a pair of birds from their perch on a mesquite tree.

The bag from Charlie's car opens with a loud zip and reveals a treasure of life-ending equipment; a couple of Sig Sauer 9MM pistols, five loaded clips, some boxes of what looks like rifle ammunition, and a large knife. There's also a pair of binoculars, some MREs, a small laptop, an iPad with a flash drive attachment, a small black iPod, and a United States passport.

"Uh," George is standing behind me, peering over my shoulder, "that should solve our ammo problem."

I pick up the passport and flip it open. There's a color photo of Charlie. Her hair is a little shorter, but equally red. She's smiling; I know that smile. I look at the name printed on the insert: Judy Bethulia.

I toss the passport to George, grab a pistol, pocket a couple of clips, and tuck the knife into my waistband.

"Check out the name on the passport," I tell George. "Use the web on my phone to Google it. I'll be back in a minute."

"Wait," George says. "You can't go alone. There are two of them."

"I've got two guns," I assure him. "You can't shoot. I'll be fine."

He nods and walks back to the car. I start jogging up the road, ignoring the stabbing pain in my leg, to find whatever it is the pickle people have that might be of use.

***

I can see the tops of the flipped SUV's tires as I run up a small rise in the road. There are voices.

"Have you alerted team two?" It's a man's voice. He sounds like he's wheezing.

"They were in team two's vehicle," says a second man, his tone shrill. "Team two isn't answering any communications. They're out of play."

I stop jogging and cross to the left shoulder, crouching behind the brush at the top of the rise. Not having gone for a good run in at least a week, my lungs burn.

To stop my chest from heaving, I breathe in deeply through my nose and slowly blow out the air. My heart rate slows and I focus on the two men standing behind the SUV. Both of them look bruised from the wreck, but seem okay. They can't see me.

"Who the hell is this kid?" the second asks. "This was not supposed to be difficult."

"You should have had him at the gas station," says the wheezy one. "You hit the wrong guy."

"Yeah," the second steps toward the first, pointing his finger. "Team three didn't have any luck either. They had him cornered in the tunnels and couldn't tag him. Team two...who even knows what happened to them."

"The file on him didn't mention anything about firearms training," the first coughs and wipes bloody spittle from his chin. The wheezing is worse.

"You okay?" The second puts his hand on his partner's shoulder. "You puncture a lung?"

"I don't know," he bends over and coughs again, spitting a trail of bloody saliva onto the road. "We've gotta get that kid. He's supposed to be dead three times now. It's like he's got a guardian angel or something."

From my position behind the brush, it's hard to tell if either man is armed. When the angry one bends over to help the wheezy one, a handgun peeps from the holster on his left shoulder. He's right handed.

"I'll call team three," says the angry one. "They're on standby. We need them in position to intercept."

"You haven't called them?" wheezes the first one. He's now on one knee, Tebowing. "They won't activate without your call."

"That's why I'm calling them now," the angry one says through gritted teeth. He balls his fist before reaching into his jacket breast pocket. Now's my chance.

I check the Sig Sauer's clip and turn off the safety. The .40 caliber holds 12 bullets. This one is equipped with a barrel suppressor. Plenty of bullets and no noise. Dropping to one knee, like the wheezing pickle person, I quickly brace my arms and extend the 9MM. With my left eye closed, I tilt my head to the right and target the angry one.

He's thumbing a number on the phone when I pull the pressure sensitive trigger.

Pop!

The bullet rips through the back of his right shoulder and he spins around, the phone flying from his hand as his arm goes limp. His guttural scream is unnerving. He's clutching his shoulder with his left hand, stumbling in disoriented pain when I send another silent shot.

Pop!

Right through his left hand at the wrist. He won't be unholstering the gun.

I stand and pull the Governor from my waistband. With a gun in both hands, and my arms fully extended, I march quickly toward to the two spooks. The angry one is writhing in his pooling blood, while the other falls back into a sitting position. He raises his arms in surrender, trying to suppress another messy cough.

"Who are you?" I demand, one weapon aimed at each man. The angry one is shivering, his color evaporating. The wheezy one says nothing.

"WHO ARE YOU?" I repeat and pull back the hammer on the Governor, aiming it across my body at the angry one's right leg.

No response.

Pow!

The shot shell sprays into the angry one's leg, peppering it with shrapnel. He curls up in a ball and wails.

"We're contractors," says Wheezy. "Independent contractors."

"You work for F. Pickle?" I level the Governor at Wheezy. I still have Angry in my peripheral vision. He's hurt, but he still has a weapon.

"Something like that," he says and wipes the back of his chin with his sleeve. Blood is smeared across his cheeks.

"What do you want with me?" Why do you want me dead?"

"We don't give a rat's ass about you," he says without a hint of expression on his face. "We're doing our job."

"What's your job?"

"To protect the interests of our clients," he coughs out in a nasty spray. "That's all you're getting."

"I don't think so." Without warning I aim the Sig at his right hand and pull the trigger.

Pop!

"What the—"

Pop!

His right foot.

Now I have two men crying for their mothers in the middle of Nowhere, West Texas. I've lost my mind. I don't know where I've found this penchant for violence. Maybe I've been pushed too far. Maybe I've always had it in me, hiding underneath the surface.

"You answer my question or a bullet finds your left foot," I stand over him, my fingers on the triggers of both weapons. I step on his foot.

"All right!" He grabs at his knee, as though that'll ease the pain in his foot. "You know too much!"

"About what?"

"I don't know!" Wheezy lays back and covers his face with his hands. "I only know what I'm told. Neutralize you. You know too much."

That's enough. It's all I'm going to get. Keeping my eyes on both men, I back up and find Angry's cell phone a few feet from the SUV and take it as a souvenir.

George and I have more work to do.

***

"That's it?" asks George. He's fidgeting in the passenger seat, having given the driver's seat back to me. "You know too much?"

A sign to the right of the highway tells me we're only four miles from the I-10 and highway 118 interchange. We'll switch to George's rental, assuming it's still behind the gas station. "They weren't much help."

"I heard a gunshot," he says. "I think it was one. The echo made it difficult to tell. Did you kill one of them?"

"No." The Governor is tucked between my legs; the Sig is in the center console. Both have their safeties on.

"Did you shoot either of them?"

"Yes."

"One time?"

"Five."

"You shot at them five times but you didn't kill them?" George's knee is bouncing. Apparently his hero tonic has worn off.

"No, I encouraged them to tell me more than they wanted to divulge."

"You tortured them." George isn't asking a question.

"Torture?" I glance at him, my jaw tensing. "I didn't torture them. What are you? My conscience? Gimme a break, George. One of them was armed. They both admitted that their mission was to kill me. If they got me, they'd have gotten you. Torture?"

If I'm being honest, I didn't need to shoot Wheezy in the hand or the foot. The shotshell to Angry's leg was probably unneeded too. I run my tongue across the top of my mouth. I can still feel the small cut left there by glass-laden baby food.

Am I no better than The Saint?

No. It's not the same thing. I'm trying to save my life. I did what had to be done. Nothing more.

"That reminds me," I pull the Governor from between my legs. "This needs another bullet. The 9MM there in the console needs a fresh clip. It's in the glove box."

George doesn't move to reload either of them. He sits there looking at me with what I guess is concern. His eyebrows are arched and pressed together. His fingers are tapping on a bouncing knee.

"By the way," he finally says. "She was an assassin too.

"Who?"

He picks up the passport from the floorboard and waves it at me.

"Judy Bethulia was a killer too?" I check the rear view mirror. There's nobody there.

"Judith of Bethulia killed the Assyrian general Holofernes as he was about to attack her home city, Bethulia," George recites. "He was interested in her because she was beautiful. That got her close to him. She got him drunk and cut off his head."

"Another woman assassin who kills a man because of political differences."

"That's a sanitized way of putting it," George says. "More like a pretty woman using her good looks to get close to an unwitting victim."

"Really?" I say to him sarcastically, the implication not lost on me. "What else does it say?"

"It's biblical stuff," he says. "There are more than a hundred famous works of art depicting her killing the dude. Many of them have her holding his head after she cut it off. Brutal."

I let Charlie, or Judy – or whatever her name was – get close to me. Her beauty was certainly what had caught my attention. What was it that kept me interested? What was it that kept her from killing me? Was there something darker we both sensed in each other that subconsciously drew us to one another?

"You really had no idea who she was?" George puts the phone in the center console next to the 9MM.

"Apparently not," I admit. "She played me from the beginning. I was a mark, a target, whatever snipers call their prey. The only thing she didn't do was put a bullet in my head."

***

It was a Saturday morning. My dad woke me up from a dead sleep.

"Jackson," he whispered. "Get up. I've got a surprise."

I was groggy when I stumbled downstairs in a T-shirt, jeans, and a pair of brand new Saucony running shoes. They were ugly but comfortable. At the kitchen table was a glass of orange juice and a plate of French toast. My dad was at the coffee pot. My mom was frying some eggs.

"What's the surprise?" I asked, plopping myself into a chair.

"Your dad has a special outing planned for the two of you." My mom was smiling. "A guy thing. I'm not invited."

"You can come," I managed with a mouth full of French toast shoved into one cheek. "Whatever it is."

"No, she can't." My dad eased up behind her at the cooktop and kissed her neck. "Besides, I am sure she has her day all planned out already."

"Maybe," she said coyly. The two of them were good parents. They loved each other a lot.

"What is it?" I took a swig of juice.

"You'll see when we get there," my dad winked, and finished sweetening the coffee he'd poured into a stainless thermos. "Your mom made lunch. Everything is loaded into the truck. Whenever you're finished eating, we can take off."

It took me less than a second to shove the rest of the plateful into my mouth, drown it with juice, and bolt for the door. I ran back to kiss my mom and shuttled back to the truck.

We were on the road for what seemed like forever, but it was probably only an hour or so. My dad swung the wheel to the right and we turned off of the highway onto a narrow gravel road darkened by the thick canopy of tall pines overhead. The rocks and pine needles crunched under the thick, oversized tires on my dad's Toyota Tundra.

"Where are we going?"

"That would only be the fiftieth time you've asked in the last thirty miles," he laughed and patted my knee. "You'll see when we get there."

The gravel road wound to the left and into a clearing. There was some wire fencing extending across the field, from one end to the other and a small iron gate blocked the road. My dad slowed the truck to a stop.

"We're here!" He adjusted the faded Los Angeles Raiders ball cap on his head. "Hop out."

I sat there for a moment, seatbelt still strapping me to the seat. I panned the horizon. It was grass, trees, rocks, and more trees.

"C'mon Jackson," my dad called from behind the truck. He'd dropped the tailgate and was fumbling with a thick canvas tarp. "I need your help back here buddy!"

I hopped out, my new shoes plopping onto the gravel, and met my dad at the tailgate. He'd peeled back the tarp to reveal a gold mine of artillery. There were three rifle bags, a crossbow, a few boxes of ammunition, a quiver of composite arrows, a backpack, and a large red Igloo cooler.

I looked up at my dad who was already looking at me. We both knew, without saying a word, what an awesome day we were about to have.

"I need you to roll the cooler and carry the backpack," he said as we lowered the cooler onto the ground. "I'll carry the weapons and the ammunition."

He led me past the gate and across the field. Neither of us said much as we trekked past the buzz of dragonflies and waist high goldenrod. The backpack clanged against my back and every few hundred yards I'd switch the arm pulling the heavy cooler.

We'd walked maybe a half mile when the clearing widened to a small lake. The brush melted into clay and dirt along the edge of the water. There was a small wooden picnic table, the remains of a campfire, and some outcroppings of rocks.

"What is this place?" I asked, dropping the cooler and thunking the backpack onto the picnic table.

"A friend of the family owns it," he told me, looking across the lake, which stretched for maybe an acre in either direction. "My dad brought me here when I was about your age."

"Why didn't we bring the truck all the way here?" I wiped my forehead with the bottom of my shirt. It was getting warm.

"Aw," he laughed. "We could've. I thought the hike would add to the suspense."

"I did kinda think we were trespassing," I told him.

"Trespassing?" Where'd you come up with that?"

"The Lord's prayer," I told him as though it were obvious. "You know, 'As we forgive those who trespass against us'?"

"I know it," he said, unzipping one of the rifle bags. "It's always good advice. To forgive and we'd like to be forgiven. Right?"

"I guess."

I watched him pull my Henry rifle from the bag. He tousled my hair with his right hand while pulling out a box of ammunition with his left.

"Here's what I love about your rifle, Jackson," he said as he started loading the gun. "I can get 22 of these small .22 short bullets into the tube-fed magazine. That's a lot of ammo."

Dad finished loading it and handed it to me before he grabbed the backpack and walked toward the rocks. I followed him to the rocks and the edge of the lake.

He pulled out five tin cans from the bag. "These are your targets. Try to pop each of them off the rocks." He set them side by side: crushed tomato, sweet corn, green beans, another crushed tomato, and a frijoles negros.

"Where do you want me to shoot from?" I asked, the Henry slung over my shoulder like a continental soldier.

"Go back about twenty yards. Next to the campfire." He checked the cans and joined me by the ashen circle. It smelled like burnt marshmallows.

"Whenever you're ready," he said, stepping behind me.

I turned to my side, left shoulder forward, and spread my feet. With my left hand I cranked the lever.

Click!

I pulled the Henry to my right shoulder and tilted my head to the right to sight the crushed tomatoes. I slowly pressed into the trigger.

Pow!

By the time the rifle kick into my shoulder the can clanged off of the rock.

"Nice," said my dad. "Now I want you to hit the other four in rapid succession."

"What does that mean?" I asked, cranking the lever again. "Like fast?"

He nodded. I nodded.

Aim. Pull. *Pow! Clang!* Corn

Crank. Aim. Pull. *Pow! Clang!* Green Beans.

Crank. Aim. Pull. *Pow! Clang!* Tomatoes.

Crank. Aim. Pull. *Pow! Clang!* Frijoles Negros.

I turned to look at my dad. He was looking at his Timex.

"Twelve seconds," he said. "Incredible!"

"Why were you timing it?" I asked. I had the Henry pointed at the ground now.

"Just checking," he said and winked.

An hour and two reloads later, the cans were peppered with holes. I hadn't missed a single shot.

My dad pulled the red cooler over to the picnic table and flipped the lid open. The plastic hinges creaked and he dug to the bottom, pulling out two cans of Dr. Pepper with his right hand. He plopped them onto the edge of the table with a pair of sandwiches and a big bag of Lay's potato chips.

"Lunch," he said. "Then something really cool."

We talked about music and classic television in between mouths full of peanut butter, raspberry jam, and white bread. My sandwich was cut into two triangles, my dad's in rectangles. I don't know why my mom cut them differently, but she did. She paid attention to the details.

I finished my Dr. Pepper and asked for another. My dad suggested too much caffeine wasn't good for a sharpshooter, so I swigged a bottle of water instead.

"You ready?" he asked, straddling the table's attached bench.

"Sure. What's next?"

"A crossbow."

"Cool! I hopped up, eager to try out the new weapon.

My dad opened up one of the rifle bags and pulled out what looked like a rifle. There was no barrel. Instead, at the front of the rifle, is a bow with cables extending from either side.

From the cooler, he pulled a bag of big yellow apples and carried them to rocks. He set five of them up in a row, almost exactly like he'd arranged the cans. He walked back with the bag in one hand and an apple in the other. He was chewing on a large bite.

"So," he said, still chomping as he picked up the matte black weapon, "this front part of the bow is called the stirrup. You point that at the ground, rest it, and load the bow from that position."

He placed it nose first into the ground and slipped his foot into the stirrup. Grabbing the string with both hands, he pulled it back until it caught. Another bite of the apple and he tossed it into the cooler.

"What I did was pull the string into the catch. That locks the tension on the string. This front part you'd call a bow is actually called a lathe."

I nodded, my eyes wide and locked on the bow.

"Now what do you think this is called?" he asked, holding up a shiny silver arrow with red feathers.

"An arrow?"

"Close," he said. "But no. It's called a bolt. When you load it into the bow, you need to always do it at the same position. There's a little groove here it sits in. See it?"

I nodded again.

"Now before you lift it up, you check the auto and manual safeties here," he pointed to them, "then you can aim and fire."

He picked up the bow, held the butt to his shoulder and aimed, his left eye squinting.

Thooop!

Miss. The bolt clanged off the rocks beneath the apples. My dad opened his left eye and smiled at me.

"You get the point," he said. "Now it's your turn."

I fired five bolts. I hit five apples.

"You've got a gift," my dad said.

My dad loved me. Both of my parents did. But I don't think I'd ever seen him beam with such pride. He seemed to skip, float almost, as he went to retrieve the bolts.

I had a gift. I was a natural.

It was a good day.

***

Across I-10, in front of the gas station where we've stashed George's rental car, is a black Lincoln Town Car limousine. Exhaust puffing from the tailpipe tells me it's running.

"Who is that?" George asks, nodding toward the car. Its rear windows are illegally dark.

"Dunno," I say, easing across the intersection and into the parking lot next to the car.

"Pickle?"

"I don't think so." I put the car in park and turn it off. The keys are still in the ignition. "They would have killed us already." We're perpendicular to the Town Car on the driver's side. I don't see anyone in the front seat.

"Or tried," George laughs nervously.

The rear driver's side window rolls down and beyond it is a familiar face.

The Saint.

"Who is that?" George looks at the man in the car and back at me.

"It's the guy who drugged me, kidnapped me, tortured me, drugged me again, and then saved my life."

"Seriously?" George rubbernecks between the two of us again. "How did he find us?"

"He has a way of doing that," I huff and get out of the car. "What do you want?" I shout in no particular direction as I round the front of my car toward the Lincoln. I'm carrying the 9MM.

"You look like bloody hell," The Saint says from his comfortable seat. "Did somebody get hurt?"

I look down at my shirt. It's a Rorschach test of blood spatter. Disgusting.

"Why are you here?" I asked again, approaching the window. "Where's your driver?"

"Well," says The Saint, "to your first question, I am here to offer my assistance. To your second, he's in the store getting a drink and using the facilities."

"What kind of assistance?" I can feel George over my shoulder.

"Why don't you gather your belongings and get inside the car? There's plenty of room."

"I don't know about this," George whispers loudly enough for The Saint to hear. "Can you trust him?"

"My dear George," says The Saint, his eyes shifting to the reporter, "you cannot trust anyone implicitly. There are degrees of trust, are there not? Right now I don't see anyone else offering you assistance."

"Where would you take us?" I ask.

"To my plane."

George is considering the degrees of trust. "What plane?"

"I have a small little aircraft," The Saint says. "You can't carry your munitions through security at a commercial airport. You might best be served on a charter flight."

"All right," I say, "we'll go. But you need to make two stops."

"Clearly," The Saint feigns magnanimousness. "I wouldn't have it any other way."

I pop the trunk and grab my backpacks and Charlie's duffel. George has the phones and the revolver. He slides into the car while I dump my belongings into The Saint's trunk. I slam it shut and join George in the rear facing seats opposite our host.

"What about my rental?" George asks.

"We've got bigger problems than returning that car," I say. "For instance, there's a trail of dead bodies between here and the observatory."

"Including the one you dumped," George snaps back.

The Saint pulls a cut crystal glass from the cup holder to his right and swirls a caramel colored liquid before raising the glass to his lips.

"A body? Dumped?" The Saint's eyes widen with his smile. "Do tell, gentlemen!" Neither of us say anything.

He swallows hard and rests the glass on his right knee. "How rude of me! Would either or you care for a drink? This is a Glennfiddich 1937." He winks at George. "I'm more than happy to share."

"Must be pricey," George says, his eyes on the knee-balanced glass in The Saint's right hand. "Only bottle in the world, and all."

"A bit," he raises the glass to his nose, closes his eyes, and inhales. "I paid twenty at an auction in 2006."

"Twenty dollars?"

The Saint bellows with laughter, slapping his knee with his left hand. "Oh heaven's no, good man. *Twenty-thousand.*" He sips from the heavy glass, and licks his lips. "Twenty dollars," he mumbles. "Ha!"

"I'm good," I say. "Thank you."

He raises the glass toward me in a toast. "To each his own,

Jackson."

The front door opens and shuts, and the limo lurches forward.

"Where's the plane? Midland or El Paso?"

"It's in Alpine at a small airstrip there," he says. "Not a long drive. So, back to body dumping. Details please."

I tell him about our meeting with Ripley, the shootout in the room, Ripley's death, Charlie and Crockett, and my attempt at coercion with the Pickle spooks. I've got nothing to lose by filling him in on what we've done.

"Impressive," says The Saint, swirling the whiskey in his glass. "You're more than I anticipated you'd be, Jackson. Every step of this journey, you prove to be surprisingly formidable."

"Charlie said something like that," I say. "It's a backhanded compliment."

"Ahhh," he nods. "Still not over the girl are we? She was a stunning beauty, I'll admit. Let's be honest with ourselves, Jackson. She was never who she claimed to be."

I turn to look out the window at the field of pump jacks, dotting the land like chess pieces on a board.

Are any of us who we claim to be?

"Enough about the siren who sent you careening into Charybdis," The Saint says. "Whose body did you dump?"

"Ripley's," George answers for me. "It's on the side of highway 118."

"Ripley?" The Saint says. He seems surprised. "I didn't anticipate that. Dumping Ripley reveals a calculating, self-preserving, almost cold-blooded side to you both. I'll have some of my friends go retrieve what you've left behind and assure the authorities are left in the dark, so to speak. That would be helpful wouldn't it, George?"

"It wasn't my idea," George says quickly.

"You didn't have any ideas," I retort without taking my eyes off the horizon. "Call it whatever you want. I was doing what was necessary."

"Please don't mistake me, good man," The Saint offers, waving his hand for clarification. "I'm not judging you. I'm applauding you. Again, you've risen far above expectations."

"Whose expectations?" I turn to look at him. "Who are you

talking about?"

"Everyone involved, Jackson." He pulls the glass to his lips and, before gulping fifteen hundred dollars' worth of whisky in a single swig, he says, "You should be dead by now."

CHAPTER 11

The airport is a couple of miles north of Alpine, Texas. It looks like a Martian landing strip. Reddish brown dirt is everywhere, and in the distance, there's a small rise of jagged hills. There's a small terminal building next to a couple of large fuel tanks. Past the terminal, which really looks more like an aluminum storage building, is a white twin engine jet. Except for a tail number, it's unmarked.

"That's your plane?" I ask, tapping the tinted window. "The white one?"

"Yes," says The Saint. "It's quite comfortable. An Embraer Legacy. I had it made to very particular specifications."

"That's *your* plane?" George asks. "It's not a loaner?"

"A loaner?" The Saint laughs. "Heavens no. It's mine. Although, I have to tell you the cost of jet fuel has skyrocketed so much, it's almost not worth it. If it weren't for the discretion it provides many of my friends, I'd likely have sold it."

"You're good with stopping in Austin first and then Houston?" I asked. "I have things I need to take care of there."

"Of course. Whatever you need, Jackson. I have to stop in Austin regardless. It's no bother." I get the feeling there's something he's not telling me.

The car stops beside the jet and the driver opens The Saint's door first. He lumbers out of the car with help and the driver moves to our door.

It's warmer outside than it was at the gas station near the

observatory. I'm glad to be in shorts and a T-shirt, regardless of the blood. I get my backpack from the driver before he loads the contents of the trunk into the belly of the jet. Its engines are on and the flip down steps into the jet are open. I can smell the jet fuel.

A slender blonde is standing to the left of the steps. She's in a tight blue skirt and tighter white blouse. Her hair is pulled tight against her head in a slick bun. She smiles with unnecessarily red lips and waves me aboard the plane.

"Please watch your step, sir," she says in a slight southern drawl. Virginia maybe, or North Carolina. Definitely not Texas. "Be careful of your head when you reach the top. Welcome aboard."

I thank her and step up and into the cabin. To the left is a wet bar with a refrigerator, a wine cooler, and a microwave. Farther left is the lavatory and the cockpit, its dual controls alit with green and red. To the right is a cabin nicer than my apartment.

Facing the rear of the jet, I see it's an ode to ivory leather and walnut trim. Along the right side of the aircraft, stretching much of its length, is a long sofa. To the left are four pairs of captain's chairs. Two face forward, and both are occupied by uniformed Texas State troopers. They might be Rangers. Two more chairs face the rear of the aircraft and all of them have walnut tables between them. At the rear of the jet is a pair of what look like recliners.

There's the subtle sound of opera playing over the speakers and the hiss of air conditioning. The Saint is lounging on one of the recliners at the rear of the cabin. He's waving at me to join him.

"Come, my boy!" he commands. "Sit with me. There is much to discuss."

I walk back to the rear of the aircraft and sit in the recliner next to him. It's incredibly comfortable. I'm physically exhausted. The smell of the leather, the plushness of the cushion, the gentle violin of the music would have me asleep if it weren't for the adrenaline coursing through my body. I drop the backpack between the two recliners.

"What do you think?" He spreads his arms, as if he's parted the sea. "Far superior to a commercial flight, don't you think?"

"It's the music that makes it," I lean my head back against the thick high back of the chair.

"It's Charles Gounod," he says affecting the French

pronunciation. "His splendid adaptation of Goethe's *Faust*."

"Is it?"

He turns to me with interest. "It was originally rejected by the Paris Opera for not being lavish enough. It wasn't until a revival years later that it became a hit."

"Did it?" I ask.

"Oh yes," he says. "Fascinating. You can interpret something one way, only to find out, much to your surprise, it was much better than you'd originally surmised."

"Fascinating," I sigh. "Now what is it you want to discuss? You seem to be hiding something from me. It's like you know a lot more than you've let on. You're playing me."

George is spinning in a captain's chair near the front of the cabin. He's on my phone.

"You are right," he says. "I have not been fully transparent with you. I should tell you that—"

"Gentlemen," says the pilot over the intercom, "we'll be taking off here in a couple of minutes on runway zero, one, nineteen. We'll travel at about four hundred knots, fly up to about thirty-eight thousand feet and reach Austin, Texas in under an hour and twenty minutes. The skies are clear, winds are calm. We don't expect any problems. If you need anything, please ask your cabin attendant Sally Anne. She's here to help."

The music resumes. My host wipes the corners of his mouth with his thumb and forefinger. "As I was about to tell you," he begins before being interrupted again.

The lavatory door pops open and out walks a familiar face.

"Jackson Quick," the man says as he struts to the back of the plane. "As I live and breathe."

I'm not quite sure how to react. He's the last person in the world I'd expect to see on this plane.

"Have you been playin' hooky from work, son?" He laughs before sliding onto the end of the sofa in his dark blue suit. He adjusts his tie, spreads his arms across the back of the sofa, and rests a black ostrich skin boot on his knee. He exhales and smiles a large toothy grin. His hair is impossibly perfect, ice blue eyes looking right through me.

"Governor," I say. "How are you?"

***

The day my life changed is seared into my mind. A perverse version of it plays repeatedly in my nightmares.

It was the day I killed my parents.

My knee was stiff. It was cold and rainy outside of my fogged bedroom window. I sat on the side of my bed and did slow leg extensions to loosen up the scar tissue. I didn't want to go to school.

Blair Loxley had been relentless that week – pushing me into lockers, sticking his flat palm into my Salisbury steak lunch and running the grease across the top of my head with his fingers.

I took it. I was rising above it. I hoped if I continued to ignore him he would eventually quit. It wasn't working. Bruised ribs, a knee operation, and situational depression were all evidence.

Action was needed.

Rather than climb back under the covers and fake a stomach flu, I got up and quietly walked down the hall to my dad's office. I opened the accordion closet doors and, behind some winter coats, found his gun safe. He didn't know I'd seen him enter the combination a couple of times and I had it memorized. Three spins and I had it open. Inside were a couple of handguns and a pair of rifles. I gripped my Henry, checked to make sure it was unloaded, and slowly closed the safe door. It clicked shut and I padded back to room to get ready for school.

Both of my parents were in the kitchen when I bolted through the front door with a quick "Goodbye!" hollered over my shoulder. It was still dark outside, and I had the Henry, butt up, hidden under my coat and behind my messenger bag. In the daylight, someone would have noticed it. In the dark of predawn, I was good.

At the track, I crouched behind a small equipment shed. There was a six-inch gap between the ground and the lower frame of the shed. The Henry slid perfectly between the two, hidden from view.

I left my prized possession under the shed and trudged to school, stepping in puddles along the way, dirtying my new white Chuck Taylors. Mom wouldn't be happy. Converse sneakers weren't cheap.

I was one of the few students in the hallways. The poor weather would have everybody running late, I was sure. It gave me plenty of time, and opportunity, to stop by Blair Loxley's locker and slip a small envelope between the vent slats.

The envelope's contents reappeared after second period, when Loxley's fist shoved an unfolded piece of notebook paper into my chest. We were in the hall near the gym.

"Really, Jacktard?" he sneered. "You ain't given up yet?"

"To you?" I laughed. "Right."

"Well," he spat, "you got it. After school. At the track." He pushed my left shoulder and strode off down the hall.

I looked down at the note, I was holding in my right hand:

Hey, Stooge. Let's end this. Today. I'll see you where you tried to end ME. I doubt you'll have the guts to show up.

He knew it was me. Who else would it be, right?

I didn't see him again until the end of a very long day. I watched, it seemed, every tick of the classroom clock as last period wound down. My heart was pounding.

I didn't tell anyone about the antagonistic note. I didn't want people around, seeing what I was about to do. I knew deep down, it was a bad idea. As I walked up the rise of a small hill overlooking the track, I could tell Loxley hadn't been as judicious.

There was a crowd of about twenty, maybe thirty, people standing around waiting. In the middle of them was the bully. He was laughing and joking around, clearly not daunted by my challenge. I'd have to leave the gun behind. There was no using it in this scenario.

I took a deep breath and walked into the arena.

***

The Governor waves at the flight attendant Sally Anne. "Can I get a coffee? Splash of cream and two sugars, please." He watched her move toward him like a lion watching a gazelle, tweaking his tie as she approached. "Oh, and darlin', add a shot of a Bailey's, would ya?"

She smiles. "Yes, sir."

"And my friend here, Jackson," he points at me while still eyeing her, "he'd like a Diet Dr. Pepper."

"Anything for you sir?" she asks The Saint. He shakes his head and shoos her to the bar at the front of the aircraft.

"Jackson," the Governor says, the words curling out of his mouth, "I imagine you have many questions."

"Why are you here?"

"You know I have a big debate tonight," he says. "Lots of pressure. A lot on the line. I needed a little *me* time." He adjusts his cuffs, tugging on each of them to reveal gold rimmed, circular cufflinks emblazoned with the Texas State seal. "But you must have more questions. Am I right?"

"Yes."

"Ask away." He flips his right wrist to look at his watch. "We've got just under an hour and twenty minutes, according to the pilot up there."

"I don't know where to begin." I look toward George. He's fallen asleep.

"Well," he says, "let's start with the iPods."

"Okay."

"You know what was on them. You looked at them."

"I suspect I know," I tell him. "But I never looked at them."

"Jackson," he turns to The Saint and licks his lips. "That's a problem for me."

"I don't understand."

"Don't play coy with me, son!" His tone sharpens with the spit flying from his mouth. "I know you hooked one up to your computer and checked it out. You had the codes saved in a file for God's sake."

"I did have the codes saved," I admit. "I never hooked it up to a computer. I've already been over this with your accomplice here."

The Governor inhales and wipes his mouth again. He leans back and studies me for a moment. He laughs heartily. I glance at The Saint. He's smiling, lips pressed together.

"We know that, son," the Governor says. He reaches over and slaps my knee. "I'm playing with you. We know you're clean. That's why Sir Spencer over here let you go. He knew you were telling the truth."

"Sir Spencer?"

"Sir Spencer Thomas," answers The Saint. "S-T. St. The Saint."

"You're a knight?" I ask, confused. "What is a knight doing with the Governor?"

"I'm with whoever will have me."

"Kinda like your Charlie girl there, Jackson." More laughter from the comical Governor. "Gun for hire. That's what we've got here. A whole bunch of guns for hire."

"So," I say, my eyes closed to visualize the flow chart in my head, "The Saint...uh...Sir Spencer works for you. Charlie works, I mean worked, for Buell. The Pickle people work for the oil companies? Ripley worked for everybody?"

"I'd say that sums it up," the Governor says. "Wouldn't you say that sums it up, Spence?"

"*Sir* Spencer," he shoots back. "No need to be *too* familiar Governor. We are, after all, bound by financial considerations as opposed to ideology. But yes, I would say young Jackson here has a rudimentary understanding of the *who*. Now he needs to understand the *why*."

"Well," the Governor says, "that's a bit more complicated isn't it? Ahh, the drinks!"

I turn to see Sally Anne approaching us with a white porcelain cup and saucer in one hand and a thin glass fizzing with ice and Diet Dr. Pepper in the other.

"Thank you, Sally Anne." The Governor takes the saucer in both hands before pulling the steaming cup to his mouth. "Hot. Like I like it." He winks at her and she hands me my drink with a smile.

The Governor blows on the coffee. I take a sip of the soda, catching a small piece of ice under my tongue.

"Anything else?" the pretty woman asks, briefly looking each of us in the eyes. We shake our heads and she returns to the wet bar. All of us watch her leave.

"Mmmm," he says before blowing on the coffee again. "Like I like it."

"The *why* then?" I ask.

"Yes," the Governor answers, his head nodding quickly up and down. He places the saucer and cup on the small polished walnut end table at the end of the sofa. "The *why*!" He makes air quotes with his fingers and adjusts his tie again. "This is a complex operation into which you've mixed yourself, Jackson. It's got many...moving parts."

"Elaborate," I cut in. "Please."

"Those iPods, they contained financial information; bank accounts, routing numbers, that sort of thing. A bit of information regarding the progress of our little project over at Rice. You know that don't you?"

"I thought I saw bank numbers on the iPod in Alaska. The contact there dropped it."

"She told me," says the Governor. "That's what got this whole ball of wax rolling so quickly downhill."

"What do you mean?" I glance at George. He's still sleeping.

"That contact was concerned about your trustworthiness," he says, picking up the coffee and taking a sip. "I assured her you were clueless, but she demanded some certainty."

"Given her financial stake in the matter," adds Sir Spencer, "we felt obliged to comply with her request."

"So, without your knowledge," the Governor says, "we had your apartment searched. That's when we found the downloaded code numbers and the iPod synchronization data."

"I didn't—"The Governor puts up his hand to stop me.

"I know you saved the codes," he says. "No big deal. They really mean nothing."

"They're significant Texas dates. That has to mean something."

The Governor takes another sip of coffee while exchanging a look with Sir Spencer. He takes a second longer draw of the hot liquid and slowly puts it back on the side table.

"Regardless," he says, "we had to know for certain if you were the one who synched the device. That's where my friend Sir Spencer enters the picture more clearly."

"That's why you drugged, kidnapped, and tortured me?"

"I wouldn't go so far as to call it *torture*," corrected Sir Spencer. "It was merely the employment of enhanced interrogation techniques."

"No," I argue, "you went all *Zero Dark Thirty* on me."

"I guess that would make you Jessica Chastain," laughs the Governor, pointing at Sir Spencer. "But yes. That is why we felt the need to question you under duress."

"You passed." The Governor gives me a thumbs up. "You clearly didn't know anything about the computer synch. We quickly determined it was your dearly beloved."

"Charlie?"

"Yes," says the Governor, his tone becoming more serious. "The more we vetted her, the less we could find about her."

"That," adds Sir Spencer, "and on the night I *kidnapped* you, she left the bar with a known soldier-of-fortune."

"Crockett."

"Yes, Crockett," says Sir Spencer. "Most assuredly a *nomme de guerre*, as was Charlotte Corday, we assume."

"It was," I say.

"When our people put Charlie and Crockett together," the Governor went on, "we put together she was the one who'd lifted the financial information. We also know she shot Buell."

"Wait," I shake my head. "She worked for Buell. She said that before she died. Why would she shoot him?"

"Sympathy," says the Governor. "It worked too. Buell's favorability rating is through the roof. Our own internal polling has him with a commanding, though not insurmountable, lead among independent voters."

"You digress," counsels Sir Spencer.

"Right," the Governor says. "We told our partners in the energy business you were clean. They didn't buy it."

"Why?"

"Because you hopped right over to Charlie's place after Sir Spencer left you in your apartment," the Governor explains. "They figured the two of you must be in cahoots."

"That's why the Pickle guys were trying to kill me? They think I was working for Buell too?"

"Let's clarify," says Sir Spencer. "They are trying to kill you. They couldn't be sure as to your loyalty. We could not convince them otherwise. I could only guide you along the way and try to watch over you."

"What's the money for?" I ask. "Why was Charlie interested in the information on the iPod?"

"Charlie and Crockett were working for Buell," the Governor

says. "And through her connections, she was able to get a job working for me. Double agent, Mata Hari kinda stuff. When she found out you were a courier for me, she latched on to you."

"And the money?"

"The money, which was not in small amounts, was payment for my help," the Governor gives Sir Spencer a look that tells me he's measuring his words.

"Help for what?"

"Survival."

"I don't follow."

"You know Buell and his Nanergetix company are working on a more efficient fuel. That fuel is made better by enhancements on the molecular level."

"You mean on the nanoscale," I correct him.

"You're right," the Governor smiles at me and looks to Sir Spencer. "He really is a smart cookie. I did good in picking you, Jackson. Yes, the nanoscale. That's more microscopically accurate."

"Did *well*," corrects Sir Spencer. "You did well in picking him."

"Whatever," shrugs the Governor. "Better fuel is ultimately *not* what our energy companies want. If every gallon of the nano-enhanced fuel goes farther, the profits go south. We're talking way south."

"So...?" I lean in, wanting him to get to the point.

"So," he says, "they paid me money to prevent that from happening. As the Governor of the energy capital of the world, I have a little influence. I have resources. Texas has its advantages."

"Ripley."

"Bingo!" The Governor points at me. "Dr. Ripley. He was the ticket. I knew he could figure out a way to magically undo whatever enhancements Buell created. And when the federal government tells the energy companies to use the Nanergetix creation in their refining process, we could, here in Texas, add our own little juju to the mix."

"They paid you to find Ripley?"

"They paid me to find Ripley, to keep the mad scientist on a leash, and to keep Texas friendly toward their industry."

"Which Buell would not do should he become Governor," I

conclude.

"Correct!"

"But our friend Ripley became unpredictable," Sir Spencer says. "He grew increasingly nervous about what it was we were asking of him. It became unbearable, apparently, when Mr. Buell learned of our effort. He tried to undermine us."

"He tried to flip Ripley into a turncoat," the Governor says. "We told Ripley to play along, to make Buell's folks believe he was flipping. They weren't convinced of his allegiance. They concocted that plan to have Charlie shoot Buell. It not only got him the sympathy vote, it also put Ripley on notice when they framed his dad."

"You couldn't do anything? You're the Governor."

"Right," answers the Governor. "As though I'm going to stick my nose into the attempted assassination of my political rival. I do anything of the sort, and it looks terrible."

"That's really why Charlie shot Buell," I surmise. "It was about the nanotech stuff more than the politics."

"C'mon now, Jackson," laughs the Governor. "You're smarter than that. Everything's about politics. Everything."

My life is upside down because I delivered iPods to energy executives. One of them thought I saw something I shouldn't have seen, and the rest of it unraveled from there.

I was collateral damage. The Governor didn't care about the danger into which he might be throwing me. Here he sits in a private jet, smugly sipping his Bailey's and coffee, telling me about politics.

Everything is about politics.

"So," I tilt my head and lean in to the Governor, "this is about the money."

"Excuse me?"

I can't tell if he didn't hear me or he's offended by the inference.

"This is about the money," I repeat. "What's the money for? I mean it has to be millions, right? What's your plan?"

"You need to speak up, Jackson," he says, rubbing his left palm on the leather arm of the sofa. "I thought you said millions."

"I did."

"Try billions, son." He leans in, his face inches from mine. I can see his eyes studying mine, like he's looking for fear. "It's billions. I don't play for pennies."

My mind races back to the discussion we had over pizza, the one about secession: *"If you talk to some financial gurus, they'll tell you that we can't survive without the billions that the federal government gives us. But that isn't true. All it takes is the start-up capital. We need a few billion to get going."*

That's the end game. He wants Texas to secede and he's using big oil money to do it.

***

Blair Loxley stood over me, taunting me, after a single hit sent me to the ground. He was buoyed by the cheers from his friends, their ring around us shrinking as I stood and regained my balance.

It was a sucker punch, launched into my chest as I extended my hand to shake on the fight. I should've known better. I thought, with the crowd, he'd stray from his guerrilla tactics. I was wrong.

He circled around me, hunched over, his fists balled tight in front of him. His face was red, his eyes narrowed and focused. He was as ready to end this as I was.

"C'mon, Jacktard," he spat. "Take a swing. I dare you."

I stepped back, and was pushed forward by one of his friends. Loxley swung at me as I neared him, but I ducked and he missed. His momentum carried him to my side and I lunged into him, knocking him to the ground. I was on top of him for a moment and managed a couple of quick jabs to his gut before he shoved me off of him.

"Get him!" yelled one of his friends.

"Throttle him!" screamed another.

We both got to our feet at the same time. I looked into his eyes again. They weren't as focused. There was doubt. In front of all of his friends, could he beat me? Would he be humiliated?

"Throttle me?" I said between heaving breaths. "You gonna throttle me, *stooge*?"

That drew snickers from a couple of people in the circle around us.

208

"Dude," somebody said. "You gonna let that fly, Loxley?"

Loxley looked past me to whoever it was that challenged him and charged at me with his arms wide open. I dropped to my back and kicked up my legs as he got to me. He tripped and flew past me into the circle, sliding face first into the grass.

I rolled over and jumped onto his back, straddling him. With one hand on the back of his head, I pressed the left side of his face against the ground. With the other, I pulled his left arm back at an uncomfortable angle. I was essentially lying on top of him, my chest pressed against the back of his neck.

Within an instant, I'd gotten the upper hand. The circle was backing up, widening as Loxley whimpered and struggled against me. I could hear the mumbling in the crowd. Nobody was cheering Loxley.

I leaned in closer to Loxley's ear. I could hear him struggling to breathe through his mouth.

"This ends now," I whispered. "You don't mess with me anymore. Do you understand?" I tugged on his left arm and he let out a muffled wail.

"Let him up!" someone said. "You're hurting him."

I ignored the call for mercy.

"It ends now," I repeated, more loudly. "Do you understand?"

Another tug. Another cry.

"You win dude!" Someone else in the crowd. "You got him! It's over."

Blair Loxley never showed me mercy. As best I can from my position on top of him, I manage to grab his thumb. He's flailing against me. My weight is in the right place. He can't overpower me.

I gain control of his hand. "It ends now!"

At the same time I push into his face with my upper body, I bend back his thumb. He's grunting against the ground; a repeated short grunt. He sounds like an ape.

The grunting stops only once I've pulled his thumb back enough to hear it pop. The grunt becomes a scream, followed by the collective gasp of the crowd.

With one last push onto his face, I roll off of him. He rolls onto his back, tears streaking through the dirt on his face. He curls into a ball cradling his hand.

I stand and look at the crowd around us. Not one of them stopped me. Not one of them, any one of whom could have easily overpowered me, stopped me from breaking his thumb.

Instead they stood there, wide-eyed and silent at what I'd done. Nobody said a word until, from behind me, I heard an adult's voice.

"What's going on here?"

I turned to see the assistant principal part the crowd. He looked down at Loxley and over at me. He knew what had happened, but probably couldn't process it.

"Jackson," he says, bending down to attend to Loxley, "did you do this?"

I took the fifth and didn't say anything.

"Jackson!" he yelled at me as he helped Loxley to his feet. "I asked you a question."

"Yes," I said and wiped my face with the back of my arm.

"I'm taking Blair to the nurse," he said. "I want the rest of you to stay here. That includes you, Jackson. The police are on their way."

"Police?" I said. "Why? This is...it's a school fight."

"No, it's not," he says. "Where is your gun?"

CHAPTER 12

For the first time since the Governor had appeared from the lavatory, I was aware of the music filtering through the cabin. It's a chorus of men singing:

Glory and love to the men of old,
Their sons may copy their virtues bold;
Courage in heart and a sword in hand,
Both ready to fight and ready to die for Fatherland!

"It's the Soldier's Chorus," Sir Spencer said when he notices I'm listening. He is gently waving his right as if he's conducting. "'Gloire immortelle de nos aïeux.' It's in Act Four. Valentin and his fellow soldiers are returning from war, singing about the glory of those who fought and died in combat. It's moving."

Glory and love to the men of old!
Their sons may copy their virtues bold,
Courage in heart and a sword in hand,
All ready to fight for Fatherland.

"You're building a private war chest?" I ask the Governor. He's summoned another cup of coffee from Sally Anne.

"I guess you could call it that," he says. "A man can't go into battle without the proper resources. Am I right, Sir Spencer?"

"Spot on, Governor," he says in response. "Spot on."

"We are warriors, Jackson. It's a battle between what's right for Texans and what's not. We're on the side of good here. Our economy feeds off the energy industry. We survived the recession in '09 because of oil and gas production. I mean, President Obama said it, 'We're the Saudi Arabia of natural gas!' We can't let anything affect that."

"He meant the United States as a whole," I say. "I don't think he was talking specifically about Texas."

"Get your head out of the sand, boy," the Governor is preaching now. "Texas *is* The United States if you're talking energy of any kind. Hell, we're ahead of the Socialist Republic of California when it comes to wind energy production. *Wind* for goodness sake. Our economy, the nation's economy would be impotent without what the energy folks do for us. Those so called 'environmentalists' are traitors as far as I'm concerned. You can't have it both ways."

Sally Anne returns with another coffee refill for the Governor. She assures him it's without Bailey's this time, and sways her hips back to the front of the plane. The Governor blows and sips from the new cup.

"I've heard you argue these points before," I remind him. "How does that justify your plans to secede?"

The Governor almost spits out his coffee and he coughs at my question. "Secede?" He clears his throat and laughs. "Where did you get that idea?"

"Secession is a key talking point on the campaign trail. You're talking about battles and us versus them. Why else would you need billions of dollars in what you called a war chest?"

"*You* called it a war chest, Jackson," he says. "I tacitly agreed with that assessment. We could never secede. It's a talking point to assuage the most conservative elements of the party. Wow. Secession?"

"Don't blame the boy for his assumption," advises Sir Spencer. "You have made it seem as though you are on the extreme end of the Texas independence movement. You've often considered the costs and benefits of such an effort. I don't think him naïve for taking you at your word."

The Governor sips from the cup. He rolls his eyes at Sir Spencer but says nothing.

"What about F. Pickle?" I ask. "The security company. Where do they fit into this? They do work for you."

"True," added the Governor. "I've used them to do some work for me in the past, some opposition research you might say. That's purely political stuff, campaign related tasks and such. I don't think they're working for us right now." He looks to Sir Spencer for confirmation.

"Oh no," says Sir Spencer. "We're not using them this go 'round, and because of our altercation in the tunnel toilet, I doubt we'll employ them in the future."

"They're working for the oil companies?"

"Likely," says Sir Spencer. "They're protecting their interests, not ours. I gather someone felt *you* were not in their best interests."

"Then what is all of this about?" I ask. "If it's not about making Texas an independent republic, and the oil companies aren't completely on the same page, why are you doing all of this? Why is my life at risk? Is it really about money?"

"Of course it's about money! It's about money and power and politics. All three of those are the same thing. I want to stay in power, the energy companies want to control the politics, Buell wants a little bit of both, and we all want MMM-O-N-E-Y." He sings the last five letters as though he were Lyle Lovett.

"Look," he licks his lips and pats me on the knee, "since you're tired, or confused, or whatever...I'll break this down for you, Jackson."

George is still asleep. Sally Anne is leafing through a magazine at the far end of the cabin length sofa. Sir Spencer seems bored, typing into his phone. I'm dumbfounded. For some reason the Governor doesn't seem to care who hears his psalm.

"Don Carlos Buell is the bad guy here. He wants my job and he wants to ruin the energy industry. On both those accounts he's interested in destroying Texas." He laughs at himself. He's *so* clever. "The energy folks hired me to help them keep their favorable environment. I hired Ripley and Buell tried to steal him. When that didn't work, Buell had your little Nikita shoot him for sympathy and then frame Ripley's dad. Ripley's dad was conveniently a secessionist. If he's tagged for the shooting, it puts pressure on Ripley and makes my rhetoric appear violence-inducing. And here we are..."

"Do you know Ripley *didn't* turn?" I ask. Charlie seemed

certain he was working for Buell.

"I don't think he did," the Governor says. "I don't know. Maybe he did. It doesn't matter. We know enough about the Nanergetix marker now."

"Here's something that may matter," Sir Spencer interjects. "Jackson, how many dead bodies did you say you'd left behind in Ft. Davis?"

"Three in the lodge – Ripley, Charlie and Crockett – and the two Pickle guys, who may or may not be dead. That makes six dead and two hurt."

"As I feared," says Sir Spencer, reading from his phone. "I've had a team cleaning up your mess. They report three in the lodge, Ripley, and Charlie as fatalities. They also confirm the two wounded F. Pickle employees. They didn't find that sixth dead body."

"Crockett?"

"Yes," says Sir Spencer. "They report he is missing."

"I thought he was dead!" I exclaimed, the implications racing through my head. "He didn't move. I thought he was dead."

The Governor tilts back the cup of coffee, inhaling the last drops. He leans back on the sofa and stretches his arms out to the side, crosses his right leg over his left and smirks.

"You thought wrong."

* * *

"We are now in our final descent into Austin-Bergstrom International Airport," the pilot says near the end of Faust's fifth act to tell us we're almost there. "The weather is beautiful. The winds are calm. We should have you there right on time. We'll refuel, which should give you some time to stretch your legs, and we'll be on our way to Houston-Hobby."

Sally Anne walks toward us, carrying a tray stacked with white towels. In her right hand is a set of silver tongs, which she uses to pull a wet, steaming towel from the stack.

"Would any of you care for a hot towel before we land?" She bends at the waist as she offers. The Governor's eyes are fixed squarely on her revealing décolletage.

"Hot," the Governor says. "Like I like it!" He seems unfazed by the conversation we've had during the flight.

"Why did you tell me all of that stuff?" I ask the Governor as Sally Anne hands me a towel. I use it first to wipe my hands even though they're clean. "I mean, why let me in on all of this?"

"Mmmm," the Governor says through the towel covering his face. "We thought you deserved to know. It's not like you're going to go running to the press with this. I mean, you're up to your neck in it. You're...what's the word I'm looking for, Sir Spencer?"

"Complicit."

"Yes," the Governor wads up the towel and puts it on the table next to his coffee cup. "Complicit. Furthermore, you're in a little bit of danger. You need our help."

"Yeah," I acknowledge with a nervous laugh. "I feel like I got the James Bond speech, where the bad guy tells him everything right before he attempts to kill him."

"What's with you and movie references?" the Governor asks. "*Zero Dark Thirty, James Bond.* I don't get it."

"Coping mechanism," Sir Spencer answers. "Quite understandable, really."

Sally Anne gently shakes George's shoulder to wake him. He opens his eyes and scoots up in the seat. She hands him a warm towel for his face and saunters to the wet bar.

"Speaking of the press," the Governor says in George's direction, "George Townsend is it? Channel 4 in Houston?"

"Uh," George pulls the towel from his face and looks at the Governor. His eyes are wide. He looks around the plane and back at my boss. "Yes, sir. I'm George Townsend."

"Well, George, your narcolepsy notwithstanding, this entire trip has been off the record. Am I right?"

George looks at me and I nod almost imperceptibly. "Sure, Governor," he says. "May I get a comment when we land?"

The Governor tilts his head as would a confused dog. "A comment about what exactly, George?"

"The debate tonight?" George answers after a beat. "What else would I want to ask you about, sir?"

"Ha! Good one, George. I like you." He wags his finger at the reporter and winks. "You're a quick thinker. Good on your feet, right?"

George doesn't answer. He pulls my phone from the desk and puts it in his lap.

"You gonna take notes, George?" the Governor asks.

"I have a video camera," he says. "We can do it right after we land, before I hop back on to fly to Houston."

The Governor looks like he's weighing whether he wants to do that. "All right. That's fine, but we only talk about the debate."

The landing gear hits the tarmac in Austin. The plane lurches when the pilot applies the brakes.

"Welcome to Austin!" he exclaims over the speaker system. "A couple of minutes and we'll be to the general aviation terminal. I'd appreciate it if you'd stay in your seats until Sally Anne has opened the exit door and lowered the steps for you."

The plane slows and the pilot guides the jet to the left toward a series of hangars. I gather my backpack and think about the task ahead. My trip to Charlie's apartment is all the more important now that Crockett is alive. As much as I want to know more about who she really was, I need evidence of her involvement with Crockett, Buell and Ripley. It's bound to be somewhere in her place.

If I can find enough material there, I can get everyone off of my back. I can break my deal with the devil and move along. It's what I'm best at doing anyhow.

"Hey, Jackson," George snaps me from my mini-trance. "Here's your phone." He tosses me his phone, giving me a look that tells me he knows what he's doing. "You've got a message."

I look down at his phone and the MESSAGES icon reads "1". I click the button that takes me to the message screen. Neither the Governor nor Sir Spencer is paying attention to me. They're engaged with their own phones.

"I love Twitter," says the Governor, thumbing the tiny keyboard on his iPhone. "Gives me a chance to connect with the people."

"I don't follow social media," says Sir Spencer. "I don't get the narcissism of it all. I couldn't care less what you ate for lunch Governor."

"C'mon, Sir Spencer, it's the proletariat connecting with the bourgeois. You should appreciate that, given your French opera blasting in the plane the whole trip."

I ignore the irony.

On George's phone, there's a single message, sent from my phone.

i need ur phone. trade w me. k? wasnt asleep. awake whole trip. ur phone recorded everything.

I erase the message and click the phone back to the home screen.

I look from the screen to George. He smiles.

Wow. Now that's a reporter for you.

* * *

Blair Loxley sat next to me in the vice principal's office. His hand was wrapped and his thumb splinted after a trip to the nurse. Neither of us looked at each other or said anything. The vice principal was on the phone. He'd already called Loxley's mother, and now he was talking to mine. I could hear her worried voice through the receiver as the vice principal explained the basics. When he hung up, he took a deep breath and exhaled.

"I'm not going to candy coat it for either one of you,' he said. "There's a good chance you're both going to be suspended, maybe expelled." He leaned forward from behind his desk and adjusted his nameplate.

"I need you to tell me where you put the gun, Jackson."

I said nothing.

"The police will be here before your parents arrive and they'll find it," he warned. "If that happens before you tell me where it is, this is only going to get worse."

Too late.

The door behind us opened and in walked two uniformed police officers. I remember both of them being tall with thick, rounded shoulders. They looked like the guys who participated in those strongest man competitions on cable. Neither of them smiled as they walked around to the front of the vice principal's desk.

"I was explaining to the boys how much trouble they're in," said the administrator. "But neither of them seems to grasp it."

"Who brought the gun?" one of them asked. "Where is it?"

The vice principal nodded in my direction. "That's Jackson.

The gun is his. He won't tell me where he put it."

"How do we know there's a gun at all?" asked the second officer. "Since nobody's seen it."

"Somebody reported seeing Jackson with it this morning on the way to school," he said. "An anonymous tip that came in late today. They said he was carrying it under his coat."

"Why's the other kid here?" asked the first officer, his Popeye arms folded in front of his chest. "What did he do?"

"They were in a fight. We're holding both of them here until their parents arrive."

The second officer knelt known in front of me and looked me straight in the eyes. "Where's the gun, kid? If you brought a gun to school we need to know where it is."

I said nothing.

"Why would you bring a gun to school?" asked the first officer. "You know that's against the law."

"Where'd you get the gun?" said the second officer, inching more closely to my face. "You know if you got it from a parent, that parent can get in trouble too."

I hadn't thought about that. My stupidity was putting my parents in jeopardy. I couldn't stay quiet.

"He was bullying me," I nodded toward Loxley and it came pouring out. "I brought it to scare him, but there was a big crowd of people around. I knew I shouldn't do it. I left it where I put it. It isn't loaded. It's hidden. I didn't point it at anyone."

The second officer looked at his partner and back at me then stood. With his hands on his hips he walked to my side and put his meat hook of a hand on my shoulder. "Come on kid, show me where it is."

"Don't you care that he was bullying me?" I asked. "I mean he beat me up and busted my knee."

"I care," said the second officer, "but that's not what we need to deal with right now. We need to get the gun so somebody doesn't find it and take it."

"He beat me up! I was defending myself," I pleaded. "I was trying to scare him into leaving me alone."

"I understand," the officer squeezed my shoulder. "We can talk about that after you show us where you hid the gun. Now what kind of gun is it?"

I sat there, my throat aching from the thick lump that had formed at the base of it. I was doing everything I could not to cry in front of Blair Loxley. A single tear would've undone the victory I scored that afternoon. I remember blinking and swallowing to fight it.

"What kind of gun is it?" the second officer repeated. He'd softened his tone again. He knew I was trying not to break down in front of my tormenter. He had to know.

"It's a rifle," my voice was barely above a whisper. I swallowed hard.

"What kind of rifle?"

If I told him what it was and where it was, I would lose my rifle. I would lose the prized possession my father had handed down to me. I'd betrayed myself.

Why did I bring the gun? Why did I do this?

"What kind of rifle?" the first officer said, stepping closer to me. "We need to know so we can help you. You don't want your parents to get in trouble do you?"

I shook my head and blinked. They'd found my weak spot.

"The more you help us," he added, "the less trouble for your mom and dad."

"It's a Henry lever action," I whispered. "It's not loaded."

"Where is it?" the second officer asked again. "Can you take us to it?"

Weak kneed, I led the two officers out of the office and toward the shed near the track.

* * *

I unlock the door to Charlie's apartment with the key she'd given me a couple weeks earlier and swing it open to the smell of the citric perfume which intoxicated me the first time I met her.

The sofa in front of me reminds me of the last time I saw her, casually dressed in her Bush-Cheney T-Shirt and those hip-hugging jeans. Inhaling, I remember the taste of her lips, the smell of her hair.

She played me. I was a pawn.

On a glass computer desk across the room, sits her laptop. I cross to the desk, drop her duffle bag on the floor, and slip into the heavy wooden chair in front of the desk.

While the computer hums to life, I open the bag and pull out the iPad, the iPod, and the small laptop. I sit the small laptop next to the more substantial one already on her desk and flip it open to turn it on.

Something's missing.

I dig through the bag and find the flash drive attachment that plugs into the iPad, but there's no drive inserted into it.

The larger laptop boots up and asks for a password. I punch in *twofacedliar.* That doesn't work. Neither does the misogynist expletive I enter next.

I decide to bypass it. I reboot the computer into Safe Mode with Command Prompt and log in as an administrator. The command prompt appears and I type in *net user.* A list of Charlie's computer profiles for the laptop populate the screen.

There are five of them. I look at their names. The first one is *Charlie Corday.* I skip it. That's the profile she'd use when I was around. It's bound to be innocuous.

Next is *Anne Parillou.* Funny. She played the part of Nikita, the female spy, in Luc Besson's cult favorite.

I scan down.

Margaretha Geertruida Zelle. Mata Hari's real name.

Judy Bethulia. Her passport identity.

The last name on the list is the profile I need to search: *Emily West.*

She was the indentured servant who, legend has it, "occupied" Mexican General Santa Ana as the Texans prepared for the Battle of San Jacinto. Because of her, supposedly, General Sam Houston's troops were able to surprise Santa Ana, defeat him, and win Texas' independence from Mexico.

She was The Yellow Rose of Texas.

I type *net user,* a new master password, and reboot. As the computer revs up again, I get up from the desk and walk to her bedroom. The pine sleigh bed is unmade, its white sheets rumpled onto one side. A yellow comforter is folded at the bottom. The ceiling fan is whirring, the pull chain rapping against the attached light fixture in a rhythm.

I get down on all fours and look under the bed. There's nothing. The nightstand next to her bed has a drawer and a cabinet door. The drawer is stuffed with earbuds, Kleenex, and a television remote. In the cabinet there's a small safe with a combination lock and a key. I try the key first and it turns. *It's unlocked!*

Inside there's a manila envelope and a flash drive. I toss both of them onto the bed and make my way to her closet. Inside, to the left, there's a built-in shelf with some of my clothing on it. I pull out a pair of jeans and a Round Rock Express T-shirt. It feels good to change clothing, even without a shower. My sweats find a home balled up in an empty shopping bag on the floor. I grab the bag to dispose of on the street, pick up the drive and the envelope and head back to the computer.

Sitting at the desk, I pull open the envelope. It's empty.

The computer is still humming, but no home page yet. I take the flash drive and slip it into the iPad attachment.

There's no code on the iPad, so I hit the icon that opens the drive. The screen fills with a .PDF document labeled *Yellow Rose*.

I knew it.

The first page reads like fiction:

YELLOW ROSE INITIAL ASSIGNMENT NGTX45617862ATX

FOR INTERNAL USE, EYES ONLY

--JOB ACQUIRED AS INSTRUCTED, INDENTITY DOCUMENTS AT DROPBOX #4

--YOU ARE TO DETERMINE EXTENT OF PENETRATION BY TARGET 1 AND EXPLOIT

--TARGET 1 IS NOT ON *KILL* LIST, BUT CLOSE SURVEILLENCE REQUIRED

--DAILY REPORT ON TARGET 1 MANDATORY THROUGH TYPICAL SECURE CHANNEL

--FAMILIARIZE TARGET 2 **NOT PRIORITY**

--GATHER INTEL TARGET 3 AS INSTRUCTED THROUGH UPDATES

--SEE DROPBOX #3 FOR UPDATES. NOTIFICATIONS THROUGH JOINT ACCOUNT

Scrolling down, I see a series of photographs. Target two is Roswell Ripley, Jr. Target three is my boss, the Governor.

Target one is me.

It's a picture of me sipping a McDonald's coffee, walking up Congress toward the Capitol. It's at least six months old.

There are schematics of my apartment, my office, Ripley's office, the Governor's mansion and his offices in the Capitol. There are phone numbers, bank account numbers, lists of restaurants I frequent. My taste in movies and music reads like the questionnaire next to the centerfold in a *Playboy* magazine.

Trying not to freak out, I put down the iPad and log into the desktop.

Notifications through joint account.

I go to the desktop and click on Internet Explorer. The home page pops up for a search engine. My guess is the search engine is also her email provider. I double click the email function. The email loads. The account is *Charliegirl@mynetmail.com*. That's probably not it, but I scan her inbox, sent items, deleted folder, and saved mail to be safe. I find nothing. I click the *TOOLS* icon on the top right of the screen. There's an option for *ADDITIONAL ACCOUNTS*. I click it and the screen repopulates with an account called *yellowrose1@mynetmail.com*.

Excited, I quickly click through her emails sent and received and find nothing. Her saved email box is empty. It's like a dummy account or something.

I find the folder marked UNSENT and click it.

It's a gold mine.

In the folder, I find a series of at least twenty unsent emails, each one revealing the progression of Charlie's operation. It appears from the language, every other email is from Charlie to someone overseeing her activities. The alternating messages are replies from that someone.

I randomly click one of them to read it more closely.

RE: NGTX45617862ATX

--TARGET 3 UNCOOPERATIVE

--REASSESSING TARGET 3

--TARGET 1 INTEL BEING INVESTIGATED

--PREP FOR HOUSTON ASSIGNMENT, SEE ATTACHED PHOTO
--MAKE CONTACT WITH OPERATIONAL PARTNER
--RESPOND BY 0600 WITH UPDATE

There's an attached image labeled DiscGreen. It's an aerial photograph of what looks like the park near the convention center in downtown Houston; Discovery Green. That's where Buell was shot.

The next email is from Charlie.

RE: NGTX45617862ATX
--TARGET 1 NO LONGER ACQUIRED. EFFORTING
--TARGET 3 REASSESS CONFIRMED
--OPERATIONAL PARTNER IN LOOP
--HOUSTON ASSIGNMENT PREP ACKNOWLEDGE

She's clearly referring to my disappearance, to Ripley's designating as persona-non-grata, and that Crockett was in the picture. She must have worked with him on the Buell shooting. *Reassess* must be code for *kill*. I look at another email from her handler.

RE: NGTX45617862ATX
--YELLOW ROSE ACKNOWLEDGE
--URGENT ACKNOWLEDGE
--REASSESS URGENT

She's out of the loop. They want her to check in.

I go back to her unsent folder and see there's another email chain.

I skip to the last email and notice it's dated this morning.

RE: WILTEDROSE
--ACKNOWLEDGE TARGET 3 ACQUISITION AND TERMINATION
--ACKNOWLEDGE REAQUISTION OF TARGET 1, CONSIDER REASSESSMENT

--REASSESS TARGET 2, ACKNOWLEDGE RECEIPT OF ATTACHMENT ASAP
--RETRIEVE NEEDED DOCUMENTS DROP #4

Wilted Rose? I have no clue what it means. All the notes in this chain are within the last twenty-four hours and are headlined RE: WILTEDROSE. Maybe it signals a change in assignment. Maybe she never checked in? Doesn't really matter, but there's a series of photographs attached to the email. All of them are different shots of the same building. Three of them show exterior views and two of them are of the interior. I vaguely recognize the building but can't quite place it.

I copy one of the photographs to the computer's desktop and insert it into an image search online.

It's the public television station in Austin.

The location for the debate tonight.

Crockett's still alive and he's going to kill the Governor.

CHAPTER 13

I'm staring at that last email on the screen, holding George's cell phone to my ear. "George, where are you?"

"I'm at the station, downloading the video off of your phone. It's almost too good to be true!" He sounds giddy. "I mean, the Governor is on camera, in somebody's private jet, baring his soul to you. It's ridiculous."

"Have you shared it with anyone yet?"

"Not yet. It's taking forever to dump this stuff from the phone onto my computer's hard drive. I've got to get it onto the newsroom server and transfer the video I shot on that camera. You know, Ripley and Charlie. It'll be a little while."

"So, you're not airing it."

"I *am* airing it," he says. "Of course I am airing it. When I am sure it's usable video, I'm showing it to my news director and the executive producer. They'll want to air it. Are you kidding me?"

"When do you think you'd put all of this on television?" I'm trying to process how this new development, the one I *should* have seen coming, is going to affect everything. I didn't take him for the jerk he apparently is.

"I dunno," he says. "Maybe tonight at ten. That would be my hope. I mean, really, Jackson, can you believe this? The story of my life fell into my lap because of you. I'm going to win all kinds of awards with this stuff."

My world is collapsing, people are dead, and he's talking about plaques and Lucite trophies. This is why people hate television news.

"You can't air it," I plead. "Not yet." I hadn't thought he'd be so quick to share it with his bosses. Sir Spencer *was* right. I can't really trust anyone when everyone has their own self-interest in mind.

"Riiight," George laughs. "We have the Governor admitting to payoffs from the oil industry, denouncing the secessionist movement on which he's built a great deal of his campaign, and essentially calling his opponent a liar capable of conspiracy and murder. I can't *not* air that! Furthermore, I've got Ripley on camera talking about his science stuff on camera. Not to mention the video I've got of Charlie confessing *something* about Buell's involvement as she died. I mean, all of this, when it's put together, it's unreal. I can't let this sit!"

"George, the Governor's life is in danger. If you air this stuff, it gets him killed for sure."

"No, it doesn't," he says. "It *saves* his life! If someone wants him dead, and this airs, nobody will touch him. I'd love to put this on the air after the debate tonight. The timing couldn't be better."

"You're going to need to get reaction from the Governor's camp and from Buell before you air it right?" I ask. "It's Buell who wants him dead. The hit's supposed to happen at the debate. This really screws up everything."

"Not necessarily. We can ask certain questions without revealing we have video. It's like we're fishing."

"The Governor *knows* you were on that plane," I remind him. "He may be a narcissistic money grubbing pig, but he's not stupid. The Pickle guys still want us dead. Buell *could* want us dead at any moment. You put yourself at risk. You put me at risk. The only people not trying to kill us right now are on the Governor's side. Do we want to jeopardize that? Nobody else is going to get this stuff. Can't you hold it?"

George doesn't say anything.

"George?" I press. "After the last two days, you're *now* abandoning me? You're putting the story first?"

"Okay," he sighs. "Here's the deal. You knew I was always in this for the story, Jackson. That's all this was. I wouldn't risk my life for anything other than that. You should have known. I'm not a spy or a mercenary. I don't *do* guns. I put up with it for the *get*.

Now I've got it."

"Are you kidding me?" I ask. "Is this a joke?"

"Jackson," he says. I can hear his leg thumping against his desk in the background. "For a smart guy, who's kind of a badass, you're unbelievably naïve."

"How naïve is this, George? Consider the fact that when your big *get* airs, we'll both be hauled in for questioning after the trail of bodies we left behind. It doesn't matter Sir Spencer had it cleaned up. *If* he had it cleaned up."

George remained silent.

"You've got at least some of the carnage on camera, George. When you air the video of Charlie confessing whatever it was she confessed, it's proof we were at the scene of a deadly accident and left without calling the cops. You've got video of a missing scientist whose body *we* dumped onto the side of the road. If Sir Spencer did clean up Ripley's body, he'll still be considered missing. There'll be questions to answer there, George. We'll be charged with, at the very least, leaving the scene of an accident, if not something more criminal. How good are your station's attorneys? Will your boss foot the bill?"

He still says nothing.

"George?"

"Fine," he sulks. "I can hold it for now." True reporter. He's all guts and glory until he needs guts for the glory. "I'm not sitting on this forever."

"Thanks. Hold it until I get back to you. When I'm ready, you can air whatever you want."

"What about the Governor? You said someone wants him dead now. Do you have any leads?"

"Yes."

"And?" He expects I'm going to help him now. Unreal.

"Does your station have a reporter at the debate?"

"We have a crew there. Our political reporter is on the panel. She's there with a photographer."

"I'll consider tipping *her* off when I see her." I hang up.

* * *

I pointed to where I'd hidden the lever action rifle, standing several feet away from the shed. I'd tried to get the gun myself, but the officers stopped me.

One of them stood behind me, his thick hands on my shoulders, holding me in place while his partner crouched in front of the gap underneath the shed. He reached into the space, slid out the rifle, and held it up as he stood.

"This it?" he asked, checking the safety. "This your gun?"

"Yes," I whispered.

"Speak up," the officer behind me said, squeezing his mitts. "Is that your weapon?"

"Yes," I whimpered. "It's mine."

"Is it loaded?" the officer holding the gun asked. "Did you put bullets into it?"

I shook my head, sniffling back the snot running from my nose.

"Speak up." Another squeeze on my shoulders.

"No!: I shouted. "I didn't load it!"

The officer holding the weapon unscrewed the spring loaded magazine beneath the barrel and checked for ammunition. Then he checked the bolt. He looked at the buttstock of the rifle and ran his thumb across it. He stared at it for a minute, his eyebrows squeezed together as though he was confused.

"What's this mean?" he asks, walking toward me with the buttstock facing me. "Who's Hank?"

On the buttstock was the nickname I'd scrawled into the wood with a buck knife. *HANK* was written in a cross between print and cursive. It was only legible because there were four letters. After I'd done it, my dad had taken a lighter and burned the etching so it blackened.

"It's the rifle," I told him, tears streaming down my cheeks.

"I don't get it," said the meat clawed officer behind me.

"It's a Henry Lever Action Rifle," I sniffled between gasps for air. "Hank is short for Henry. My dad gave me the gun. I named it 'cause it's mine now."

"Not for much longer," said the cop behind me. "That gun's evidence. We're gonna hold on to it for you and your dad." There was condescension laced with disgust in his voice.

"C'mon," said the other officer. "We've got to get you back to the school. When your parents get here, we'll take you down to the station."

"You're arresting me?" I squeaked.

"Nobody said that," the first officer, the one holding my gun, was trying to keep me calm. He understood I was a stupid, frustrated kid at the end of his rope. He knew the gun wasn't loaded. "You have to understand this is very serious, Jackson."

I did understand. I was terrified about the consequences as much as I was angry at myself for letting the bully get the better of me. Loxley was the instigator. He'd tortured me for months. Now he was getting a slap on the wrist and I was about to get expelled and have a dark blotch stain my permanent record.

The officers were walking me up the slight rise to the front of the school when I saw the assistant principal hurrying through the twin metal doors at the entrance. He was moving like those speed walkers who swing their hips unnaturally, to gain speed without running. Something was wrong, something other than my imminent academic demise.

The officers didn't notice it, I don't think. They were talking to each other about the amount of paperwork about to be required of them, despite their shift ending. One of them had a date. The other one mentioned having to call his wife to "advise her he was detained".

The vice principal approached, out of breath as he spoke, and their attentions turned from their lives to mine.

"We've gotten a phone call," he said, beads of sweat blooming on his wide forehead.

"And?" the married officer asked. "What about it?"

The assistant principal put his hands on his knees. "I'm sorry, I'm trying to catch my breath. I didn't want to say any of this inside."

"Who called?" asked the other officer, the one holding my gun.

"It was one of your colleagues," he answered after letting out a deep breath through his mouth. "He knew you were here. He wanted me to tell you there's been a horrible accident."

"What kind of accident?" the married officer asked, a worried look on his face.

The assistant principal glanced at me for a split second and avoided eye contact. I knew it involved my parents. He didn't want to tell me, but he had no choice. He had to be the bearer of bad news.

"Um," he said without looking at me, "a car accident. A bad one. It happened maybe twenty minutes ago. I think two or three cars were involved. I'm not sure. The officer said it involved... involved Jackson's parents."

The officer with meat hook hands changed his grip around my shoulder. It softened while at the same time maintaining its hold on me less aggressively. He pulled me imperceptibly toward him.

"What do you mean it involves my parents?" I asked, pulling away from the officer as he tried to comfort me. "What does that mean exactly?"

The administrator still wouldn't look at me, and addressed the cops. "Your colleagues quickly identified who was in the wreck from license plate and driver license information. The names rang a bell because of what's happening here, and so..."

"What?" I pressed, hardly keeping my composure.

He finally looked me in the eyes. He was breathless, sweating, and uncomfortable. He pulled loose his tie and unbuttoned the collar of his short sleeve dress shirt. "Your parents aren't coming to pick you up, Jackson," he said. "Neither of them."

* * *

Do I really want to stop Crockett from killing the Governor?

It's a legitimate question. If the Governor dies and Crockett gets caught, how does that help me?

The Governor clearly doesn't care about me. He faked it. He used me. He had me kidnapped and interrogated. He's no loss.

He also doesn't want me dead. That's a rare trait these days. Maybe he can impress upon the oil companies the benefits of leaving me alone. If he dies, Buell could become Governor. That's not good for me.

Walking out of Charlie's building, I turn left toward the bus stop. The phone in my pocket vibrates. It's an unlisted number.

"Hello?"

"Jackson, good man," says a cheerful, familiar voice. "How are you?" I'm not surprised he found me. Even with someone else's phone, he never has any trouble tracking me down.

"Sir Spencer," I answer. "Or Saint. Or whoever you are...what's up?"

"Where are you headed?"

"To stop the Governor from getting killed," I tell him. "He's a target."

"Whatever do you mean?" He laughs and his muffled voice tells someone, "He says your life is in danger."

"Crockett is alive, right? I've got some information which leads me to believe his next target is the Governor."

"Where are you getting this?" Sir Spencer isn't laughing now.

"There was some stuff on Charlie's computer..."

"You went to her apartment?"

"Yes."

"Why?"

"I *told* you I was going there. I wanted to find out—"

"Who she really was?" There's a lilting sarcasm in his voice. "Oh, dear boy."

"Irrelevant," I say, trying not to raise my voice. There's a woman standing next to me at the bus stop now. "You need to be aware of the threat."

"Do you have any suggestion as to when or where this threat might be?"

"The debate. It'll happen at the debate or after the debate. I saw building diagrams."

He sounds less dubious of my warning now, "We'll make certain there is additional security."

I step onto the blue city bus. "I'm coming there anyway. I know what he looks like."

The bus driver looks at me as I step past him and into a seat a couple of rows back. The bus is half full so I'm able to sit alone.

George's phone is basic, but it does have internet browsing capability. I open the browser and type in 'FT DAVIS OBSERVATORY DEAD' and hit the search button. The list populates on the screen but there's nothing about shootouts or car crashes, no news of dead bodies lying on the highway. Maybe it's my search terms. I type FT DAVIS CAR BLOOD SHOOT

POLICE. Nothing. HIGHWAY 118 MCDONALD BODY INVESTIGATE. Nothing.

Maybe Sir Spencer did have the scenes cleaned up. That might mean the oil companies don't know I'm alive and Buell is unaware Charlie is dead. Unless, of course, Crockett is in contact with him.

The bus lurches as the driver brakes. There are still a few stops until I'm at the television station. A couple of people shuffle past me to exit and a few more climb on board.

None of them have any idea what's about to happen. They're all oblivious to the plotting and the scheming and the killing. My life is full of conspiracy and betrayal. I'm waist deep in blood and oil. They're listening to their iPods and texting on their smartphones, happily unaware of the mayhem.

Ignorance is bliss.

* * *

The crowd is already gathering when I step off of the bus at a bland looking complex of three buildings that essentially comprise the University of Texas media center. Toward the southeast corner of the complex is the local PBS television station KLRU. Inside their portion of the building is studio 6A.

I've been here before. Inside 6A, they tape a public affairs program called *Civic Summit*. The Governor has appeared two or three times.

A small group of protestors, at least that's what I think they are, are holding poster boards and chanting. There are UT police at either end of their rally.

"No more blood for oil," they harmonize, unaware of the irony. "Wind, solar, and water that boils." A couple of them are wearing overplayed Guy Fawkes masks which make them look comical rather than politically witty. Their signs read CLIMATE FRAUD and MOTHER FRACKER.

I walk past a row of bicycles and up a small ramp toward the open plaza that bridges two of the complex's three buildings. There's a rope line for people to enter the television station that leads to a pair of walk-through metal detectors. In front of the detectors are two collapsible tables, onto which people are emptying their pockets and dropping their jackets. Burly, barrel-chested men in dark suits are rummaging through handbags and turning on cell phones.

On the other side of the detectors stands more muscle, presumably Texas Rangers, holding black wands with the name Garrett written in neon yellow. Those who don't make it through the first sentry unscathed get a T.S.A.-style pat down and a wave of the wand.

I recognize one of the Rangers from the Governor's detail and approach him at one of the tables. He looks like the actor Tim Roth. He could be his twin brother.

"Hey," I nod. "How's it going?"

"Fine," he says without looking up from a bag he's searching. "The line starts back there." He picks up his head, and only then recognizes me. "Oh! Sorry. Didn't know it was you. You're Quick, right?"

"Yeah," I smile. "You're Rushing?"

"Right." He slides the purse past the detector to its owner on the other side. "What's up?"

"I need to get inside, but I don't have time for the line. Is there a staff entrance or something?"

"Aren't you a little underdressed?" He eyes the jeans and baseball jersey.

"I am. Charlie Corday has my suit. You know her right?"

"Tall red head?" Everybody knows Charlie. Nobody knows she's dead. "Looks like Nicole Kidman before she redid her face?"

"That's her," I smile. "She's got my clothes and she's already in there. Can you help me out?"

"You have your staff I.D.?"

"I think so," I fish around in my jeans pockets, knowing I don't have it. "Uh, I guess I left it at home. Been a really crazy day, you know?"

"Yeah," he says. "Okay. Cut in line here and go through. Give me your backpack. I'll check it."

I hand him the backpack and start to slide past the man to my left when a woman, his wife maybe, blocks me. She's glowering at me and my baseball jersey.

"Where is he going?" she huffs, pointing at me. "We've been in line for thirty minutes. He walks up and gets a pass?"

"Ma'am," Rushing steps toward us, "he's with the Governor's staff. He's running late, and I'm giving him a pass."

She folds her arm and doesn't move.

"Ma'am," Rushing takes another step and pinches the bridge of his nose in mock frustration. "I'm sure you don't want to do this right now. Please move aside and let the young man past you."

She gives me a disapproving glare, shares it with Rushing, and moves aside with the help of a gentle tug from her husband.

"Thank you," I slip past her and through security. Rushing hands back my bag.

"Figures he works for the Governor," the woman sneers. "Exactly the sort of thing that has me voting for Buell."

I ignore her and start looking for anything out of place.

The crowd is filtering into the studio, which has room for maybe a couple of hundred people. Most of the guests are still in the large lobby.

I recognize a few of them as having paid visits to the Governor's mansion over the last few months. Others are well-known philanthropists, and maybe one or two political types. Mingling amongst the growing crowd, trying to remain inconspicuous, are the Rangers.

They're easier to spot than they'd like to be, with their earpieces winding their way around their ears and down the jackets of suits that cost a third of most of the guests' shoes. I spot five of them.

I circle back through the crowd to the studio where a dozen people are seated now. Bathed in light in the middle of the studio sits the debate moderator at a round table. A couple of other people are sitting with him and they're chatting softly, going through notecards. Opposite them are two empty chairs.

There's a member of the production crew with her hair tied back in a ponytail, a pair of headphones around her neck. She's biting a fingernail on her left hand, and scanning a clipboard in her right.

I recognize a man standing near the crew member. He's part of the Governor's policy team. His name is Kelly. I don't know if that's his first or last name. We don't like each other, but I need his help.

"Kelly," I call to him as I walk past the first row of seats in the audience. He's scrolling through his Blackberry. "Hey, what's up?"

"Nothing," he says. He looks up from his phone and smirks. "Aren't you underdressed for this, Quick?"

I look down at the jersey. "Need to go change backstage. Do you know where the Governor is?"

"Yes," he says returning his attention to his email. "I do."

I don't have time for his crap. "Where is he?"

"He's through that door over there, down the hall to the left, last door on the right," he nods in the direction of the door. "But he's busy."

"Rethinking your policy advice I imagine." I turn to the door without waiting for his reaction. "Big debate tonight, Kelly. Hope you didn't hang him out to dry."

He shouts something crude in my direction and I scoot through the door, down the hall, and to the last door on the right where a Ranger standing is watch.

"May I help you?" "Yes," I offer my hand. "I'm Jackson Quick. I'm an aide to the Governor. I need to see him."

"Jackson Quick," he repeats.

"Yes."

He raises his left wrist to his mouth and speaks in a soft voice. "I have a Jackson Quick here to see the Governor, says he's an aide." He pauses. "Just a moment," he tells me. "They're checking."

The phone in my pocket buzzes. It's George. I ignore it. I've got nothing to say to him.

The door opens. It's my boss. He's all smiles.

"Jackson," he reaches out and grabs my shoulder. "Good to see you. But *oh my*! You're a little underdressed for the occasion."

"So I hear," I say. "Ran out of time."

He pats my shoulder and pulls me into the room. "It's not a problem. Now come on in and sit with me. We have a few minutes until the debate starts."

In the room is the Governor's wife, a couple of high level assistants, and a uniformed Austin police officer. The Governor nods in the officer's direction.

"This here's the extra help you thought I might need tonight," he laughs. "All is well with the world."

Everything seems as it should be. It's not, I know.

Crockett is here. Somewhere. If I don't find him the Governor's as good as dead, along with my chance at a normal life.

* * *

I don't remember much in the hours, days, or even weeks after the vice principal told me why my parents weren't coming to get me. They were dead.

I learned later they'd traveled in my mother's car. She was driving. The uninsured driver of a pickup truck ran a red light and plowed into them. I was always told they died instantly and felt nothing, but I don't know if that's really true.

I do know it was my fault. They died together. The last thing they knew about me was that I was in trouble at school.

If I hadn't taken Hank to school, they wouldn't have raced to come deal with it. If they hadn't been dealing with it, they'd still be alive. If. If. If.

If I had a dollar for every time that word had dominated everything in my life.

My life. For a long time after my parents died, I didn't have much of one.

After their funerals, I went to live with an older cousin. She was my only family and didn't have much time for me. She was decent but absent.

My parents had life insurance. She spent most of the payout on herself. Thankfully, they'd put money in a trust she couldn't touch.

The criminal charges against me were dropped. The prosecutor said I'd been through enough already. Still, I was expelled for bringing the gun to school and was sent to an alternative school. It was there I learned Blair Loxley was nothing compared to real bullies. It was brutal. I learned how to take care of myself.

After two years at the alternative school, my cousin got tired of me. She grew weary of the weekly teacher conferences. I wasn't doing homework; I wasn't paying attention in class; I got into fights. When I was at home, I dove into music and television. They were my escape. I wasn't willing to change.

She sent me to a small boarding school in Chatham, Virginia. Somehow, my cousin and the alternative school talked the boarding school into giving me a scholarship. I was a hard luck case or something. I never found out how it worked, except that I had to maintain a C average and participate in at least one extracurricular activity per semester. I chose cross country and the technology/audio visual club.

I kept my grades up. I ran. I learned about electronics and computers. I was angry and alone, but not stupid. I knew a second chance when I saw one, so I grew up and made it work.

My roommate was a nice guy, but apparently my violent dreams were too much for him. I slept through them. He complained I would cry and talk about my parents. Once he asked me who Hank was. I didn't tell him.

After a few months he asked for a transfer to another dorm. The school granted it. I roomed alone for the rest of my time there. It was me, my music, and late night television. David Letterman and the Velcro wall is still one of the funniest things I've ever seen, even if it was in reruns.

It was like I was surrounded by zombies. All the other students were there with me, but they never engaged me. They knew I was different. They sensed it. Maybe I sensed something in them I didn't like. Either way, I was a loner.

I survived it, and because I was young enough when I got expelled, it didn't go on my permanent school record. After four years of good grades and no trouble I got into college. N.C. State. My dad's alma mater. Sometimes I'd go watch the rifle team practice. They didn't have a home range on campus, but I'd drive to a nearby range in Holly Springs to see them. It made me feel close to my dad. I never picked up a gun. I couldn't do it.

I'd listen to the pop of their .177 air rifles and with every trigger pull, flash to a memory of my dad smiling.

You're a natural.

The coach noticed me after a few of my visits and introduced himself.

"You wanna shoot?" He'd asked. "We've got an extra .22lr small bore you can use."

I'd thanked him but declined. It was the last time I went.

College flew by, and before I knew it, I was a man with a trust fund. Still, I needed to work. I bounced around. No roots. No ties. No love for anywhere or anyone.

That is, until I got the job with the Governor and he put his trust in me. Until I met Charlie and she said she loved me. Austin was becoming home. Those roots were starting to take hold. I told myself I was happy. I was normal. I was special.

I wasn't naive. I wanted to believe it. I didn't see the truth because I wanted to believe the lie.

Not again. I'm on my own. I've got my own back to watch, my own life to save.

CHAPTER 14

The phone buzzes in my pocket. It's George again. I ignore it again.

From the back of the studio I can see the Governor and Don Carlos Buell seated next to one another, the moderator across from them. The other two journalists are writing on notepads. The debate is about to start. The production crew member with the ponytail points to the moderator.

"Good evening, I'm Devon Smith. On behalf of Austin's PBS television station, I'd like to welcome you to tonight's debate which is being presented as part of KLRU's Civic Forum series."

The audience is engaged, all eyes on the five people at the center table. Buell and the Governor are doing their best to avoid looking each other in the eyes. Except for the moderator's voice, the room is silent.

"The discussion will focus on a series of public policy and political issues likely to confront the state of Texas and its Governor during the next four years. Both participants have met the criteria to participate tonight. They've both received their respective party's nomination. They've both raised at least two-hundred and fifty-thousand dollars according to their latest filings with the Texas Secretary of State's Office. They have an active staff in at least four of the following five cities: Austin, Dallas, Houston, San Antonio, and Corpus Christi."

To my left, a remotely operated camera swings a few inches to focus on the panelists next to the moderator. It zooms in on one of their faces and pulls out to reveal both of them.

"I'd like to introduce our panel of journalists," the moderator says. "Samantha Recuerda from 4 News Houston." The audience applauds. "To her left is Luke Omala, a reporter from The Dallas Morning News." The audience applauds again. "They will be responsible for asking the candidates a series of questions. I, as the moderator, will ask the follow up questions and keep us on time tonight. I hope." The audience laughs politely.

The automated camera pedestals to the left and refocuses on a wide shot of the table. There's another camera on the other side of the studio swinging into position for shots of the candidates. Kelly, the policy aide, is next to the camera, as is Rushing. Rushing has his hands clasped in front of him, standing guard.

"We'd like to begin with the candidates' opening statements," the moderator announces. "Each will have one minute. By coin flip, Mr. Buell will go first. Mr. Buell?"

Buell clears his throat and looks straight into the camera next to Kelly. I glance up at an overhead monitor to watch his remarks.

"Fellow Texans," he begins with a smile, "thank you so much for allowing me to come into your homes tonight and share with you a vision for a better, brighter Texas." He shifts in his seat and awkwardly moves his injured shoulder. "I entered this race, not out of some grand ambition or need for power, but because I see a better path than the one we're taking."

A third camera shifts into position and focuses on the Governor. On the screen above me, there's a split image; Buell talking, the Governor listening.

"As I've spent time with so many of you across this wonderful Republic, I've talked a lot about how this campaign," Buell reaches out to the camera, toward the viewers at home, "how *our* campaign, is about Texas values and American idealism."

On the Governor's side of the screen, my boss is no longer looking at Buell. He's focused on the notepad in front of him. He's writing furiously and shaking his head.

"I've told you, I believe as God has blessed me, he has blessed each of you. He has given you the ability to shape your future, to choose your path. I want to be the one who harnesses that capital that exists within every one of you. With your help we can, together, improve the lives of our families and neighbors. We can lift up those who need help without sacrificing that which we've worked hard to accumulate."

The image on the screen above switches back to a single shot of Buell. He's polished. His double Windsor knotted tie sits perfectly in the space between his starched white collar, a dark suit framing him smartly, save the slight bulge of a bandage on his shoulder. His eyes are gleaming.

"As you pledge your allegiance to the Old Glory of the United States and the Lone Star of Texas at schools and at ballgames, please remember I, Don Carlos Buell – D.C., as my wife calls me – I pledge allegiance to you, the people of this glorious state."

Three of the four cameras shift again as the moderator thanks Buell. He reminds the audience not to applaud until the debate concludes.

"Now, Governor," the moderator says. "You have one minute for your opening statement."

The Governor smiles broadly, thanks the moderator, and locks his eyes on the lens of the camera next to Kelly and Rushing.

"I certainly want to begin by thanking the good people here at KLRU television and the University of Texas for their hospitality. I also want to thank the man sitting next to me for his interest in my job," the Governor laughs and draws a muted approval from the audience. Buell plays along and smiles.

"The poor man ain't qualified," the Governor shakes his head. There's a surprised murmur from the audience; Buell retains the fake smile. "I'm sorry. It's true."

Buell's smile disappears when he realizes the Governor is foregoing platitudes for a brutal hammering right out of the gate. He obviously wasn't expecting it. A camera swings into position to capture his reaction on a split screen.

"He's a wealthy man," the Governor says. "He is. He's a successful executive who got filthy stinking rich in the oil fields without ever getting his hands dirty. He might not know petcoke from tar sands if you put them in front of him, but he played the oil game and won.

"Then what does he do?" The Governor shifts away from Buell and points at him. "What does this filthy, stinking rich oil baron do next? He abandons the oil game for the environmentalist wackos who are trying to destroy the energy industry. His company, Naner-whatever-it-is, wants to do away with carbon-based fuel."

It's Buell who's taking notes now. He's not looking at the Governor. With every word my boss utters, I swear Buell's pen digs deeper into the paper.

"You have here a man who refuses to dance with the one that brung him. You have a man who wants to undo the very fabric of this great state. What are we without energy?" The Governor slaps his palm on the table, startling Buell and the journalists. He laughs.

"He wants to 'harness the capital within you'? Right! He'll harness it only if it's carbon free, renewable, and pledges allegiance to global-warming, environmentalist wackos."

Kelly's smirking. The camera to his right slides into its new position. Kelly shifts his stance next to the camera so as not to get run over by the robot.

Rushing isn't there anymore. There's a different ranger standing there. He's taller than Rushing with short hair, looks military. I don't recognize him, but something about him seems uncomfortably familiar.

My phone buzzes. A third call from George. I don't answer it.

I'm at the back edge of the studio, so I easily work my way closer to Kelly and that ranger. As I get closer, maybe thirty feet away, I notice the ranger's jaw is bruised, and he has a gash on the back of his nearly shaved head.

From twenty feet I can tell he's not a ranger. There's no earpiece. Then I see it.

On his hand.

Semper Fi.

* * *

I'm fifteen feet from Crockett, in the darkened rear of the studio. He doesn't see me. He's too focused on his target.

My phone buzzes again. This time George leaves a text:

Jackson. It's urgent. Charlie was playing two sides.

I take the bait and reply.

What do u mean 2 sides?

I look back toward Crockett. He's biding his time.

i listened to tape when she died. was able to understand her last words.

I text back: *So?*

An immediate response: *she said she quit buell. he wanted you dead. she was working for governor.*

I text: *r u sure?*

George responds: *yes. exact words: "i quit buell. he wanted to kill you. i flipped to your boss. be careful. trust." exact words.*

I think back to the series of unsent messages in her email. There were a bunch of them sent under a coded name, the last of which she never acknowledged.

Buell was looking for her.

There was another series sent after I'd ditched her on my way to the airport under the mission *Wilted Rose*.

She was no longer *Yellow Rose*. She'd flipped. She was working for the Governor at the end. George was right.

If that was the case, if she'd flipped and Crockett was working with her, it was the Governor who wanted Ripley dead. It was the Governor and Sir Spencer who tipped her off to our whereabouts in West Texas.

It means the Governor isn't Crockett's target.

It's Buell.

Thx. I send a final text to George and slip the phone back into my pocket.

If the target is Buell, and he wanted me dead, why do I care if Crockett kills him? It's a fair question. In good conscience, I can't let it happen. I've got to stop it.

I look back toward the spot where I'd spent the first part of the debate. My backpack is on the floor, against the wall. There is nothing in there that can help me.

Back to Crockett. He's not moving.

What happened to Rushing?

There's not much time. Crockett could go off at any time. I slip back to grab my backpack and out a side door at the rear of the studio.

Buell's voice is echoing down the empty hallway through the speakers in the ceiling.

"This state needs a lot more than the promise of a better future.

We need to undertake the sacrifices that will make it happen. The Governor likes to talk. He doesn't act."

The hallway leads back toward the lobby. From there, another hallway leads to the Governor's green room. I walk quickly toward the end of the hall and push open the door with my shoulder. Rushing is sitting in a chair in the corner of the room staring straight at me. He has two bullet holes in his chest. I rush over to him, knowing there's no point.

"Rushing?" I touch his shoulder. He's limp. I open his jacket and find his shoulder holster empty.

Think, Jackson. Think!

I'm distracted by the belief that I'm staring at a dead ringer for Tim Roth when it hits me.

In Quentin Tarantino's movie *Reservoir Dogs*, Tim Roth's character Mr. Orange is an undercover cop. He carries two weapons, a revolver in his pocket and a Beretta 950 .25 Jetfire in an ankle holster.

I check Rushing's ankle. *Bingo!* He's holstered a Glock 36 with six rounds in stack magazine. I start to tuck it in the front of my jeans when three blasts explode above my head. I shrink to the floor and look up. It's the ceiling speaker.

Gunshots!

I'm too late.

There are screams from inside the studio before I rush back down the hall. The ceiling speakers amplify the cries, creating a cocoon of audible pain around me.

Before I pull open the studio doors, they explode outward, the patrician crowd climbing over itself to get out of the line of fire. I push my way inside, the Glock 36 comfortable in my hands. The automatic safety is off.

The crowd parts in time for me to see Don Carlos Buell's head snap back and recoil forward. Crockett is maybe five feet from him. The Governor is sitting with his hands up, surrendering to the man he hired.

Crockett steps to the Governor, points the gun straight at his head and says something I can't hear through the chaos. The Governor squeezes his eyes shut and clasps his hands above his head, pleading. This was not part of his plan.

Without thinking I yell across the studio, "Crockett! Crockett!" I level the Glock, and load the chamber in one seamless move.

The Governor opens his eyes and looks toward me, a look of fear and confusion on his pale face. Crockett, his weapon still pressed against the Governor's forehead, turns and the bullet rips into his chest, below his neck.

The force of the .45 caliber bullet spins him to the left, opening him up and widening my target. I take two steps toward him, the Glock still level and squeeze the trigger again.

The second bullet finds the center of his chest. A third tattoos him right beneath his left eye and he falls back onto the table. His limp body slides onto the floor in a heap.

The Governor is frozen, his hands still above his head. He's whimpering. The two journalists and the moderator are hiding under the table. I take another step toward them and there's a fourth gunshot. Next to my backpack strap, the slam of a baseball bat powers into my back, followed immediately by a hot, searing pain in my right shoulder. My arm goes numb and I drop the Glock.

"Drop your weapon!" somebody shouts from behind me.

To my right there's a ranger with his weapon aimed at me. With my left hand I reach to grab my right shoulder.

"Do what he says!" says the ranger. "Drop your weapon! Get your hands up!"

They think I shot Buell?

"I dropped my gun!" I yell. "I can't raise my right arm."

"You hit him," says the ranger I can see. He's moving toward me carefully, barking at what must be another ranger behind me. "He's hit."

I've been shot, I discover. That's what's wrong with my arm.

"Governor!" I yell as I drop to the floor, hitting my bad knee. "Tell them who I am. Tell them who I am!"

I roll onto my back and try to keep focus. The pain is intense. It burns like an iron is pressed against my shoulder.

"He's okay," the Governor says as the fog rolls over me. "He's okay. He saved my life."

Somebody calls for a paramedic. Someone else talks about casualties, about the shooter, Buell, and two rangers being down. A police officer is hurt too. The thickening fog of pain and exhaustion takes over and I black out.

CHAPTER 15

For the second time in a week I wake up in a hospital bed. The television hanging from the ceiling is tuned to cable news. I sense someone sitting next to my bed, and hear them slurping a drink.

"H-hello?" My throat is dry. I swallow against what feels like sandpaper.

The figure next to me turns his attention from the television. My eyes have trouble adjusting to the bright fluorescent light, but even through the slits of my eyes I can tell it's the Governor when he speaks.

"Howdy Jackson!" he drawls. "You sure took one for the team. I owe you, you know."

There's a dull throbbing in my right shoulder, my head hurts, my bad knee aches, and there's an intravenous line leading into my wrist from a bag hanging next to the bed.

"You're a lot more than I bargained for, son," he says. "I mean, wow, right? I was sure that nut was gonna kill me." He stops to take a slurp from a Starbucks cup.

"You knew him," I say accusingly. The rasp in my voice makes the words sound foreign.

"I knew who?" The Governor tilts his head and arches his eyebrows. He sets the cup on the small table next to the bed.

"The shooter." I clear my throat. "His name was Crockett. You knew him."

"Never saw him in my life," the Governor says, crossing his legs. "You must have hit that head pretty hard." A fake laugh follows.

"Yeah, maybe. Sir, is my backpack anywhere around here?"

"I think so, why?"

"These lights are hurting my head," I squint. "I have a pair of sunglasses in my backpack. Could you get them for me?"

The Governor nods and pats my leg as he gets up. He's out of view for a few seconds and returns with the shades. He puts them on for me, slipping them carefully over my ears. I adjust them with my left hand and touch a small tab above my ear as the Governor sits back down.

"You might not have known his face," I remark, steering the conversation back in the right direction. "But you knew who he was and why he was there."

"I know he was a killer," he says. "He was there to kill me."

"You hired him to kill Buell."

"Ha!" The Governor laughs. "Why would I do that?" He doesn't deny it.

"Charlie flipped."

"I don't understand what you mean," he thumbs his tie and reaches for the Starbucks.

"Charlie was working for Buell," I remind him. "You told me that on the plane."

"Agreed."

"Something happened after she shot Buell. I don't know if he wanted me dead, or if he didn't pay her what she wanted. I don't know."

"Where are you going with this? Get to the point."

"You had Buell killed."

"Those are dangerous words," the Governor says, lowering his voice and leaning forward. "I'd be careful with wild allegations, Jackson."

"He said something to you..." I try to push myself up in the bed but my right side is too weak. "The shooter, Crockett, said something to you when he put the gun to your head."

The Governor doesn't say anything, but through the tint of the glasses I can see the tension in his jaw.

"What did he say?" I ask. "You *owe* me," I added after he didn't respond.

He flinches against those words and exhales. "He said..." the

Governor swallows. "He said I killed his partner."

"What else?"

"He said," the Governor's glare had softened. He was back in that moment with the gun to his head, "he said he owed her, his partner. He blamed me for her death. He said I was responsible for the Ripley job. I ordered it. It was my doing. He wanted me to pay."

"Why did you want *Ripley* dead?" I asked, pressing my luck. "He was helping you with your bid against Buell's nanotech. He was the one doing all the work and he stayed loyal to you."

The Governor was looking past me, still somewhere else. I'd hit a nerve.

"Loyal?" he snapped. "Nobody's loyal. Nobody. Everyone is a partner of convenience. My donors love me if I can push through legislation that helps them or hurts their enemies. The energy companies love me if I can deliver. My staff is loyal as long as I win reelection. I couldn't lose the election. Buell's ridiculous ploy in Houston was working. He was winning. Our internal polling was trending the wrong way. He was a sympathetic character. So—"

"So you had him killed?"

"It was perfect. He'd already been targeted once," he said, his eyes gleaming with the brilliance of his plot. "Another assassination attempt was completely believable. It's already all over the news that your man, Crockett, was sympathetic to Ripley senior. Investigators found all sorts of incriminating evidence in his vehicle. It was almost too easy."

"But Dr. Ripley—"

"Ripley was a cog in the wheel," he snarls, putting a hand on my right leg. "He was a frightened little nerd. He couldn't handle the pressure. We couldn't risk him flipping and we had everything we needed from him anyway. We can duplicate the marker. He became expendable."

He squeezed my leg with that final word. It was a sign. It was a warning.

"Everyone is expendable given the right set of circumstances," he hissed. "I thought you'd become expendable. You proved to be...."

"Loyal?"

He releases his grip on my leg and slaps it. "Right! Loyal."

"I'm not kidding."

"Neither am I," he says, shaking his head. "You're valuable right now. You've got some cachet."

"What do you mean?"

"Well," he picks up the Starbucks and slurps the last of the coffee, "you have a lot of information. Information which people don't want made public. Right? So, as long as that information remains right where it is, in that banged up head of yours, you remain valuable."

"Is that a threat?"

"Oh no," says the Governor. "I agree you're loyal. But, you know, loyalty is relative."

"So..."

"Don't poke the bear, Jackson." The Governor sits back and smiles, chuckles. "Don't poke the bear."

"I understand sir."

A nurse appears in the doorway behind the Governor carrying a bedpan.

"Excuse me," she says. "I'm sorry Governor, but I need a little privacy with Jackson here."

He stands from his seat and bows to the nurse, who moves to my bedside.

"Good to see you awake, Jackson," she says. "My name is Nurse Helen. Do you think you can stand and go to the bathroom?"

I nod.

"Do you need those sunglasses?" she asks. "I can take them from you."

"I'm finished with them." I look at the Governor as nurse Helen slips them off of my face, blinking at the light as my eyes readjust. "Governor, sir, thanks for coming by. I really appreciate how loyal you are to all of us on your staff."

"My pleasure," he says and turns to leave. "I'll be keeping an eye on your recovery."

"I'll keep you posted I'm sure, sir."

The Governor leaves the room, his boots clicking down the hall. Nurse Helen is checking the fluids in the bag next to the bed.

"Can I make a phone call from the phone here?" I ask her, gesturing to the one on the table next to the Governor's empty Starbucks cup. Nurse Helen nods and hands me the cordless receiver.

I dial a series of numbers and listen to it ring a couple of times.

"Hello?" answers a tired, worn out sounding voice.

"Is this George Townsend?"

"Yes," he says. "Who is this?" He must not recognize my gravelly voice.

"It's Jackson Quick."

"Jackson?" His voice perks up. "How are you? *Where* are you?"

"I'm in the hospital. I'm calling to give you the okay."

"Okay," he says. "I have to admit something."

"What?"

"We're going with it tonight. I couldn't wait anymore. Not with what happened at the debate last night."

"Well, you might wanna hold off for a few more hours."

"Why?" He sounds skeptical, ready to argue.

"I've got something that will supplement the video you already have." I look over to the glasses next to me on the bed. They're still recording.

EPILOGUE

"Some people look at me and see a certain swagger, which in Texas
is called 'walking'."
--George W. Bush, 43rd President of the United States

The yellow-walled Gibson lounge at Maggie Mac's in Austin is
almost empty. It's me and maybe twenty others listening to Birdlegg
and The Tight Fit Blues Band. Birdlegg's in his fedora, dancing
around the front of the small stage. The three piece band behind
him is keeping time, riffing with his unpredictable phrasing.

His long sleeve white shirt is soaked through with sweat, a too
thin tie flapping back and forth across his shoulders. He tips the
fedora back on his head, eyes closed. Birdlegg feels the music.

Tuesday nights aren't big on Sixth Street. For most of the few
who venture out, they're a way to help bridge the gap between
Saturday and Thursday. For me it's safer to be out on a night with
fewer people to watch. From the high backed chair in the corner, I
can keep everything and everyone in front of me.

The club soda I have been nursing for the last hour sweats on
the side table next to the chair. I don't really want to be here. I
wouldn't have picked Birdlegg, as good as he is, to entertain me, but
I had to get outside.

My new apartment is nice enough, but the four walls felt smaller
today than they did yesterday or last Tuesday.

I picked Maggie Mac's because of the privacy in the Lounge,

because I haven't been here in a month, and because it reminds me of Charlie.

The bar is named for a nineteenth century prostitute who was known to pleasure her clients before fleecing them. She worked in Liverpool at a place called The American Bar. Eventually she was caught and sent to a penal colony in Australia.

At least that's what it says on the bar's website.

My club soda is flat. Most of the ice has melted. I catch a sliver between my teeth and flip it around on my tongue before it melts. I raise my hand and the waitress waves back. She's helping somebody near the stage. It'll be a minute.

Birdlegg pulls out his mouth harp and starts blowing. He could go for three or four minutes like this, with his harmonica wailing, crying almost to the rhythm of the drums. The bass and six string are silent while Birdlegg eases up to the microphone and works his hands back and forth. The small crowd claps and hoots their approval.

For me, Stevie Ray Vaughan recorded the definitive version of the song. Ray Charles was good too. Birdlegg equals them both with his passion.

His eyes are squeezed shut against the beads of sweat streaming from his dark face. Against the light, the droplets look like sequins. He's possessed and his bandmates nod their heads in approval.

I almost miss the waitress standing next to me, a beer in her hand.

"This is for you," she says and replaces my club soda with the mug.

"I didn't order that." I rub the ache in my right shoulder.

"I know," she whines through her onyx nose ring. "Some British dude bought it for you. He asked me to bring it over."

Past the waitress, on the far side of the lounge, near the stage, Sir Spencer is perched forward on a small stool. Between his legs and Oxfords is a cane, his left foot tapping to the rhythm of the blues. He smiles at me, his teeth glowing against the stage lights.

I look back at the waitress. She's shifted her weight to one hip, clearly impatient.

"Okay," I relent. "I'll take the beer."

She rolls her eyes, slaps a cocktail napkin on the table next to me and follows it with the mug. The head sloshes over the rim and dissolves into the napkin.

The last time I drank a tap beer in a bar, my life fell into a rabbit hole. Sir Spencer was the Mad Hatter. Maybe he was the Cheshire Cat.

The audience claps their approval. Birdlegg steps back to the drums and grabs a bottle of water. Sir Spencer presses against his cane to stand. He seems older, more tired than the man who's been harassing me since that last cursed beer.

He finds his way to the chair next to me and eases into it. His legs crossed at the ankles, he rests the cane between his legs, leaning on it.

"Jackson," he says, "how are you my good man?"

"Fine."

"Fine?" He arches his eyebrows. "Not a ringing endorsement of your life at the present, is it?"

"It is what it is."

He hands me a folded copy of the *Austin American-Statesman*. He's probably the only person who reads newsprint anymore.

The headline reads *Governor Vows to Fight, Despite Video Evidence*. A secondary above-the-fold article proclaims *Governor's Connections to Big Oil Questioned*.

"Turn the page," Sir Spencer says dryly. "There's more of your handiwork."

More articles fill page 3A: *Investigators Looking For Video Source, Reporter Won't Divulge; District Attorney: Evidence Points To Bloody Conspiracy; Governor, Energy Execs Could Face Multiple Federal Charges; Secessionist Suspect Ripley Cleared Of All Charges, Released From Custody.*

I hand back the newspaper without bothering to read the articles' contents. I get the gist. It's not complicated. I'm a target, and everyone's aiming at me.

"I surmise you are burdened with a great deal of worry," he says, leaning back and adjusting the cane, which he uses to point to the crowd around us. "Any of these people could be your undoing. Anyone, at any time really, could be the one looking for you. You cannot be certain when they'll find you. You'll become a man constantly on the run. You'll never rest."

He's repeating what I've been telling myself for the last month. It could come at any time. My end.

"The Governor is none too pleased with his current predicament. He has nasty friends, as you are already well aware. I can fix that," he says, as though he's got the cure, the antidote that will return my world to what it was. "I can ensure your safety."

"So you say," I look at the beer, the foam almost gone. "How can you be sure?"

He leans forward again and rubs his palms on the handle of the cane. "I have a great deal of influence. When I choose to wield it, the influence can benefit any number of causes."

"So," I ask, leaning toward him, "who are you?"

He laughs. "I am part of that power which both eternally wills evil and eternally works good."

A deal with the devil to extend my life.

What options do I have?

"You have skills I find of high value, Jackson," he presses. "You could supplement my efforts to..."

"To what?"

"To make the world a better place." His face is earnest, no hint of the sarcasm I'd expect.

"Seriously?"

"With all seriousness, my good man," he nods. "With all seriousness. I do what is necessary. I believe you said that once, didn't you?"

This is a sales job. This is Darth Vader trying to persuade Luke to join him on the dark side. There's no other choice. Maybe he *does* do what he does for good, in the grand scheme of things.

I reach for the mug on the table and grip the handle. It tastes warm. Not bitter. Over the rim of the glass, Sir Spencer smiles broadly. He's definitely the Cheshire Cat.

"I think..." I have him hanging on my answer with that smile.

"Yes?" he says, almost too eagerly.

"I think I'll take my chances." I set the beer down on the table. "I've gotten this far on my own."

His eyes study mine. Sir Spencer miscalculated, I can see it in the twitch of his brow, the almost imperceptible change in his smile.

I stand and sarcastically genuflect. This is where I climb back out of the hole.

"You know you won't last long by yourself," he warns. "I cannot protect you. There are too many who want you dead."

I want to tell him where to get off. I want to tell him he's wrong and I can handle this, that I'll survive without his hellish arrangement. I don't.

Instead, I smile a ridiculous grin, turn my back on Sir Spencer and walk out. Slipping in a pair of earbuds, I press play on my iPod. The music starts. I carefully adjust the 9mm tucked into my waistband underneath my untucked shirt.

I am alone. Again. As it should be.

ACKNOWLEDGEMENTS

First and foremost I must thank my beautiful wife and children for their support, encouragement, and unshakable belief in me.

My appreciation also extends to Michael Wilson, Anthony Ziccardi, and the team at Post Hill Press in New York and Nashville for their confidence in my work and their tireless efforts to put these stories into the hands of readers.

I have to give a big high-five to my editor, Felicia A. Sullivan. She took on this book despite an already difficult workload and improved both its content and flow. Her efforts were invaluable.

Equally priceless is the help I've received from so many wonderful authors: Steven Konkoly, Graham Brown, Bob Morris, Lisa Brackmann, Richard Stephenson, and others. They've provided a guiding light along an arduous path.

Jason Farmand is a graphic genius. His cover for this book (and for my first novel SEDITION) exceeded what I envisioned. He has given life to my stories without using words.

I could not have written the prologue without the expert help of the good folks at snipercentral.com. They provided wonderful technical assistance.

Dr. Scott Tinker and Dr. Matt Laudon were very patient in answering my questions about nano science. Their clear explanations of the complicated, wide-reaching field were critical to the book's plot.

Thanks are due my trusty beta-readers: Tim Heller, Gina Graff, Curt Sullivant, and Steven Konkoly. They are fearless souls who waded through typos and omissions, continuity errors and redundancy, to give me outstanding constructive criticism.

My appreciation also extends to my parents, Sanders and Jeanne, my sister Penny and brother Steven, and my in-laws, Don and Linda Eaker, for their undying support and shameless promotion of my work.

CPSIA information can be obtained at www.ICGtesting.com
Printed in the USA
LVOW13*1453060314

376322LV00002B/15/P